MURDER JAMBALAYA

Borgo Press/Wildside Books by LLOYD BIGGLE, JR.

MURDER JAMBALAYA

A J. PLETCHER & RAINA LAMBERT MYSTERY

LLOYD BIGGLE, JR.

Edited by Kenneth Lloyd Biggle
and Donna Biggle Emerson

THE BORGO PRESS
MMXII

MURDER JAMBALAYA

The following business firms and places are wholly fictitious:
Pointe Neuve; Gator Inn; Hotel Maria Theresa; Club Edie;
L'Endroit Bar; Ently and Company; Forsythe Galleries; Storril's;
DeVarnay's; Golden Sunset Motel; MidAmerican Airline;
Sierra Western Airline; Pacific Northern Airline; Nusiner and
Company.

FIRST EDITION

Published by Wildside Press LLC

www.wildsidebooks.com

DEDICATION

To the courageous citizens of New Orleans,
whose pride in their beautiful city
inspired a visiting author

CONTENTS

CHAPTER ONE

I knew something was wrong the moment I stepped out of the arrival gate at the New Orleans International Airport. It was a dreary, drizzly morning in mid-November, and Raina Lambert was there to meet me. Even in good weather, she doesn't make a practice of meeting airplanes or anything else, and I rarely see her when we are working on a case together. She had her red hair piled up in a new style that would have seriously interfered with her halo if she'd had one, and at seven in the morning, in a situation where beauty and glamour were entirely irrelevant, she managed to look both beautiful and glamorous, not to mention stylish. Stepping off a plane after a night of cramped travel, I was none of those things.

"What is it now?" I growled.

She took my arm and walked with me to the baggage area, and we talked in low tones along the way.

"There's a rumor that Marc DeVarnay was seen by someone a few days after he disappeared," she said.

"Where was he seen?" I asked.

"In a little fishing village called Pointe Neuve. This has to be verified at once. A man named Charlie Tosche is waiting outside for you. He'll take you to your hotel so you can check in and leave your luggage, and then he'll drive you down to Pointe Neuve."

It was an order. In the firm of Lambert and Associates, Investigative Consultants, Raina is the Lambert and I am one of the associates. She is not merely the chairperson of the board;

she is the board.

Even so, I consider it my duty to temper her more irrational edicts with logic. "According to Confucius, or maybe it was Karl Marx, the best rumor is half a lie," I said. "Who claims to have seen DeVarnay?"

"Maybe no one. A family friend who knew DeVarnay was missing heard it from someone and told DeVarnay's mother. We've got to find out quickly whether there's anything in it."

"Who is Charlie Tosche?"

"A local man I hired. A game warden. He knows the area and the people there, and he'll give you any help he can."

"I'll tell you what I think," I said. "I don't believe there is any such person as Marc DeVarnay. He's a figment of everyone's imagination. I've just finished the most preposterous wild goose chase you've ever involved me in, and now you're sending me down to the swamp and bayou country to start the whole thing over again."

She gave me a severe look. "You did a good job in Savannah. Even the client admitted it. What are you groused about?"

"All the time I was there, I was counting on a few free days to enjoy the place. Instead, I've been slogging across the country to no effect whatsoever, and now I'll be mucking around in a God-forsaken fishing village where it'll start raining pitchforks and alligators the moment I arrive. That's today's official Southern Louisiana weather forecast—pitchforks and alligators. I've checked it. The forecast for Savannah calls for pleasantly warm temperatures and bright sunshine. I've checked that, too. Ten to one Pointe Neuve won't even have rudimentary modern conveniences like sidewalks and indoor plumbing, and it'll be thirty miles to the nearest McDonald's."

"You can go back to Savannah when this is finished," Raina said. She added apologetically, "I'm not through in Minneapolis. I'm flying back this morning. Hopefully, another day or two will do it. By then you should be able to tell me how you're going to find DeVarnay and how long you expect it to take. If you turn up anything at Pointe Neuve, use this phone number and tell Lieutenant Keig about it. That's Lieutenant George Keig. He's the New Orleans police officer in charge of the DeVarnay case. It shouldn't take you more than a couple of hours down there."

"If it's a fishing village, it can't be very large," I said. "Forty-five minutes should do it."

"It'll be spread out along a bayou. Better allow two hours. Maybe even three. When you get back to your hotel, remember you're not here to play. You have no excuse for investigating anything at all on Bourbon Street. DeVarnay never went there."

"Poor boy," I said. "His mother must have kept him in a straight jacket."

My suitcases arrived, and we went outside to meet Charlie Tosche, a tall, lank, sunburned man with disconcertingly blue eyes. He was wearing a khaki jacket, khaki trousers, and a khaki billed cap that bore the motto, "Cajuns Are Better Lovers." His natural habitat was the swamp and bayou country, but his battered jeep looked like a relic from Desert Storm.

Raina introduced me. "This is J. Pletcher, one of my investigators."

Tosche nodded politely and shook my hand. He said nothing. When I got better acquainted with him, I learned that he usually said nothing. He was invariably polite and soft-spoken when he did speak, but that was seldom.

I took my leave of Raina, and Tosche drove me toward downtown New Orleans.

I marveled, as I had on previous visits, that a city with such a variety of fascinating places could look so humdrum along its main traffic arteries.

Since there was nothing worth seeing, I occupied myself with trying to imagine what a fugitive New Orleans millionaire and businessman could find to do in a tiny fishing village—except, perhaps, fish, and there had been nothing in his dossier to suggest he had the slightest interest in that. I couldn't even hazard a guess.

At least I was able to do my imagining without interruptions.

Between the airport and my hotel, Charlie Tosche didn't utter a word.

We reached Canal Street, whose 171 feet of width accommodates four lanes of traffic on either side of a tree-lined center strip reserved for an additional two lanes of busses, all of which gives it high ranking among the world's broadest main streets. Locally, it isn't even the widest street in New Orleans, but it certainly is one of the most important. It marks the boundary of another dimension. Beyond it one encounters different architecture, different people, different kinds of businesses. Crossing into the French Quarter is like going from one country to another. Even the streets can't pass that Canal Street frontier without changing their names.

The French Quarter, the Vieux Carré or old square, is the city's premier tourist attraction, a fascinating blend of residences, businesses, entertainment establishments, historical monuments and legends, and artistic and musical activity, all housed in lovely old buildings that are Spanish in origin rather than French. At that hour of a damp, gloomy morning, however, it looked bleak and deserted and as unlike a mecca for tourists as a back alley in New York City. Its streets, cluttered with the debris of last night's merrymaking, badly needed the washing they were about to get. The tourists were still in bed nursing hangovers.

Hotel Maria Theresa, a small, family-run establishment, had a lovely, gallery-surrounded courtyard—balconies are called galleries in New Orleans—and, since I had no idea when I would see it again, I gave myself a treat and stood on my own private, second-floor gallery for all of ten seconds to admire the view. In the courtyard below, amidst a stylish arrangement of potted tropical plants, there was a heated swimming pool surrounded by a clutter of tables, chairs, and chaise lounges, all deserted at that hour except for a custodian who was rearranging the clutter in a disinterested manner. I quickly changed into the most appropriate clothes I had for a visit to a fishing village in threatening weather, slipped several photos of Marc

DeVarnay into an inside pocket, and hurried back downstairs.

"Here I go again," I said to Tosche, not cheerfully. "Wild goose chase the second."

He made no comment.

During my flight, I had wondered whether the predicted bad weather would dampen my enjoyment of New Orleans. The question was no longer relevant because I would shortly be contemplating an entirely different kind of wildlife. I could see only one bright side to the stupid case I was trapped in. If we got completely bogged down, which seemed likely, we would still be in New Orleans for next spring's Mardi Gras. At least I could work with something to look forward to.

By the time we reached the lengthy Greater New Orleans Bridge over the Mississippi River, rain was coming down hard. We headed toward a landscape that made my fleeting glimpse of the Vieux Carré seem like a drizzly hallucination.

Pristine, lush beauty fills the Mississippi Delta except where corrosive touches of civilization, in the form of factories, shopping centers, housing developments, warehouses, oil depots, offices, trailer camps, and bars advertising cutesy drinks called "Sex on the Beach," or "Jungle Juice," or "Cement Mixer," ooze into it from the New Orleans metropolis. When we finally put the corrosion behind us, we entered a different world—and a very wet one.

I had thought I knew all about swamps and bayous. Now I discovered how different the two things are. A swamp is a swamp. A bayou may look like a wide canal with low banks and carry an enormous quantity of shipping, or it may look like an almost overgrown stream leading into a wilderness.

Where there are roads, this is a land of bridges. Water laps the edges of embankments, and thick vegetation conceals the swamps just beyond. The bridges carry the roads over bayous. Looking about me, I became increasingly skeptical that the cultured, highly educated, extremely wealthy Marc DeVarnay would have ventured into this soggy landscape or that I could find a trace of him if he had.

My guide and chauffeur remarked that the water level was up half a foot. I looked about me—gray sky pouring rain, grayer land, gray water where it was visible—and pondered the difference another six inches of wet could have made.

Road signs suddenly got exotic, with drawings of alligators and advertisements of swamp tours. An unlikely looking restaurant, a shack in the middle of nowhere, called itself the Gator Inn and bragged about its alligator dishes. There was one glimpse of history in a reference to the Jean Lafitte National Park, Lafitte being the pirate-*cum*-hero who is alleged to have won the Battle of New Orleans for General Andrew Jackson in 1815—a truly notable achievement since he wasn't there at the time.

I asked Tosche about the gourmet qualities of alligator meat.

"Some think it tastes like chicken," he said.

"You don't think so?"

"Tastes like duck to me. You should cook it the same way you cook duck."

"At the airport, I heard a tourist say alligator was very good, but she might have enjoyed it more if she hadn't known what it was. I thought alligators were an endangered species."

"Not any longer—not in Louisiana. They're protected, but they're not endangered. Regulated hunting is allowed to control the population."

"Sounds like fun," I said.

He shook his head. "You couldn't qualify. You have to own the place you hunt and live there."

He lapsed into silence. As the road became lonelier, the soggy landscape showed fewer and fewer contours. White herons patrolled the water at the edge of the embankment. They were the wrong species, but they somehow seemed symbolic of this new wild goose chase I had been launched on. The entire watery wilderness unrolled before us like a vast plagiarism. The further we penetrated into it, the samer it looked. Eventually we turned onto a side road—I had thought we were on a side road—and reached the fishing village of Pointe Neuve.

The road paralleled the bayou, which was at least a hundred yards wide there, and the village consisted of a scattering of houses strung out along the two of them. Those on the bayou side of the road were built on the edge of the water, with large front yards that haphazardly displayed heaps of junk as well as boats in varying stages of salvage or disintegration. Across the bayou, and almost out of sight around a bend, an industrial wasteland had flowered in the wilderness, thrusting up a clutter of warehouses, derricks, and the ungainly shapes of oil tanks. Barges and good-sized ships as well as a tug or two were tied up at its docks.

Most of the ships docked at the village were shrimp boats with high booms suspending nets. The houses, which ranged from neat, well-built cottages to shacks, were constructed on posts that raised their living floors six or eight feet or more above the ground. Those along the bayou extended out over the water, and the lower level served as a double garage, housing a boat at one end and a car at the other. Across the road—and on higher ground—a few bold souls had houses that were supported on pillars of cement blocks or bricks that raised them only two or three feet.

Tosche summarized the area's economy succinctly—fishing (for shrimp, fish, crabs, and oysters); oil (the industry was a huge presence throughout the delta as well as offshore, with reminders everywhere); and the hunting, fishing, and trapping carried on by visiting sportsmen as well as residents.

When I commented on the elevated houses, he grinned. "That's a lesson Cajuns learned. In storms, the tide can be raised six or seven feet—or even more if a hurricane was to hit directly."

Corrugated iron streaked with rust was the "in" thing for fishing village roofs. The generic Pointe Neuve home had a high peaked corrugated roof, a slightly pitched corrugated extension over the front porch, and a similar extension over the rear porch if the owner enjoyed the luxury of having two. Those who lived along the bayou could fish from their rear porches.

Midway through the village, we passed the only business establishment I saw there, a combination grocery store, café, and gas station housed in a long, shack-like building. The sign said, "Community Store and Café." The gasoline side of its business went unadvertised except by its two weathered-looking pumps.

At the far end of the village and somewhat remote from the other homes, several rustic palaces were set far back from the water, each with its own dock and boathouse. The boathouses looked more homelike than some of the shacks I had seen elsewhere in the village. There were cabin cruisers parked at the docks and sport cars parked in the driveways. The docks had shelters built over a picnic table. These were summer or year-around retreats for families whose wage earner—or earners—had lucrative jobs in New Orleans.

On one of the docks, children sat under the shelter watching two small radio-controlled boats race down the rain-swept bayou. When an enclosed tourist boat came into view, they sent the toy boats speeding to meet it. Then both radio-controlled boats raced the tourist boat, outdistancing it easily.

Having shown me the village, Tosche turned around and started back. He asked, "How do you want to proceed?"

I hardly knew myself. The bayou was more of a main thoroughfare than the road, but only about half of the houses were located there. There was no observation point from which one could see everything that went on in the village. "I don't suppose there's an elderly resident who sits around all day watching to see who comes and goes," I said.

Tosche shook his head. "No. There's no one like that."

"I'm sorry to hear it. I live in hope that someday, right at the beginning of an investigation, I'll discover a witness with unlimited time on his hands who keeps a log of everyone and everything that passes by. Sherlock Holmes never had any trouble finding one, but it doesn't happen to me. What about an indolent housewife with excessive curiosity about her neighbors?"

He shook his head again.

"I'll even settle for a business establishment where someone keeps a lookout for prospective customers."

"There are a couple of businesses located on the bayou. They mostly sell stuff fishermen need, like bait and gas, and most of their customers come in boats. Otherwise, the only business establishment is the store and café, but no one there bothers to look outside unless someone buys gas. There is one thing you should consider—people in these parts get suspicious if anyone seems overly interested in what they're doing. Especially strangers." He paused. "If you don't mind my asking—what are you trying to find out? Maybe I could be more helpful if I knew."

"Didn't Miss Lambert tell you anything about it?"

"She hired me to bring you down here and give you any help I could."

Along the way, he hadn't asked a single question. Obviously he had a remarkable reticence. "There's a man missing," I said. "Someone heard someone say he'd overheard someone else mention that someone or other had seen him down here."

Tosche turned his intense blue eyes on me. "That's a bit vague, isn't it?"

"Extremely so. Like most rumors, it probably doesn't amount to anything. On the other hand, since there haven't been any other clues, it has to be checked carefully."

"If it isn't classified information, who's missing?"

"A man named Marc DeVarnay. He owns and operates an antique store on Royal Street in the New Orleans French Quarter. Comes from an old and prominent New Orleans family."

"Never heard of him," Tosche said matter-of-factly, dismissing all of the old and prominent families of New Orleans with one eloquent shrug. "We get plenty of that kind down here fishing and hunting. I suppose it was one of his own crowd that saw him. Locals wouldn't have known who he was."

I made no comment. I still didn't know enough about DeVarnay to know the sort of a crowd he ran with.

"How long has he been missing?" Tosche asked.

"About two and a half weeks."

"When was he supposed to have been seen here?"

"That's as vague as the rumor. Maybe a couple weeks ago."

"All we can do is ask, but it'd be better if you let me do the asking. Everyone down here has a secret or two, and a snoopy outsider wouldn't get very far. I suppose that's why Miss Lambert hired me. Do you have a photo?"

"Of course."

He parked at the end of the village, and we got out. The rain was coming down harder, now. I was wearing a raincoat with a hood, but that did nothing to protect my shoes and trouser legs. Tosche was still in his khaki jacket and trousers, but there was an all-weather look about him. He seemed to shed water. Fortunately Marc DeVarnay's photos were in plastic sleeves, or they would have got as wet as I did.

We began going from door to door, marching up to one house after another and knocking. When there was any response, Tosche, who was Charlie to everyone and knew everyone's name, displayed one of the photos and asked if this *étranger* had passed through Pointe Neuve in the past couple of weeks.

DeVarnay's name wasn't mentioned. I drew a few suspicious looks, but it was Tosche who was asking, and he got straight answers. All of them were spelled N-O if in English or N-O-N if in French.

We tackled the houses along the road first because zigzagging between them and the bayou houses would have quadrupled the distance we had to cover. After the tenth negative, Tosche turned to me with a frown. "Maybe we should talk about this before we go any further. Did the rumor say anything about what this guy was doing down here?"

I shook my head. "A friend of the family who knew he was missing heard about it tenth or twentieth hand and told DeVarnay's mother. That's as much as we know."

Tosche pondered this for a moment. "Both the missing man and the person who saw him could have been in boats that passed on the bayou. In that case, people living here wouldn't have seen him at all."

"Maybe so," I said. "But regardless of where he was or what he was doing, we have to inquire."

Tosche shrugged indifferently. "We might as well get on with it, then."

We continued knocking on doors, taking a stretch of houses along the road and then crossing to check houses by the bayou. I got wetter and wetter.

Out on the bayou, a flotilla of oil pipes hoved into sight. The pipes looked huge—maybe two feet in diameter and twenty or thirty feet long. They also looked old and rusty. Evidently a pipe line had been disassembled and the components were being moved elsewhere. Several lengths of pipe had been placed side by side on special floats. There were a number of such units arranged end-to-end, with tugs interspersed, and they made a long and thoroughly tedious procession. We were half way through Pointe Neuve before the flotilla disappeared from sight.

Watching it gave me something to occupy my mind with. As for the investigation, it was already a washout, and the only other thing that could be said about it was that we'd picked an appropriate day.

The rain suddenly gathered intensity, as though someone had turned the volume up a notch. I huddled in my raincoat and listened to Tosche ask the same questions and get the same answers while I thought, for no reason at all, about the historic parks and squares of Savannah and the splendid weather it was having. If a flock of wild geese had flown over, I would have been severely tempted to join up.

Eventually we reached the Community Store and Café. Like the nearby houses, it was set on cement block supports. There were only three small, high windows visible from the road. The paint was peeling and the corrugated roof was a mass of rust. The two gas pumps were in the open. Some of Pointe Neuve's buildings had seen better days, but the Community Store and Café had the defeated air of always having been a wreck. A notice tacked to the side of the building had once read "Pizza," but half of it had blown away.

"Could you do with coffee?" Tosche asked me.

"About four cups," I said. "Maybe a sandwich, too. The breakfast I had on the plane was about as substantial as this rumor we're chasing."

We entered. There was no one in sight, but a cowbell clanged when we opened the door. Half of the long room was given over to the café, with a counter at one end, a few tables, and two booths, one on either side. The other half was the store, with a cabinet for frozen foods, one for refrigeration, and a couple of rows of shelves containing cans and boxes. It wasn't much of a store; but then, it wasn't much of a café, either. There was one unlikely ornament: Against the wall, on the boundary between café and grocery store, was a video poker machine.

A door opened behind the counter, and a tired-looking, very faded blonde rewarded our presence with a disinterested glance. The door closed again for a few moments, and then she came out. She was of hefty build, big-bosomed and big-armed, and her face and arms looked reddened by the wind. She had the look of having spent the previous night hauling on shrimp nets. She was wearing jeans with a frilly blouse.

She said, "Hi, Charlie."

"Hi, Eva. Coffee pot functioning?"

"It's the only thing I sell much of," she grumbled.

We sat at the counter. She placed cups of coffee in front of us, and we ordered sandwiches. When she brought them, Tosche asked, "Seen any strangers around recently?"

"How recently?"

"In the past couple of weeks."

She shook her head. "Just the usual hunting and fishing crowd. Some of 'em are pretty strange, but they aren't strangers." She giggled.

I slid DeVarnay's photo across the counter. The instant she saw what it was, she decided not to recognize it. She was already shaking her head when she took a quick look, and she kept on shaking it.

Resignedly I pulled the photo back.

"Just a minute," she said suddenly. "Lemme see that again."

I handed it to her. She squinted at it, eyes narrowed with effort.

"Old Jake," she said suddenly.

"What about him?" Tosche asked.

"He was in here with this dude. At least—I think it was this dude."

"When?" I asked.

Her eyes narrowed again. She reflected for a moment. "Wasn't last week. Must have been two weeks ago. Monday or Tuesday. Early in the week, anyway. What day does Old Jake surface? I never keep track, but he shows up regular once a week. Buys a few staples like oatmeal, and bread, and canned stuff. And beer—plenty of beer. Then he disappears for another week." She paused. "Come to think of it, I haven't seen him since. Maybe that's because he bought so much stuff that day."

"Are you certain this dude was with him?" I asked.

"As good as," she said. "They sat over there in that booth." She pointed. "Old Jake always sits at the counter and has nothing but coffee. That time he sat in the booth with this dude or someone a lot like him." She nodded at the photo. "The dude was wearing a tourist cap that said 'New Orleans' on it, but he took it off while he was eating. Looked just like the picture. Same build, too. Pretty good looking chap, actually. They had the special, took their time eating, and the dude talked a blue streak but in a low voice. Old Jake mostly listened with a silly grin on his face, which was odd for him. Normally he won't shut up and listen to anyone, but the dude was buying, so he listened. When they were half finished, he ordered a pizza to go, and the dude paid for that, too, and also anted up for the groceries Old Jake bought."

"What was the dude talking about?" I asked.

"Don't know. Whatever it was, he didn't want me to hear. Kept his voice down almost to a whisper." She seemed piqued about that. "There was something funny about him," she went on. "I mean—something really strange. He was buying for Old

Jake, which was odd enough. And he was acting a part—he'd put on old clothes for it, but they were new old clothes, see what I mean? And he talked and talked like he was promoting something, which was screwy. Who with any sense would try to con Old Jake?"

"Did this dude have a car?" I asked.

"Didn't see or hear one. They left together in Old Jake's boat—I'm sure about that. You know the racket it makes. I heard it start up, and I looked out and saw them heading up the bayou."

"Did anyone else see them that day?"

"Don't know. If anyone was around the dock when they came or went, he must have seem them. Ask Bert—he may have been working on his boat."

"Thanks," Tosche said. "We will."

We gulped the sandwiches and finished our coffee. We were in a hurry, now, to see whether there were any more witnesses. The elusive wild goose had suddenly laid a golden egg.

CHAPTER TWO

Bert, whose full name was Bertram Comereau, took some finding. We sloshed from one end of the village to the other, finally locating him in a garage playing poker with three characters who looked very much like him—wiry, weathered-looking chaps with blue eyes and dark hair.

They laid their hands down and looked at us inquiringly when we walked in. Tosche asked his question. Bert, the youngest by a number of years, nodded his head and said, "Yeah. Old Jake did have someone with him, but that was quite a while ago."

One of the other men nodded. Tosche later identified him as Jacques Deslande—not even a close friend would have dared call him Jack. "It was week before last," he said. "I saw them, too."

I passed the photo to Bert. He squinted at it the same way Eva had. "Could be. Guy was wearing one of those caps with a long bill, so he didn't look exactly like this. But—sure. This must be him."

Bert handed the photo to Jacques, who glanced at it and nodded. "That's him. I saw him with his cap off. It was a hot afternoon, and he was sweating. He took it off and mopped his forehead. He was looking for property to buy, Old Jake said. There isn't any for sale, but they walked up and down the road looking at places. Then they went in the store."

One of the other men, Ed, who had the unlikely surname of Smith, said, "I saw Old Jake about that time with someone in his boat."

I offered him the photo, but he shook his head without looking at it. "They were way out in the channel. Old Jake's beard ain't hard to recognize, and anyway, I know his boat, but I never got a close look at the other guy. City slicker on his day off, I would have said. Wasn't anyone who belonged down here."

"Is anything wrong?" Bert asked.

"He's missing," Tosche said. "Someone said he was seen here, so we're checking."

"Oh." Bert shrugged. "Well—he certainly was seen here, but that was a couple of weeks ago. Tuesday or Wednesday, I think. It don't put no label on where he is now."

"Right," Tosche said. "But at least we know where to ask about him. Maybe Old Jake can tell us something."

He turned to me. "Do you want to talk to Old Jake?"

"Where can we find him?" I asked.

"He's got a *cabon*," Tosche said. "Little place over on Squirrel Bayou. It belongs to an Orleanean named O'Harran, he used to use it as a fishing and hunting lodge, but he hasn't done much of that for years. He lets Old Jake stay there for keeping the place up."

"Old Jake don't do much up keeping," Bert said with a grin. "Fact is, he don't do any. He didn't even replace the glass when he broke a window. I suppose if the roof blew off, he might do something about that."

"How far is it?" I asked.

"Half an hour in a motor boat," Tosche said. "If we can find a boat."

"Take mine," Ed said. He tossed a key to Tosche, who thanked him and the others, gave me a nod, and marched out. I paused to add my own thanks and then squished after him.

The rain had let up—which was just as well, because the boat lent to us was not a cabin cruiser. It was an open boat with an outboard motor that seemed to produce more sound than movement. As we headed out into the channel, we were passed by a sizeable ship Tosche identified as an offshore crew boat, one that took workmen and supplies to the oil platforms in the

Gulf. Pointe Neuve slipped astern, and on one side of the bayou a forest closed in. On the other were occasional buildings—a house or two, a cluster of warehouses, a dock with boats and a derrick. Tosche pointed out the trading post where the Cajuns sold alligator hides and furs during hunting seasons.

Eventually the forest took over both sides of the bayou, but even that didn't shield the place from civilization's corrosive touch. We passed one wreck after another—old barges and ships that were half sunk in the shallows and rusting to oblivion, which unfortunately was a slow process.

We turned into a smaller bayou lined with tall live oaks. These are evergreen oaks, a beautiful, massive tree of the American South that puts out enormous branches close to the ground. Festoons of Spanish moss added their own touches of hoary beauty to the grayness of the day. This was Tosche's natural habitat, and he relaxed and became almost articulate as we penetrated further and further into it. Several times he shouted remarks above the din of the motor about something we passed. Once he pointed out an armadillo burrowing along the bank. Another time it was a tree stump that marked an alligator den.

Sitting there a foot or so above the water, it suddenly occurred to me that our small boat offered very little protection against a rampageous gator.

I called to him, "Is it possible to outdistance an alligator by swimming?"

"Not unless you can do better than twenty-five miles an hour," Tosche shouted back with a grin. He added, "You can't outrun one, either. They've been clocked up to thirty-seven miles an hour on land."

"If one gets you in its sights, you're done for, eh?" I asked lightly.

"Naw. All you have to do is jump out of the way. They have short legs and can't turn sharply. Anyway, they can only travel twenty-five feet or so before their legs give out. They don't often bother people in the water, but it's probably wiser not to share a swimming hole with one. Snakes are a lot more dangerous than alligators. They can drop into boats from trees."

It hadn't occurred to me to look for danger overhead. This sounded like a gag someone thought up to scare a tenderfoot with, but Tosche seemed serious enough.

It was a land of brackish water, freshwater mixed with sea water, and both fresh and salt water fish were taken here. On the shore in an occasional clearing, low palmetto palms could be seen. Tosche called them swamp cabbage and said Cajuns used them like coleslaw. A shallow backwater was crowded with the flower-tipped stalks of arrowroot plants, whose roots were another important Cajun food and medicine source.

Finally we turned into a bayou as narrow as a creek. Trees lined the shore, and arching limbs trailing strands of Spanish moss formed a roof over us. The water was absolutely still until our boat passed. Civilization seemed unimaginably remote, but even this charming place hadn't completely escaped the corrosion. I counted three beer cans floating near the bank.

When Tosche cut the motor, the silence had the same impact as a door slamming. We drifted around a bend, and ahead of us on the right was a dock. When we came closer, the roofline of Old Jake's *cabon* could be made out through the trees.

Tosche seemed puzzled. "Old Jake's boat is gone," he remarked. "His pirogue is gone, too."

"Pirogue?" I echoed.

"Cajun canoe. It's a small, flat-bottomed boat, doesn't draw much water, so it's useful in a swamp. Old Jake may be out fishing, but I don't know why he would take his pirogue." He hesitated. "I suppose there's no point in calling on him if he isn't there."

"Might be a good idea to find out whether he has a house guest," I suggested.

Tosche seemed doubtful, but he used a paddle to turn us toward the dock. I jumped out and tied the boat to a post. Tosche watched disapprovingly but said nothing. Together we went up the path to the *cabon*.

It was built on a hump of high ground between the bayou and a swamp—a weathered wood shack on high posts with a corrugated iron roof that was in the process of rusting away completely. We mounted the steep steps to the open porch. An old wreck of a lounging chair stood in one corner. The battered table beside it had a couple of charred tobacco pipes, a large coffee can that served as an ashtray, and a clutter of empty beer bottles. I paused and read the labels with raised eyebrows: *Blackened Voodoo Lager Beer.*

"Local brand?" I asked Tosche.

I thought I was joking, but he said, "Yeah. Dixie Brewing Company."

He called loudly, "Ho, Jake!" Then he banged on the warped door. There was glass in one of the two windows that looked onto the porch. That one was closed. The other was opened permanently, no glass, but there was a new screen tacked into place over the opening.

Tosche banged on the door again. Then he opened it. "Ho, Jake!" he called. "Anyone—"

He broke off and halted. The stench hit us an instant before we saw what was on the floor. A man lay face down in the center of the room with the end of a long, gray beard showing beside his head. Tosche started forward, but I grabbed his arm and very firmly moved him back out of the way. In the presence of a corpse, he was no longer the expert guide.

I knelt beside the man on the floor. Obviously he had been dead for weeks. To be exact, two of them. If the *cabon* hadn't been so well ventilated, the stench would have kept us from entering.

I got to my feet. "I don't want to turn him over," I said. "I'm assuming it's Old Jake because of the beard."

"Also, the clothes," Tosche said. "Also, that scar on his hand."

"What does this area use for police?"

"The Parish Sheriff's Department."

"I'll wait here while you get help. How many hours away are they?"

"They have cars on the road. One drives through the village a couple of times a day. Figure half an hour for me to get back there and telephone, fifteen minutes to half an hour for them to respond, and another half hour to get back here."

"Make certain they understand the situation—use the word 'murder.' I'm sure they would send a doctor in any case, but they'll also need technicians and lab work."

"Are you sure it's murder?"

"That dent in the back of his head wasn't self-inflicted," I said.

"Maybe he fell."

"He had to land on something to acquire a dent like that, and there isn't anything here. Also, a man who bangs the back of his head badly enough to kill himself usually isn't found lying on his face. Call it murder. It'll put them in the proper frame of mind. If they want to correct your spelling later, that's up to them. One more thing."

I got out my memo pad and wrote down the telephone number Raina Lambert had given to me. I added Lieutenant George Keig's name and ripped out the page. "After you call the sheriff, call this number," I said. "Ask for the lieutenant. If he's not there, tell whoever answers that this information is for Miss Lambert and Lieutenant Keig. Several people claim to have seen Marc DeVarnay in Pointe Neuve two weeks ago with Old Jake, and we found Old Jake lying on his face with the back of his head bashed."

"Shall I tell the lieutenant it was murder?"

"No. Miss Lambert likes to draw her own conclusions, and the lieutenant probably does, too. Does Old Jake have a last name?"

He thought for a moment. "I think it was Hemlie or Harmlie or something like that."

"On your way," I said. "This is going to be a long day for both of us." He left in a rush.

As the motor started up, I began my own quick inventory of the *cabon*'s two small rooms. The one I stood in served as a combined living room, dining room, and kitchen. The old stone fireplace had the charred remnants of a log on the grate, but it had been used for heating only. Old Jake did his cooking on a propane camp stove that stood on a rickety table in one corner. There was a covered, new-looking pan on the stove. A straight-backed chair stood nearby. An old bureau served as a cupboard; on its scarred top were half a loaf of moldy bread in a wrapper, some cans, a couple of pans that were minus their handles, some cracked plates, and three cracked mugs, also without handles, one of which was ornamented with the message, "Sands Hotel Casino Las Vegas." The only other furnishings were an old sofa and a battery radio.

A cardboard carton packed with groceries had been left on the floor under the table. On top of the carton was an unopened pizza. Old Jake had been dead for two weeks, and the fact that he hadn't unpacked the groceries DeVarnay bought for him probably meant he had been murdered shortly after they returned to the *cabon*.

I looked again at Old Jake's bashed head. If he had been alive when his skull was dented, the blow certainly killed him. I couldn't learn more without turning him over or going through his pockets, and that might mess things up for the homicide technicians. If I waited patiently, they would tell me more than I could find out myself.

Walking carefully, I moved to one side of the room and followed the wall until I reached the doorway to the tiny back room. The floor was far from clean. Old Jake, or someone, had scattered burnt matches around and ground out an occasional cigarette, and there was spilled food in the kitchen area, but there was no months-old coating of dust to take footprints. Old Jake had swept the floor not too many days before he died. Or his visitor had.

The back room was the bedroom. It contained two new-looking camp cots, each with a new sleeping bag. Near one cot was a wreck of a chest of drawers. Near the other was a suitcase on a rickety chair. Through the window I could see an outhouse in the rear and an open shed with a stack of wood.

The suitcase was an expensive leather job, and this was the wrong address for it. In those shabby surroundings, it was as unlikely as a new forty-inch TV set would have been. I took one step through the doorway, which moved me close enough to identify the initials on it—MDV. I had never seen it before, but I recognized it at once. I had tracked it—and Marc DeVarnay— across half the country before the trail fizzled out in Seattle. How it had got back here, and why, would supply food for cogitation while I waited.

I retreated cautiously, again following the wall. As I passed the kitchen corner, the pan on the camp stove caught my attention. It was a sturdy, stainless steel container with a copper bottom and a curved designer handle, and it looked brand new. It was another unlikely item for that address. Out of curiosity, I used my handkerchief and lifted its lid. The contents were covered with a mass of mold. A large spoon that lay on the table near the stove also was covered with mold; obviously it had been used to prepare the food. I took my pen knife and cleared the mold from a small surface area in the pan. I recognized the dish immediately from previous visits to New Orleans. It was a seafood jambalaya. I was able to identify shrimp and crawfish, rice, celery, and green pepper without stirring the contents.

For all I knew, every backwater Cajun had a personal repertory of favorite jambalaya recipes. The dish also can be thrown together without a recipe using whatever is at hand—ham or sausage instead of, or in addition to, seafood; a few chopped vegetables; rice; and all of the cook's favorite spices. Even so, it seemed like an overly elaborate dish for Old Jake's table, and that gave me one more thing to meditate.

I swiped three bottles of Blackened Voodoo Lager Beer from the carton of groceries, handling them with my handkerchief so as not to offend the fingerprint gurus. I managed to convince myself that Old Jake was a hospitable coot who would have approved. In any event, he wouldn't be needing them himself. I took the beer outside, where I sat on the porch in Old Jake's chair and sampled a bottle. It was heavy, dark, and full-flavored. It matched my mood perfectly. I was feeling heavy and dark myself. I had never experienced a case with such a damnable twist to it.

The MDV on the suitcase had to stand for Marc DeVarnay, the suitcase matched the description I had been given of the luggage the missing man had carried with him from New Orleans to St. Louis and then to Seattle, and there were at least three witnesses who had seen him with Old Jake. I sat there for a time sipping beer and trying again to imagine what Marc DeVarnay, a millionaire businessman who had no interest in either fishing or hunting, could have been doing down here in the swamp and bayou country. How had he managed to get acquainted with Old Jake? More to the point, *why* did he get acquainted with Old Jake? What business, either professional or personal, could a prosperous antique dealer have been conducting in Old Jake's *cabon*? If his curiosity about Pointe Neuve real estate had been genuine, DeVarnay would have gone to a Realtor. Wandering about the area with Old Jake and asking passersby if any property was for sale would have been totally out of character for him.

As an exercise in deduction, this was like trying to work through a maze of one-way bayous, each of which wandered off into a swamp and vanished. They not only took me nowhere, but I kept losing my starting point. I could see only one certainty about the case. If I were to have the quiet, confidential conversation with Marc DeVarnay I so desperately needed, I would have to find him quickly. His mother was furious because the authorities were investigating his disappearance with what she considered ineptness and indifference. That was why she had hired expensive private detectives.

Even if it were true, it was no longer relevant. The moment the police learned DeVarnay had been seen with Old Jake, they would start looking for him in earnest. He would still be missing, but he also would be wanted for murder.

CHAPTER THREE

The idea of millionaire Marc DeVarnay hiding out in a fishing village had been startling enough, but it was nothing compared with the thought of him hobnobbing with Old Jake. After that, Old Jake's body had provided the final, jolting climax, but it was actually just one more surprise in what now seemed like an endless series of surprises. The first had come a week earlier. I had gone to bed that night in Savannah, Georgia, replete—as the poets say—with plans for enjoying a lovely city I had never visited. Years before I had read about its intriguing pattern of squares, its historic waterfront, and its splendid old homes and gardens, and the place had fascinated me ever since. Finally my work had taken me there; unfortunately, it also kept me flitting about the suburbs with nary a glimpse of the central city.

The case involved missing heirloom jewelry, an unlikely assortment of heirs as suspects, a clutter of family feuds, and assorted nasty complications. One of the finest feats of my career was to deftly remove suspicion from a dearly hated daughter-in-law, a sweet girl who intensified the client's enmity each time they met by having a mind of her own, and pin the crime on a much loved and trusted servant who had been with the client for twenty years.

I then brought off a much more difficult achievement by persuading my boss, Raina Lambert, to give me time off to enjoy Savannah. I planned my sightseeing agenda with more care than General Sherman had used in capturing the place in 1864, and I added several maneuvers the general hadn't thought of such as discovering which bar served the best mint juleps and comparing dialects of southern fried chicken and candied yams at various restaurants.

I fell asleep thinking of appropriate elaborations such as the substitution of baked ham for the chicken and the extension of my research to pecan pie. When the phone rang, I stirred myself resentfully, picked up the receiver, and groaned, "Go away."

Raina Lambert's voice said, "I've made reservations for you. You can catch a night plane if you hurry."

"I'm not going anywhere," I told her. "Just this morning you gave me a week off. Remember?"

"That was then. Now you're needed somewhere else. A New Orleans businessman has disappeared."

"Not to worry," I said. "Everyone disappears in New Orleans, but no one stays missing very long. People get confused by the fact that the bars there never close, and they lose track of time. Have you checked Bourbon Street?"

"The man's name is Marc DeVarnay. He's been gone for two weeks, and no one has any idea what could have happened to him."

"Two weeks is a bit long for a binge," I conceded.

"He has no vices at all. He even drinks with severe moderation."

"Then he's gone to heaven, which is outside our jurisdiction."

Raina spoke in the firm tone bosses always adopt when they think an argument has gone on long enough. "Here's the information on your flight reservation. I'll have Mara Wilks meet you at the St. Louis airport with DeVarnay's dossier and photographs."

"St. Louis!" I exclaimed. "I thought you said New Orleans!"

"St. Louis," she said firmly.

However remarkable the Gateway Arch may be, it is paltry compensation for losing both Savannah and New Orleans in one stroke. Resignedly I wrote down the details.

I made my plane with minutes to spare, but I had ample time during the remainder of the night, on planes and in airports, to mentally review all of the attractions I wasn't going to see in the fascinating city of Savannah. At eight o'clock the next morning, instead of strolling down Bull Street to admire its historic squares, I was landing at the Lambert-St. Louis International Airport, fairly launched on the wildest of wild goose chases, though I didn't know that yet.

Mara Wilks, a thirty-five-year-old mother of three who could have passed for a high school student with some artful neglect of makeup and dress, was there with a thick envelope of material that had been faxed to her. A selection of photographs had been sent by overnight express.

"I'll circle past the office and see if they've arrived yet," she said.

While she drove, I occupied myself with reading about Marc DeVarnay. His credentials were the sort that make mothers of marriageable daughters drool—he was single, he was handsome, he was popular, he was successful in a business he loved, he came from a prominent old New Orleans family, and he was sole heir to ten million dollars.

Fate had been almost excessively kind to him. As if wealth, good looks, and popularity weren't enough, he had founded his own antique store six years earlier, and it was hugely profitable. He was young—just thirty-two—with excellent health. He was intelligent, he was liked by his friends and even by his employees, and he had the respect of his competitors, most of whom were willing to concede, however grudgingly, that he was a very, very good antique dealer. Not only was his family highly respected in New Orleans, but if there had been a French equivalent to the Mayflower, the DeVarnay ancestors would have arrived on it.

Unfortunately, he also was missing. Had he suddenly crapped out after rolling sevens and elevens all his life? No one knew. On a Wednesday night two weeks earlier, he had left for St. Louis to attend an auction. He telephoned his widowed mother to tell her he was about to start for the airport—he always called her at least once a day. Shortly after that, he called a cab. Then he called back and cancelled the cab.

An expensive leather suitcase, a gift from his mother, was missing from his home, as were his toilet articles and some clothing. Obviously he had packed for the trip and left home with his suitcase. A quick check in St. Louis revealed that he arrived there, claimed his reserved hotel room, and attended the auction. He made a purchase at the auction and had it shipped to his store in New Orleans. All of that was as expected.

The one significant irregularity was that he failed to telephone his mother on Thursday or at any time after that. This had never happened before except when he was in Europe. She hadn't heard from him since the call he made Wednesday night just before he left for the airport. He checked out of his St. Louis hotel on schedule early the next morning, Friday, but he missed his return flight to New Orleans, and neither he nor his suitcase had been seen since.

Jolitte DeVarnay, DeVarnay's mother, was severely critical of the way the police had handled the case, but most missing men eventually show up again, screaming for help when they sober up or run out of money. DeVarnay hadn't.

As far as anyone could discover, he had no enemies, no business or personal crisis to run away from, no secret life about to come unraveled. He was as open and above-board as the heir to ten million dollars could be. Even so, the police figured he had his own good and sufficient reasons for dropping out of sight for a week or two, and eventually he would be heard from.

His mother informed anyone who would listen that the police were idiots. Marc was a good son, he was close to his mother, and he wouldn't have gone off of his own volition without saying anything to her about it.

Jolitte DeVarnay was not only a wealthy pillar of New Orleans society and politics, but she had long since promoted herself to duchess. She took her case to a series of higher courts—first the police commissioner, then the mayor, and finally the governor. It went without saying that she was on a first name basis with all three. Each in turn gave the police a prod or two but refused to call out the National Guard or ask the president to declare New Orleans a disaster area. By that time DeVarnay had been missing for two weeks, no one seemed to be giving his disappearance the serious attention his mother thought it deserved, and she was desperate.

On the recommendation of several wealthy friends, she made one more telephone call—to Lambert and Associates. Probably the fact that we call ourselves "Investigative Consultants" influenced her decision. She sounded like the kind of person who would feel humiliated if she had to engage a detective. Once she agreed to a retainer that would make even her bank account wince and indicated a willingness to accept a final bill in accordance with her status as millionaire and duchess, Raina Lambert took her complaint very seriously indeed and gave it the highest priority.

Meaning that she telephoned me in Savannah and dumped it into my lap.

"What do you make of it?" I asked Mara.

"It's an either-or case," she said.

"Explain yourself."

"Either something drastic has happened to him, or there are secrets in his life no one knows anything about."

"Or both," I suggested. "The place to begin looking for a missing New Orleans businessman should have been New Orleans, not St. Louis."

The photos had arrived when we reached her office, and both of us took time to study them. Marc DeVarnay certainly was a fine-appearing man. He was clean-shaven, his thick, dark hair had just the right stylish suggestion of a wave, and—as the fact sheet indicated—he appeared to be in robust good health. He also appeared to be the intense type of person who takes himself and life much too seriously, but a shy smile in one of the photos made me wonder whether he might be concealing a sense of humor. He looked much too open and forthright to be a successful businessman, but that could have been an asset for him.

We started at his hotel. Since there already had been inquiries by the St. Louis police at the request of the New Orleans police, our visit surprised no one. The attitude was a resigned, "Here we go again." His photo was duly studied and identified; his registration card, a copy of which we already had in his dossier, was displayed. The signature matched as well as signatures usually match. He had stayed there several times before but at long enough intervals so that no one remembered him. The hotel staff couldn't say whether he had behaved normally, but it found him a pleasant guest who caused no problems and tipped generously. He had checked in late that Wednesday night, he was out all day on Thursday as far as anyone knew, and he checked out and left early Friday morning.

DeVarnay had taken a cab to the airport, and the St. Louis police had located the driver and talked with him. He recognized DeVarnay's photo and also the description of the leather suitcase. The one thing he remembered vividly was that when they reached the airport, DeVarnay had given the skycaps the brush-off and entered the terminal building carrying the leather suitcase himself—which surprised the cab driver. DeVarnay obviously was capable of carrying a suitcase, if he wanted to, or even two or three of them, but he had seemed like an affluent type who would disdain such drudgery.

Our next stop was the auction house. The Forsythe Galleries were a trendy art merchandising establishment. I disliked them the moment I walked through the door, and I disliked Jeremy Forsythe, its owner/manager, even more. He was the prissy kind of businessman—small mustache; small smile; small, evasive eyes. His galleries seemed to be hugely successful, but I wouldn't have bought anything at all with confidence there, not even a da Vinci cosigned by Michelangelo with an attestation of authenticity from Rembrandt.

He was candid enough with us. "I know all about it—the police were asking," he said. "Certainly DeVarnay was here. I remember him only too well. Since he was going to disappear anyway, I wish he'd done it earlier—before he screwed up my auction."

We asked him what he meant by that.

"DeVarnay has a reputation," he said. "He's rich, he's built a very nice business in a short time, and he's maybe the country's foremost Mallard collector. Supposedly he's also an important authority on Mallard. I'd never met him before, but I'd heard all about him."

Both Mara and I wanted to know who or what Mallard was.

"Prudent Mallard was a famous nineteenth-century New Orleans furniture maker," Forsythe said condescendingly. "We don't see much of his work this far north, but he's very popular with New Orleans collectors. I'd managed to pick up five exceptional items, all in excellent condition, along with a few minor things, so I put them in a private auction with other pieces I'd been holding back. It was a special sale for serious Midwest collectors—admission by invitation only—and I invited DeVarnay and a few other out-of-state dealers and collectors I knew were interested in the type of things I was offering. The Mallard items were so good I thought DeVarnay would bid up the prices, in which case our local collectors, seeing how interested a big wheel like him was, would try to buy them themselves. Instead, he did very little bidding—he made a few cursory passes at the main Mallard pieces and then dropped out. That was his privilege. Unfortunately, I'd made the mistake of puffing him in advance, and because the out-of-town expert obviously wasn't interested, the local people thought there must be something wrong with the items, and they wouldn't bid, either. It was almost a disaster. Just to add insult to injury, DeVarnay suddenly came to life almost at the end and bought a small nightstand, a throwaway item, for more than it was worth."

"You say you'd never met DeVarnay?"

"No, and I hope I never meet him again. The police showed me his photo," he added when Mara pulled one out of her envelope. "That's him. He was here, but I can't imagine why he came. He thoroughly screwed up my auction by an almost total lack of interest even though he did buy one item."

"How did he pay for it?" I asked.

"In cash, and he arranged to have it shipped to his store in New Orleans. Then he left. Where he went from here was no concern of mine and still isn't."

Back in the car, Mara paused before starting the motor. "He could have been preoccupied by something—the question of whether he was going to disappear, for example. Or where he was going to disappear to. That would account for the inexplicable behavior."

"Perhaps so. But in that case, why bother to attend the auction at all?"

"Because he was expected to. Or because he hadn't made up his mind."

"There's another explanation. Forsythe had DeVarnay set up to make a sucker of him. DeVarnay was supposed to function as a shill and bid the prices up, and if he wanted something himself, he would have to pay through his nose. DeVarnay saw what was going on and refused to play. Buying a nondescript nightstand at the end was his way of thumbing his nose at Forsythe. That's one possibility. It's also possible that DeVarnay really is an expert, and those fine items weren't nearly as good as Forsythe represented them to be."

"What would that have to do with his disappearance?"

"Perhaps nothing. Up to the point Friday morning when he entered the airport terminal carrying his own suitcase, he hadn't disappeared. He was right where he was supposed to be. His disappearance happened after that."

"I suppose he could have rented a car or met someone—"

"Or taken a different plane from the one he was supposed to take. This is where we go to work."

How much of a problem you have finding traces of a person who passed through a place two weeks earlier depends on the place. With a village on the edge of an outback, which sees on the average one strange face a month, you probably won't have much difficulty. With an airport serving a metropolis, with thousands of people passing through it daily if not hourly, you'll have a job on your hands.

No one we talked with remembered Marc DeVarnay. Eventually the airlines' computers saved us, but it took time. It was early afternoon before we established that he had left St. Louis on a MidAmerican flight to Denver, traveling under his own name, shortly before he was supposed to depart for New Orleans. He bought his ticket with cash.

At that point I needed instructions. I telephoned Raina Lambert at her work number in Minneapolis and dictated a report to her answering machine. It wasn't a long report, but I had to call her back twice in order to get it finished between the beeps. Then Mara and I went back to her office to wait for Raina to telephone.

When she did, she greeted me with a question. "If DeVarnay went on to Denver, why are you still in St. Louis?"

"There are odds and ends that need cleaning up here," I objected. "Did something happen that sent DeVarnay winging into the blue? Did he meet someone? It would be a great help to know why he's on the run."

"Tell Mara to give it another day and then report directly to me. I have something else for you. DeVarnay was carrying traveler's checks, and he's cashed some of them. Four that we know about. He always carried a small reserve of money in traveler's checks when he traveled, five hundred dollars in fifty-dollar checks. They're issued by a New Orleans bank, and four of them have been returned to the bank in the usual way."

She dictated the names and addresses of the four firms that had cashed them and the dates they were cashed. When I finished writing, I looked at the list and whistled. Three of the checks had been cashed the day he disappeared: One in Denver, one in Reno, and a third in San Francisco. One was cashed in Seattle on the following day.

"Do you still want me to go to Denver?" I asked. "Obviously Seattle is the last place he surfaced—as far as we know—but that was two weeks ago. Today he may be cashing checks in

Nome or Beijing."

"I have someone trying to pick up his trail in Seattle. See what you can find out along the way."

By then it was late afternoon, and the people DeVarnay had encountered in his travels would no longer be on duty. I stayed overnight in St. Louis, working with Mara in a vain attempt at finding out how DeVarnay spent his one free evening there.

The next morning, taking the same flight DeVarnay had, I was off on the next lap of the great DeVarnay goose chase. In Denver, no one at the gift shop that had cashed his traveler's check remembered him. I asked about the shop's procedure with traveler's checks. The check had to be no larger than fifty dollars, and DeVarnay had to purchase something, show his driver's license, and sign the check in the clerk's presence.

He had parted company with MidAmerican Airlines when his plane landed, and no employee remembered him. After more recourse to airlines computers, I placed him on a Sierra Western flight bound for Reno. Again he paid for the ticket with cash.

He had taken an afternoon flight to Reno, and so did I. I spent the flight pondering his unnatural preference for small airlines. In Reno, he had cashed another traveler's check—this time in a downtown casino where gamblers cash checks of all kinds as fast as they run out of money. He had shown his driver's license and endorsed the check in the presence of the cashier. No one remembered him. I hoped he had taken time off from his frantic dash west to play a few slot machines. Otherwise, he wasn't getting any more fun out of this trek than I was.

He had taken a Sierra Western night flight to San Francisco, and so did I. He had checked in at the Golden Sunset Motel near the airport, paying for one night with a traveler's check plus some cash. I stayed at the same motel.

Early the next morning, which was a Saturday for me, I caught a Pacific Northern Airlines flight to Seattle, the same one DeVarnay had taken on Sunday two weeks earlier. The last traveler's check we knew about had been cashed at an airport gift shop in the Seattle terminal.

Mort Morris, the Seattle agent for Lambert and Associates, met me at the airport. He was a big, bristly man with a disarming smile, and it was said he could talk his way through a brick wall. He had already done the obvious.

Marc DeVarnay had not booked any flight under his own name, nor had he rented a car or stayed at any hotel or motel near the airport or in downtown Seattle. We set about systematically eliminating everything that was left. That done, we started over again, and the next step was harder. Instead of merely asking about a name, one of us had to call personally and see if anyone recognized DeVarnay's photo.

We had an almost nibble from a bus driver on the Los Angeles run. At first he thought he'd had DeVarnay as a passenger. Then he changed his mind.

And that was all. When we finished, Marc DeVarnay was just as thoroughly missing as he had been in the beginning. All we had established was that he now was missing from a different place.

On Wednesday night, precisely one week after she had cancelled my Savannah vacation, Raina Lambert telephoned. She listened to my report without comment. Very little can be said about a long, extremely thorough list of negatives.

"What do you think?" she asked finally.

"Is there any insanity in the DeVarnay family?"

"Not that I know of. What does that have to do with it?"

"There is now. No one but an insane person behaves this way."

"So what do you suggest?"

"I still think this search should have begun in New Orleans. DeVarnay very neatly led us all the way to Seattle and left us here. Then he went wherever he intended to go all along, using an assumed name."

"So why look in New Orleans when he was last seen in Seattle?"

"Because the reason he disappeared is in New Orleans, not here."

"Maybe so," she mused. "All right. Come to New Orleans."

"I didn't say I wanted to look for him in New Orleans. I'd rather go to Savannah. If DeVarnay wants to disappear that badly, let him."

"Catch a night flight if there is one," she said firmly. "Call me back and give me your flight information."

She was still the boss. I hung up and dialed an airline.

So I arrived in New Orleans and was immediately launched on a second wild goose chase. During the three hours I spent sitting on Old Jake's porch, guarding his corpse and communing with undiluted nature, I had ample time to ask myself why I didn't find a job that occasionally made sense.

CHAPTER FOUR

The police took an unconscionable amount of time getting there, and it seemed much longer than that because I had nothing to do but wait. They also took their time in getting around to dealing with Tosche and me, and we almost had to find our way back to Pointe Neuve in the dark.

They weren't quite finished with us then. A deputy met us at the dock, and, after we had refilled the motor's gas tank and located Ed to return his key, we were escorted into the presence of the sheriff himself. He had set up a temporary headquarters at his parked police car, and he was directing the questioning of every Pointe Neuve resident about the stranger Old Jake had been seen with.

He looked more like a folksy used car dealer than an officer of the law, but he certainly was no one's fool in police matters. He already knew all about me from reports his men had radioed, but he wanted a peek for himself.

From his questions, I gathered that all of the local residents except the witnesses we had already talked with were disclaiming any knowledge of either Old Jake or the stranger.

First he cross-examined me on my testimony. Then, as though he half suspected I might have dented Old Jake's skull myself, he turned his attention to my own movements two weeks previously.

"Jay Pletcher?" he asked finally, giving me a searching look. "Is that J-A-Y?"

I'd had a long, exhausting day, and I definitely had not

received my money's worth for the time invested. The deputies at the *cabon* had been downright miserly in passing along information.

"It's 'J'," I said. "The letter 'J.' I was named J-A-G-D after my German great-grandfather, but no one can pronounce it, so I just call myself 'J'."

He decided to ignore that. "You're staying at the Hotel Maria Theresa?"

"I haven't stayed there yet, but I'm registered there."

"Just so we know where to find you. Better plan on sticking around for awhile."

"I'll be here a lot longer than that," I promised.

Tosche and I trudged back to his jeep. Fortunately it had stopped raining.

"This pretty much nails down the rumor about DeVarnay being seen down here, doesn't it?" Tosche asked as we drove off.

"The police certainly will take it that way," I said. "To me, it's just one more damned complication. The fact that a man's suitcase is there doesn't automatically prove he arrived with it. It would help to know what was found in the *cabon* in the way of fingerprints, but I'll get that eventually. If DeVarnay left them all over the place, that, of course, settles it. If not, there are other possibilities, and all of them will have to be looked into. The most urgent problem right now is to find out what could have taken a millionaire antique dealer down to Pointe Neuve in the first place. According to his personal history, it wasn't hunting or fishing, and from what I saw of Old Jake and his *cabon*, it couldn't have been business." I thought for a moment. "I'll have to talk to a customs officer."

"You mean—he could have been smuggling something?"

"It's a possibility. I don't know enough about the sources of antiques to know whether there would be any profit in smuggling them. Or in smuggling something else, such as drugs, under the guise of importing antiques. I'll have to ask about it. A customs officer is the logical place to start."

"You'd want a special agent," Tosche said. "My brother knows one."

"A special customs agent?"

"Yeah. Dick—that's my brother—sometimes comes up with tips for him."

"What's your brother's business?" I asked.

"That's hard to say. Mostly he buys and sells. He knows where and how to dispose of things. You show him something, he knows who might be interested. He sells some of the stuff himself in the flea market at the New Orleans French Market."

"Can he make a living that way?"

"He seems to. He isn't getting rich, but he gets along all right, and he enjoys what he's doing. If you have any investigating you want done in the French Quarter, he knows it inside out. He can arrange for someone else to look after his tables at the market when he's busy with other things, and it'd give him something different to do. My brother gets bored easily. Until he started this buying and selling kick, he never held a job long."

"If he's available, I'm sure I can use him," I said. "Just for a start, I'd like to meet this special customs agent as soon as possible. If DeVarnay has stuck his foot in something, I want to know about it."

"I'll call him now," Tosche said.

We stopped at a gasoline station, and he called his brother. When he came back to his jeep, he announced, "He'll give his friend a call and see if he's available tonight. Either way, he'll be waiting for us in your hotel lobby."

Neither of us had much to say for the remainder of the ride. Eventually the lights of New Orleans appeared on the horizon, and we crossed the Greater New Orleans Bridge and plunged into them.

The streets of the New Orleans French Quarter are not the world's best-lit thoroughfares. Streetlights are infrequent and sometimes oddly placed—they may be located some distance from intersections where one would expect to find them. The French Quarter's numerous galleries, or balconies, further complicate the lighting. If the lamps were located at the height common for them in most cities, French Quarter sidewalks would be deeply shadowed by the galleries. Perhaps this is the reason the lights are placed lower than usual, but that further reduces their effectiveness.

The principle streets are well-lit despite this because each business establishment lights its own store front and the adjacent sidewalk with floodlights attached beneath the building's second floor gallery. On side streets, however, such as the one where the Hotel Maria Theresa was located, gloom may prevail.

Although the hotel was small and family operated, its security was commendable. The lobby's outside door was kept locked at all times. One rang the bell; the duty clerk pressed a button that sounded a buzzer and released the lock. Then he checked to see who was entering. We passed the test and left the dim street for a small, warmly lit lobby, where we found Tosche's brother, Dick, waiting for us. If it hadn't been for Dick's height and sturdy build, he would have looked like a high school kid. His blue eyes, slow grin, and rugged good looks echoed those of his brother. The only clashing note was produced by his long hair, which made him look like an exceptionally robust hippy. He gave his brother an affectionate hug, and then he very politely shook hands with me.

"He'll tell you all about it," Charlie told him. "I've got to run."

They exchanged hugs again, Charlie turned at the door, gave us a wave, and disappeared into the gloom outside. I hadn't offered to pay him. He had made his deal with Raina, and I had no idea what it was, so I left the obligation for her to settle.

In that casual fashion, I found I had switched guides. Dick said, "The customs agent will be waiting for us in a bar near here."

"Does the bar serve food?" I asked. Since the skimpy airline breakfast, I'd had only the sandwich in the Pointe Neuve café and the three stolen bottles of Blackened Voodoo Lager Beer I consumed while I waited for the deputies.

He said of course.

"What about jambalaya?" I asked.

He thought jambalaya would be straining the bar's resources at that time of night, but probably it could manage almost any kind of Po-Boy sandwich I could think of.

"Good," I said. "I'm hungry enough to take on a live alligator, but I may never be able to face jambalaya again."

The thought of food made me feel immensely better. I asked for my key at the desk, discovered that neither Raina Lambert nor anyone else had left a message for me, and invited Dick Tosche up to my room while I changed.

I'd had adventures enough for one day. All I wanted was a bite to eat, a quiet talk with the special customs agent, and then a good night's sleep. Unfortunately, Fate had my future programmed differently.

As I mentioned earlier, my room was on the second floor with a gallery overlooking the hotel's charming courtyard. Because I have lived in hotel and motel rooms much of my adult life, I know all the quirks there are concerning locks and doors, and when I left my luggage that morning, I had found out which sort I had to contend with at the Hotel Marie Theresa. As a result, I unlocked the door and opened it in one smooth movement, at the same time motioning with my head for Dick Tosche to enter first.

He did—at a run. He tore into the room and just failed to nail a fleeing figure that went out the door to the gallery in a flash and disappeared over the railing. It wasn't an enormous drop to the ground if one first hung by one's hands from the gallery floor, and of course that is what the intruder did. The only impression I got was of an unusually tall, lank, shabbily dressed male.

Tosche didn't hesitate; he followed him, and I chased after the two of them, noticing as I passed through the room that one of my suitcases was lying open on the bed where I certainly hadn't left it. When I reached the railing, the intruder, running with immensely long strides, was vanishing into a doorway.

Tosche was ten feet behind him. I would have been a poor third, so I went to phone the desk.

A few seconds passed before anyone responded. I was still blinking because I hadn't expected my flea market buy-and-sell expert to be such a peerless man of action. I explained the situation to the night clerk: There'd been an intruder in my room. He had exited by way of the balcony, and my friend had chased after him.

"They just ran out through the lobby," the night clerk said. He hesitated. "Should I call the police?"

"I really do think they might appreciate it. This character seems to have a facility for getting into hotel rooms. If he does that often, he'll give New Orleans a bad name."

"Right," the clerk said. I was just about to hang up when I heard, over the phone, the outside bell ring and the buzzer sound as the clerk responded. He announced, "Your friend just came back."

"Alone?" I asked.

The clerk sounded surprised. "Yes. Alone."

"Then he didn't catch him. I'm sorry to hear that. Send him up."

I turned to the open suitcase. As far as I could determine without touching anything, we had interrupted the intruder just as he was getting started, and nothing was missing.

Tosche arrived muttering angrily to himself. "There was a car waiting down the street for him."

"Never mind," I said. "You get an A plus for effort. You have super reflexes. Did you get a good look at him?"

"Good enough. I know the guy. He's a street character—goes by the name of Little Boy. Maybe because he's so tall and gawky. I also got the make of the car that picked him up, but they had the license number covered."

I gave him my sincere congratulations. "Some people live out their entire lives without ever finding out what fate intended them for," I said. "Thanks to this little adventure, that won't happen to you. You're a natural-born witness. All of this will interest the police exceedingly, and the more interested they are, the less they're inclined to hurry. You'd better telephone the bar and let your friend know we'll be late."

A short time later the police arrived along with the manager. When they learned that Tosche had recognized the intruder, they suddenly had visions of solving a number of similar crimes at one swoop. They sent for a fingerprint expert and assigned one of their number to take a detailed statement from Tosche. Another officer huddled with the hotel's manager and tried to figure out how the intruder had gotten into the hotel and then into my room.

As far as I was concerned, these were the wrong questions. I wanted to know how he knew which room was mine.

When a sergeant arrived, I gave him time to take in the situation, and then I briefed him on my earlier adventures. For confirmation, I referred him to his colleague, Lieutenant George Keig.

"Do you think this may be connected?" he asked.

"If you've ever doubted that the night has ears, this is your proof. The sheriff announced to anyone within hearing that I was staying at the Hotel Marie Theresa. Obviously someone did hear and got curious about me."

"But you came directly back."

I said patiently, "One keeps stumbling onto all kinds of unexpected modern conveniences in the hinterland, and one of them is the telephone. It would be stretching credulity—mine, anyway—to suggest that Little Boy's breaking into my room at this particular moment was only a coincidence. One of those clannish Cajuns overheard the sheriff and informed someone by telephone that Charlie Tosche and a stranger, name of Pletcher, had been making inquiries about Old Jake and his companion, after which they went to Old Jake's *cabon* and found his body. Pletcher was staying at the Marie Theresa Hotel. Almost any Pointe Neuve resident with an insistent curiosity could have picked up that information and passed it along. The only thing that puzzles me is why anyone would bother."

The sergeant nodded at my opened suitcase. "What did he

find out?"

"Nothing except my name on the ID tag. We must have interrupted him just as he was getting started. He didn't even have time to mess up my wardrobe."

"We know all about Little Boy," the sergeant said. "His name is Griff Wylan. The 'Griff' probably is short for something, but no one knows what, not even Wylan. At least, he says he doesn't. He had a long juvenile record, but he's supposed to be going straight, now."

Dick finished his statement, I made a brief one, and then we claimed urgent business and left the room to the fingerprint expert. The manager followed me down the hall, fervently promising to have the lock changed on my room at once.

I doubted that it would make any difference. Little Boy must have entered the room through the door—he wouldn't have risked climbing onto the gallery from the well lighted courtyard—so he certainly owned an effective master key. Probably it would work just as easily on any replacement lock the management had. It was more important to find out how he knew which room was mine, but the police would be looking into that.

I bade the manager good evening, told him I probably would be out late—which certainly wasn't unusual behavior for a New Orleans hotel guest—and left him.

Outside the hotel door, we found the street marked off by a blaze of light at either end of the dim block: In one direction, Royal Street; in the other, Bourbon Street. Scatterings of tourists were drifting past on their way from one to the other. Even at that distance, a blare of music reached us from Bourbon Street. New Orleans jazz can be good, indifferent, or thoroughly bad, but it is always loud.

We turned toward Royal Street, where the sidewalks were jammed with tourists casually shopping or avidly discussing restaurant menus. We struggled through the crowds for two blocks and then escaped into a side street.

L'Endroit, a bar and night club located between Bourbon and Royal Streets, was convenient for any kind of French Quarter rendezvous. Further, it was large, dimly lit—with dangling ceiling ornaments shaped like musical instruments that threw convenient shadows—and throbbing with exuberantly loud live music that made it difficult to hear one's own conversation, let alone overhear someone else's.

Dick introduced me to "John," a heavy-set man with a large, good-humored face and a thick but neatly trimmed beard. He wore a beret, a vest with sparkling ornamentation on it, and, in one ear, a gold earring with a small diamond. One glance at him shattered any stereotype I might have been fostering concerning customs agents.

We took places on either side of him and ordered drinks. I thanked him for waiting and gave him my card. He glanced at it and murmured into my ear during one of the band's less noisy passages, "Dick said you wanted to see a special agent."

Dick was sipping his beer and watching the crowd. I leaned close to John's ear—the one without the earring—and described my day's adventures. The steady, blaring beat of the music began to get on my nerves long before I finished, but John seemed to ignore it. He listened intelligently and didn't interrupt with questions.

Finally he asked, "Are you buying it that DeVarnay really was the man with Old Jake?"

"I'm regarding it with extreme skepticism," I said. "The waitress was a convincing witness, and the men weren't bad, but before I can chew it thoroughly and swallow it, I'll have to know what a person with his background could have been doing down there."

"Did he fish or hunt?"

"Not according to what I know about him. I'll have to find out for certain. In the meantime, I'm wondering whether there would be any money in smuggling antiques. He seems to have built a highly prosperous business quickly. Since smugglers play rough, it might explain his disappearance. He could have been done away with, or he could have found it expedient to go into hiding."

John meditated for a moment. "I'm certain stolen antiques find their way into the New Orleans market all the time," he said. "These would come from surrounding states, some of them peddled illegally by heirs without other heirs knowing about it. Of course my department wouldn't come into that. An antique dealer shops around and picks up things at second hand stores, or discard sales where the owner doesn't know their true value, or anywhere at all. Depending on his personal standards of honesty, he also may have contacts that steer stolen goods his way. It's all in the day's work to him.

"But I've never heard of any activity in smuggled antiques, and I don't know of any instance where a legitimate firm in the French Quarter has brought contraband into this country by way of imported goods or antiques—hidden in hollowed out pedestals or some such thing. Handicrafts and jewelry have no duty if they're imported from any of a list of disadvantaged countries, so there would be no point in smuggling anything from there. We do have to watch the possibility that goods might be sent to one of those countries from Europe and then shipped from there to the U.S. to avoid duties."

"Antique stores frequently deal in jewelry," I remarked. "Sometimes it's difficult to tell whether it's old or new. Does anyone smuggle jewelry these days?"

"Rolex watches are a problem right now, but these most commonly are smuggled in by individuals. They've bought one and don't want to pay the duty on it. If DeVarnay is smuggling anything, it wouldn't be antiques—jewelry or whatever. If a thing is a hundred years old, it's duty free anyway, so why smuggle it?

"But it might be profitable to smuggle in expensive new jewelry disguised in some way. Another possibility is antique art. There's a big underground market for pre-Columbian art from Central and South America. Pieces are stolen from archeological sites, or native temples, or even from museums. If they're authentic, they can bring huge prices. They aren't often brought in through New Orleans, though. The most common route is across the Mexican border with a tourist trying to pass the item off as a fake picked up cheap. There are plenty of fakes around, so sometimes it works. It's illegal to take those things out of the originating country, and we have agreements to cooperate on this end, which makes the operation illegal all the way—and that results in scarcity and higher prices. Ivory goods are another profitable item. Anything relating to endangered species can't be brought in legally, so the smuggling of fancy ivory carvings is highly lucrative.

"Except for those few things, I can't see your antique dealer profiting from smuggling. Of course his store could be a sideline or a front, and his business down in the bayou country could have had nothing to do with antiques except that he uses them as a cover for his smuggling profits. We had a case here where two businessmen with legitimate operations went into drug smuggling to get rich quicker. They bought barges and leased them to smugglers. When caught, they claimed they were businessmen innocently leasing barges. Since they were on the scene at three in the morning, the court didn't buy that."

"I hadn't thought of DeVarnay's business being a blind," I said. "I haven't looked at the store, yet, but from what I've heard, it certainly sounds respectable."

"It would," John assured me.

"Then his smuggling—if he's doing any—may have no connection with antiques?"

"The antique business would provide an excellent cover. Antiques come from odd places, some of them shady though perfectly legal. The markups can be tremendous on valuable items picked up cheap, so the store could be used to disguise the profits on something like drugs, which can be tremendous, too."

"How would it be managed?" I asked.

"That depends on where your antique dealer stands in the hierarchy. Usually there's a mother ship. Drugs are transshipped—maybe to something inconspicuous like shrimp or fishing boats or to a special small boat that's fast and doesn't draw much water. It may be extremely expensive with the very latest in electronic equipment, costing a couple of hundred thousand dollars, and the operators would have no compunction about abandoning it if circumstances require that. The profits are so huge they can write it off as one of the costs of doing business. They would need a safe place to take the drugs to, so it wouldn't be unusual for them to have a way station down in the swamps."

"Something like Old Jake's *cabon*?"

"Right, but they would prefer a place where the drugs could be picked up by truck as well as by boat. The more options they have, the better. Or they might take them to a dock where there's plenty of legitimate all-night activity and it wouldn't be unusual for a truck to be picking up a load at two in the morning. There are all sorts of angles, and these people are ingenious."

"And ruthless," I suggested.

"Especially ruthless. There's so much money involved. Down in the bayous, the smuggling business can easily get mixed up with legitimate business. It's a cash operation, but so is fishing. People have their own boats, they set their own hours, and they have their own private fishing territories. They have no legal title to them, but they defend them as though they did. If they find someone else poaching, they may resort to gunfire.

A few years ago, there was a problem with Viet Nam refugees. The refugees had been fishermen in Viet Nam, so when they arrived in the U.S., they started fishing, and actual gun wars resulted when they encroached on someone else's territory. No one down there is going to be concerned about how you make your money, whether it's by fishing, or some kind of import business, or by smuggling. As long as you don't interfere with them, they won't interfere with you. An outsider could quickly get into trouble. You'd better know the people down there, and make sure they know you, before you start any kind of operation."

"Then DeVarnay could have got in over his depth."

"It's possible. It's even likely if he was trying to operate there without taking the necessary precautions."

"But his antique business has been flourishing for years. If it's founded on illegal imports, he must have been at it for some time. Presumably he would be established there by now. And if he got in over his depth, I suppose he might have been abducted, but why was Old Jake killed?"

"DeVarnay could have been trying to shift his territory or expand it, but of course all of this is sheer speculation. I don't suppose you have a bit of evidence that he was anything but an especially shrewd antique dealer."

"That's true," I admitted. "But in that case, what was he doing down in Old Jake's *cabon*?"

John grinned and shook his head.

"You aren't impressed with my antique dealer as a smuggler?" I asked.

"Not on the basis of what you've told me. If you turn up any real evidence, we'll be glad to work on it."

He gave me a telephone number I could call if I wanted to see him again.

Dick Tosche and I walked back to my hotel.

"Have there been any rumors about DeVarnay?" I asked.

"You mean among the street people? Most of them know about him. Not only is he a prominent antique dealer, but he pays well for tips on where to find antiques. Information like that circulates with the speed of light."

"Are there any rumors about him being involved in something shady?"

"I haven't heard any. Do you want me to inquire around?"

"Please do. Just for a start, I'm curious to know whether he has a street connection—a person or persons who work for him regularly."

At the hotel, we asked the night clerk whether the police had made any progress. He told us someone belatedly remembered that Little Boy—under his real name, Griff Wylan—had worked for the hotel for a short time a couple of years before, and several of the employees knew him. Following that up, a detective figured out what had happened. Little Boy had contrived to get himself admitted through a rear employees' entrance by pretending to call on a custodian who lived at the hotel. From there he made his way to the front, got my room number from the register when the duty clerk had to leave the desk for a moment, and entered with a master key.

That answered everything except what he had been after and why, thus leaving the puzzle just as murky as it had been before.

"How can I get in touch with you?" I asked Dick.

"Sister Merlina will take messages for me." He paused and then added, "She's a witch. Certified. Nice girl, too. She runs a little curio and witchcraft shop out on Decatur." He dictated the phone number.

"That sounds splendid," I told him. "Before this is over, we'll probably need her."

CHAPTER FIVE

Raina Lambert telephoned me at seven the next morning, Friday, and I had to go to a pay phone and call her back. She adamantly refuses to speak on any telephone line that passes through a switchboard, a principle based on past bitter experience, but it sometimes results in our holding conferences in odd settings. Her first move in any strange city is to arrange for a private phone with an unlisted number.

But she wasn't in this city, she was in Minneapolis, and she was wary about my hotel's switchboard. I braved a gloomy morning and the French Quarter's debris-cluttered but otherwise deserted streets to stroll down to a small, self-service, twenty-four-hour laundry that was calling itself a sudsomat.

Along the way, I noted that two street people had already taken up positions near the hotel. One was a white man in his middle thirties, pleasant looking and neatly dressed in jeans and a flowered sport shirt. He'd even had his hair cut within recent memory, and he could have passed as a tourist almost anywhere in New Orleans. He certainly didn't look like a beggar, but he had a battered mug in his hand, and he rattled coins at me as I approached.

"Change?" he murmured. "Spare some change?"

I looked him squarely in the eye and shook my head. He reacted with a grin and a nod. Probably all street people have to be philosophers in order to survive.

The other street person, a buxom black woman with an odd looking arrangement on her head, was leaning against a building on the other side of the hotel. She had a paper cup in her hand, so I assumed that she also was collecting change.

The coin laundry was a good place for a confidential telephone conversation. There were already a few customers there, but with several washing machines and dryers pounding away, I wasn't likely to be overheard. I called Raina's Minneapolis number on the laundry's pay phone and reported. She listened in total silence, which meant she was as flabbergasted by what had happened as I was.

"How good are the Pointe Neuve witnesses?" she asked.

"Eva is first-rate. There's no doubt whatsoever that she saw someone who closely resembled DeVarnay. Old Jake and his friend were in the café for some time. She took their orders and served them, and she seems to have kept an eye on them. She may even have been curious enough to refill their water glasses a couple of times on the chance of overhearing what they were talking about. She's that type. Then she waited on them again in the store. I'd call her a credible witness whether she's right or not. Bert is just so-so. He was working on his boat and probably didn't give the visitors more than a passing glance or at most two. The other man, Jacques, exchanged a few words with them. He also saw Old Jake's friend without his hat. He's not as good as Eva, but he would be convincing. Taken together, the three of them make a case."

"That's what I was afraid of," Raina said. "What do you know about Old Jake?"

"No one knows very much about Old Jake. To be fair, until yesterday, no one had ever wanted to know very much about Old Jake. He'd been around for years, picking up a bit of change now and then as a kind of guide for fishermen and hunters. The locals—the Cajuns—regarded him with scorn because he was an interloper and really not much more than a tenderfoot himself. Other than that, he kept to himself and bothered no one, and most people considered him harmless. As I mentioned, the police down there weren't talking—at least not to me. Maybe you can use whatever political clout our client has and pry something out of them."

"What's your next move?" she asked.

"I'll need to be a lot better informed about DeVarnay's antique business before I can even start making sense out of this thing."

"I'll see what I can arrange," she said. "I'll call you back. Stay there."

"Just a moment," I said. "Did DeVarnay have any hobbies?"

"His mother didn't mention any."

"Did he do any cooking? I don't mean outdoor burn-it-yourself dogs and burgers. Did he ever prepare special dishes for his friends?"

"I'll ask."

"If he did, I'd like to know what he cooked."

She called back seven minutes later. "The store opens at ten o'clock. A man named Doug Kallenor will meet you there. Kallenor is Jolitte DeVarnay's accountant and financial advisor. When she found out her son was missing, she asked him to perform an audit and then keep an eye on the business."

"She's an unusually astute mother. I'll see Kallenor at ten. What about the cooking?"

"He never did anything elaborate. No formal dinners, but he had favorite dishes he would sometimes cook up for special occasions—gumbos or jambalayas."

"That's what I was afraid of."

"What does his cooking have to do with it?"

"A jambalaya is a mixture of ingredients of which the principle one is rice. Other than that, the cook uses whatever comes to hand in the way of meat and vegetables, and he adds his own personal blend of spices."

"I know that. I've eaten it many times."

"It's a mixture of ingredients," I said again. "One of the synonyms for 'mixture' is 'mess,' which is what we've gotten ourselves into. I'll explain later. Are we still keeping it under our hats that DeVarnay is missing?"

"With the police looking for him? Don't be silly."

"Very well. I'll try to make discreet use of it."

I strolled back to my hotel. The black woman with the odd headdress eyed me from a distance. The young man rattled his cup at me again. This time I ignored him, but as I walked past, my subconscious did a sudden flip and reminded me that street people do not normally go out begging at seven in the morning when there is no one in the streets. Beggars on side streets are rare at any time.

I carried the thought into the hotel with me and meditated it while I enjoyed a light breakfast. Complementary croissants and coffee were being served to the guests. I substituted café-au-lait for the coffee. With that, and the croissants, and the charming courtyard, I almost managed to convince myself that I really was in New Orleans and not stranded in some oasis down in the bayou country.

When I emerged, the day was still gloomy, but at least it was not raining—yet. Sunshine and mild weather were predicted for Savannah. The young man gave his cup an anticipatory jingle the moment I came out of the hotel. I wanted a closer look at the odd headdress of the other beggar, the black woman, so I turned in her direction. She was wearing three billed tourist caps, one on top of the other. She must have sewn them together to keep them in position. The topmost hat displayed the Tabasco Sauce logo. This popular Louisiana product is featured on a number of tourist items, from aprons to shoe laces. Various small souvenirs were dangling on strings from the woman's three hats—a key ring; an ear ring; an alligator foot; a miniature Mardi Gras mask; a package of matches from Broussard's, a famous restaurant; a cluster of alligator teeth; a coin purse; several things I couldn't immediately identify.

The woman rattled the coins in her paper cup at me. I stopped, examined the change in my pocket, deliberately selected a penny, and dropped it into her cup. She said, "Bless you," with a complete poker face. Normally I do not poke fun at street beggars, even when I suspect they are frauds, but I wanted this pair to know I was onto them.

I turned onto Royal Street, thinking again about Bull Street in Savannah, but at the same time I had to admit that Royal Street wasn't a bad substitute, even on a dull day. Because of its many galleries, tourists sometimes call it "the street of balconies," and New Orleans galleries have their own special attractiveness. They project over the sidewalk from the second and sometimes the third stories, supported by posts, and they feature elaborate ironwork wrought like lace in black or white along with hanging baskets of greenery and artfully arranged planters.

The effect is stunning, and it isn't restricted to Royal Street. It can be enjoyed throughout the French Quarter. Upper story residents use galleries in the same way those on the ground floor use the beautiful courtyards. They furnish them with tables, chairs, lounges, and all of the clutter of comfortable outdoor living, sometimes even including birdhouses, with panels to provide an iota of privacy from occupants of adjoining galleries.

DeVarnay's, at 337 Royal Street, was a deceptively simple-looking store in the French Quarter's Antique Row, where there are a number of such stores in a two or three block stretch. The name was presented in crisp, gold lettering across the front. DeVarnay did not own the building. He leased the first floor; the upper two floors, each with a gallery, were divided into apartments. DeVarnay lived elsewhere in the French Quarter and had no connection with the upstairs tenants.

Antique stores have a select clientele, and if they choose to do so, they can operate on hours most bankers would envy. DeVarnay's was still closed at twenty minutes to ten, although there was someone at work inside cleaning and getting the store ready for business. I arrived early on purpose so I could form a few impressions of it and also of the neighborhood.

It seemed deceptively simple-looking because the occasional price tag I was able to glimpse through the window suggested all manner of irrational and totally indiscernible complications. For example, a simple porcelain figurine, eight inches high and allegedly a bit more than a hundred years old—which some collectors wouldn't even consider antique—was going for

$3,700.

The missing man had owned and operated this store, dealing in "antiques, fine arts, jewelry, paintings, and collectibles," as a sign in one of the windows said, and that seemed to cover the subject adequately. Everything on view was displayed with good taste: jewelry; furniture; assorted articles of silver including candelabras and fancy tea service sets; china dishes that looked hand-decorated; and paintings in a delicately modern impressionistic style that I liked.

I would have enjoyed owning the paintings. Otherwise, I didn't see a single item on display in the two DeVarnay windows that I was willing to invest my life savings in or any money at all, even at 50% off, which nothing was. That was no reflection on the merchandise. I lack the collector's instinct and have no interest in acquiring things I haven't any use for just for the pleasure of owning them.

I strolled along the street, looking about and examining the windows of some of the other antique stores. Opposite the 300 block stores is an impressive-looking building with ornamental columns and a portico, formerly the Bank of Louisiana building. Now, after a checkered career as auctioneers' exchange, court building, and the site of various governmental offices, it houses the Vieux Carré Commission Headquarters and also the area's police headquarters. It is marked off by a low cement wall along the sidewalk, topped with an iron fence.

The wall protrudes almost a foot beyond the fence, just far enough to be comfortably sat on, and two street beggars were doing that. At the corner—where a fast retreat was possible if any of the many police officers passing were to challenge his presence there—was a middle-aged black non-musician. He had a cheap recorder, a straight flute, in his hands, and occasionally he blew a shrill beep on it. The cap at his feet had a sign beside it. I crossed the street for a closer look. The sign said, "I know I need lessons, but I can't afford them. Please help."

Thus far, no one was helping, but there were few passersby at that hour of the morning, even on Royal Street.

At the other end of the wall was an elderly, shabbily-dressed, excessively hairy white man. His tangled gray locks hadn't received a barber's attention for years, nor had his long, drooping, gray mustache. He wore dirty jeans and a dirtier T-shirt, both with mismatching patches, and on his feet were enormous, old-fashioned overshoes. A begrimed hat lay on the sidewalk in front of him. He had no sign, no patter, no act. The hat testified to his need.

It seemed like thundering coincidence that the only beggars I had seen that morning had taken up positions from which they could watch my hotel and DeVarnay's business. I know coincidences do happen, but I decided not to believe that one.

Back at DeVarnay's, a middle-aged woman with thick glasses, stylishly dressed but also prim-looking, arrived at ten minutes to ten and opened the front door with a key. Then she turned to me.

"I'm Selma Garnett," she said, giving me a worried look. "Mr. DeVarnay's assistant. Are you Mr. Pletcher? The detective Mrs. DeVarnay hired?"

"I'm with the firm of detectives she hired," I said.

"Oh. Yes." She seemed apologetic—as though anyone who knew Mrs. DeVarnay should have known she would never hire a single detective. "Yes. Of course. Mr. Kallenor said you would be meeting him here. Please come in."

She offered me a chair in the office, but I preferred to wander about the store. The problem with antiques, I quickly decided, is that one never knows whether to consider them museum pieces or something functional for the home. The beautifully inlaid piano on display was an excellent example. Should it be viewed as a musical instrument or as an oversized ornament? Was the exquisitely-carved chair something to be sat on or a knickknack to be looked at? I would develop all kinds of complexes if I had to live surrounded by antiques.

Doug Kallenor huffed and puffed his way into the store. He was a man about sixty, short and grossly overweight with suspiciously black hair, and he looked like everyone's favorite uncle.

If you wanted a favor, he had it. He also looked like a man who never turned down an invitation to dinner or a drink. He greeted me with a broad smile, invited me into the office, apologized profusely to Selma Garnett for usurping her headquarters, and then firmly closed the door on her.

He pulled up a chair for me, collapsed into the massive reclining, pivoting, rolling throne behind the large desk where Marc DeVarnay worked when he wasn't missing, mopped his face with a handkerchief that already had done its share of mopping that morning, and announced, "What a tragedy!"

"Why?" I asked blankly.

He stared at me. "Marc's disappearance, of course. I couldn't say anything to Jolitte, but I can to you. Marc wouldn't disappear like this. Absolutely and positively, he wouldn't do it. It's inconceivable. Something must have happened to him." He didn't actually wring his hands, but it would have been in character. Some accountants are happiest when presiding over a bankruptcy. Despite Kallenor's friendly manner and smiling face, he hadn't seen the bright side of anything since he became a C.P.A.

"I understand Mrs. DeVarnay asked you to perform an audit," I said. "When was it done?"

"Early this week—Monday and Tuesday."

"With what result?"

"There's money missing, of course."

"What do you mean—'of course?'"

"Considering the mysterious circumstances surrounding Marc's disappearance, I expected to find something wrong, and I did."

"How much money?"

"Approximately forty-five thousand dollars. He may have taken some of it with him in cash, so it's difficult to say for certain."

"Wouldn't he have left some kind of memo as a record?"

"If he took any substantial part of that sum with him, I'm sure he would have."

"But he didn't?"

Kallenor shook his head.

"What does Miss Garnett have to say about this?" I had noticed she wore no engagement or wedding ring.

"She knows nothing about it. Of course I asked her the moment I discovered the shortage."

"That's a large sum of money to suddenly fall through a crack and vanish. Maybe you'd better tell me something about the business and how its money is handled."

"Well." He rubbed his hands together. "It's a peculiar kind of business. As with any retail establishment, before Marc could sell something, he had to buy it. The antique business is unusual because in order to buy it, he first had to find it. Quality antiques aren't easy to find—unless you do your shopping in other antique stores." He giggled. "But that isn't much help because the antiques in other stores have already been found. If you're in the business, you have to look for some that haven't been found yet. In fact, you have to search constantly."

"I understand."

"Marc was an absolute genius at it. This store went from nothing to fifty thousand net its first year, and he's been increasing that ever since. Last year he paid his mother back a hundred thousand on the money she loaned to get him started, he took a hundred thousand in salary, and he still had enough net left to keep building his stock. In addition to this store, he has a warehouse with a craft shop to make repairs, frame pictures, or whatever. He was able to sell a lot of antiques because he found a lot. In the process, he developed an excellent clientele."

I didn't like the way he kept referring to the missing man in the past tense. I prefer to wait for a death certificate before I write the obituary. Until then, I keep my misgivings to myself.

I said nothing, but I couldn't resist a subtle correction. "How does he manage to find so much?" I asked.

He insisted on keeping Marc in the past. "He used informants. Pickers. Runners. Tipsters. Spies. Agents. Snoops. Not every antique dealer resorts to them, but many do, and they have different names for them and use them in different ways. Marc referred to them as his 'contacts.' He had what must have been an unusually large number of them. They scouted out antiques for him, and Marc paid them well, but he didn't trust them to make any decisions. He did all of the actual buying himself."

I must have looked as blank as I felt. The notion of someone paying money for a hot tip on an old chair was something my imagination had to grope for.

He chuckled. Then he paused to mop his face. "I don't know all the details, but the system probably worked something like this: Marc's contacts—the ones who brought him the most business—had a knack for getting invited to people's homes. They would make friends easily, and because people enjoyed their company, they would be asked to stop by and have a beer, or come to dinner, or whatever. Once in the house, they kept their eyes opened, and they might spot an old bureau their host inherited from his great-grandmother. Or his wife inherited from her great aunt. Or an armoire, or a cut-glass dish or whatever. Marc's contacts weren't experts, but they quickly learned enough about antiques to have a fairly good idea of what was valuable and what wasn't. The contact would drop a hint that the old piece of junk in the corner might be worth money to the right person. If the owner seemed interested, Marc would be informed. If Marc bought it, the contact received a nice commission for no more effort than using his eyes and making a phone call."

"That's how Marc finds a lot?" I insisted on keeping him in the present.

"Probably I'm oversimplifying, but that certainly was one of the ways Marc found merchandise. Of course he attended auctions—all over the country, like the one in St. Louis. People sometimes came in and offered to sell him things because he was a well-known dealer. There also were estate sales, and garage sales, and flea markets, and I don't know what all. No doubt it's possible to pick up bargains in a lot of places if you know the business—and Marc certainly did. A good antique dealer goes anywhere and everywhere he thinks there's a chance of finding anything, and the deals he makes are always cash deals. For that reason, Marc had to have instant access to quantities of money so he could take advantage of opportunities whenever they occurred."

"So Marc buys cheap and makes huge profits," I suggested, again returning him to the present.

"He bought fairly," Kallenor said, stubbornly keeping him in the past. "If you're a dealer, you want the people who sell to you to be satisfied enough to recommend you to a friend who also has something old to sell. That's one of the ways Marc's business grew. He also paid his contacts well."

"Valuable antiques must be expensive even at bargain prices. Are you sure Marc didn't take all of that forty-five grand with him to spend in St. Louis?"

"Marc was a reputable dealer, and at that particular auction, where he certainly was well known, I'm sure he could have paid for anything he bought by check if he'd wanted to. But there's no way of knowing what his intention was, and without asking him, there's no way to find out whether he took all of that money with him or none of it."

"But the one item he bought was paid for with cash," I observed.

"Really? What did he pay for it?"

"Seven hundred."

Kallenor shook his head. "That doesn't tell us anything about how much money he took with him. Maybe he would have paid by check if he'd bought something expensive."

"Would he be keeping forty-five grand in the office safe?"

"That's certainly possible if he had sizeable deals in the offing, and Miss Garnett says he did."

"Does she have access to the safe?"

"There are two safes. One is Marc's personal safe. The other is for general business records. She has access to the second— she would have to in order to run the store in Marc's absence."

"Do you have access to both?"

"Of course. I'm his mother's representative. Please understand—I know the money is missing. I don't know where it vanished from or where it went. I add up columns of figures. Income minus outgo ought to equal cash on hand and in the bank. When they don't, there's a problem. I can't say whether the money disappeared from his safe, or from the general safe, or if an employee appropriated it, or if he took it with him."

"But you must have an opinion."

"Yes. Well—I would think it unlikely that an employee could have got away with that much money. Not in a small establishment like this where the owner kept an eye on everything. There's no evidence of any tampering with either safe. So I think Marc took it, but I haven't any idea of why he would want to."

He went over the accounting records with me, and it was evident that the store was a gold mine. Whatever Marc's technique was for finding things, it was hugely successful.

"One more thing," I said. "Did you notice anything odd or unusual about his behavior during the time just before he disappeared?"

Kallenor mopped his face again. "Interesting that you should ask that. Normally I didn't see Marc very often. He had his own accountant, and I represent his mother's interest. It's a complicated legal situation that resulted because of the money she advanced to get the business started. So I performed an annual audit and otherwise saw him socially once in a while. But the night before he disappeared, I was showing the French Quarter to a visiting relative, and I saw Marc on Bourbon Street."

"What was odd or unusual about that?" I asked. "Marc lives in the French Quarter himself, and Bourbon Street can't be more than a couple of blocks from his home. He must have had errands that took him in that direction occasionally."

"You didn't know Marc. He hated Bourbon Street—or so he said. He considered it a blight on the French Quarter, distracting all those tourists with alcohol and frivolity when they might otherwise have been shopping for antiques. He never went near it—or so he said. But there he was, on Bourbon Street, and I saw him go into a girlie show. He always let on that he'd never been to one and detested the things."

"That *is* interesting. Did you tell the police about it?"

"Certainly not. What Marc chose to do for amusement was none of their business."

"Ah—but it was. And is. Everything is their business when a man disappears. What time did you see him?"

He thought for a moment. "Seven o'clock. Maybe a little before."

"Shortly before ten he called a cab to take him to the airport, and then he called back and cancelled it. And of course he did fly to St. Louis that night. But it certainly is interesting that he spent time at a girlie show on the night he left—especially since he claimed to detest them."

I had one more question. "When you went through the safes, did you see his passport?"

He gazed at me blankly. "I just don't remember. I suppose I wasn't looking for anything like that."

"Look now," I suggested.

We both looked, and in Marc DeVarnay's private safe we found his passport. I leafed through it. His last foreign travel had been an extensive trip to Europe more than a year before. At least he hadn't planned to leave the country when he left for St. Louis, and that was important.

Kallenor had nothing to add, so I thanked him and promised to bother him again if I needed more information. We left the office together. He gave Miss Garnett a wave on his way out; I wanted to talk with her, so I waited until she finished with a customer who had just come in.

It was a good-looking blond man, casually dressed but not in the flamboyant fashion some of the tourists affected. I would have guessed his age at thirty-five or thirty-six. He wore his blond hair shoulder length, and he had a neatly-trimmed beard—a goatee, actually—but no mustache. Miss Garnett evidently knew him. She greeted potential customers with polite formality, but she gave him a friendly nod and tossed a "good morning," at him. I took him to be a French Quarter resident.

"Hi," he said. "Boss back yet?"

She shook her head.

"Really? Still not back? That must be some buying trip!"

She made no comment.

"Look—I've been holding a couple of good tips for more than two weeks. Do *you* want them?"

She shook her head again. "You know I haven't any authority for that."

"I suppose not," he said. "I hope Marc gets back soon. These things don't keep forever. Someone else may grab the stuff." He hesitated. "Sorry to bother you, but I have some money coming."

"I'll check the book," she said.

She went into the office and returned with a ledger. She opened it, found the page she wanted, and pursed her lips thoughtfully. "There's one unpaid item here. Do you want it now?"

"Please," he said.

She counted out a hundred and twenty-five dollars, and he signed a receipt, thanked her, and stuffed the money into his pocket. "Would you write a memo to Marc and ask him to get in touch with me the moment he gets back?"

"I will," she promised.

He left with a casual wave. She made an entry in the ledger. Then she wrote a message on a memo pad and tore off a sheet. She returned the ledger to the office and left the memo on Marc DeVarnay's desk under a paperweight.

"What can I do for you?" she asked when she returned.

"Answer a few questions. Does the store handle art work from Central or South America?"

"No. Not at all. That's a specialized field, and the really valuable pieces would be extremely difficult to acquire. Most of our business is concerned with American antiques, though Mr. DeVarnay has had good success with European buying tours."

"Then you've never handled anything from Central or South America?"

"Just a moment," she said.

She went to one of the safes in the office, opened it, opened a drawer, and took out a figurine about four inches high. She brought it back and held it up for me to see. It was smoothly carved from dark green stone, but the facial features were crude and the head bulged oddly as though to represent hair piled up on top.

"It's jade," she said. "Mr. DeVarnay acquired it almost by accident with an assortment of curios, and he thinks it may be Olmec, in which case it could date back to five hundred B.C. or even earlier. But it also could be a forgery. It is similar to Olmec figurines, but the Olmecs rarely used this kind of jade. Mr. DeVarnay has been trying to get it authenticated. Unfortunately, there's no provenance at all—no evidence of where it could have come from. So it may be extremely valuable, or it may be—" She shrugged. "A trinket. This is the only item we've ever had of pre-Columbian art."

She returned the figurine to the safe and closed and locked it.

"What about ivory carvings?" I asked.

"There isn't much available. New carvings are illegal, and those who have old carvings are hanging onto them. We've never been offered any."

"Try thinking back to the last day Mr. DeVarnay was here," I suggested. "Did anything unusual happen?"

"No. It was just an ordinary day. We weren't very busy in the store, but Mr. DeVarnay was busy getting things in order because he wouldn't be here the next day."

"Was he here right up until closing time?"

"Yes. We left together, and that was the last time I saw him."

"What mood was he in?" She looked puzzled, so I added quickly, "Did he seem happy, was he looking forward to getting away for a short time, or did he act as though he were worried about something?"

"I don't recall anything unusual. He always has a great many things on his mind, and sometimes he seems absent-minded or forgetful, but he really isn't. It's just that he'll start thinking about something else. When he turns his attention back to the present, he's always very sharp and alert. He's a brilliant man."

I noticed that she kept DeVarnay in the present. "Do you enjoy your job?" I asked.

She smiled. "I adore working for him. I've been so worried that something might have happened to him."

"That's understandable," I said soothingly. "Everyone who knew him is extremely worried. Did he have any enemies?"

"Not exactly enemies. Some people were jealous of him, of course, because he made a huge success of his business so quickly. He got along well with most of his competitors, but there were a few—one in particular—who were always accusing him of unscrupulous business practices. None of that was true, of course."

"Who is the one in particular?"

"Harold Nusiner. He's an antique dealer with a store over on Magazine Street."

"Then you wouldn't call him a friendly rival."

"Certainly not! He was furious because Mr. DeVarnay bought some antiques he thought had been promised to him. When that simmered down, he kept after Mr. DeVarnay to go in with him on some kind of cooperative scheme for buying antiques. Mr. DeVarnay wouldn't have anything to do with it. Why should he? He does very well doing his own buying. But Mr. Nusiner kept after him anyway. He telephoned twice on the day Mr. DeVarnay left, and he's called several times since then. When I told him I didn't know when Mr. DeVarnay would be back, he swore at me on the telephone."

"He doesn't sound like a gentleman," I observed.

"He isn't!"

"When you left the store together on the night Mr. DeVarnay went to St. Louis, did he have any last-minute instructions for you?"

"No. He came back later, though, to finish some work, and he left a note for me."

"Really? Does that happen often?"

"Quite often. Evenings may be the only time he can call on

a family that has something to sell. That's what happened the day he disappeared. He followed up a tip, bought a table and chairs, all in very nice condition, and had them picked up at once and taken to our warehouse. Then he came back here and left a memo and the receipt for payment so I could take care of the paperwork the next morning. By the way, it was Francis who found those items for him."

"Francis?"

"Francis Dassily. The man who was just in here. I'll show you the ledger." She went and got it. "The memo that Mr. DeVarnay left for me showed a commission due Francis of $125, and I entered it the next morning. Francis was in last week, and also the week before, probably expecting to be paid and give Mr. DeVarnay the new tips he has, but Mr. DeVarnay hadn't returned. He usually deals with the contacts himself, so of course Francis didn't like to ask me for the money. But another week has gone by, and by this time he may have needed it badly, so today he asked for it."

"Could I see the ledger?" I asked. "I'm curious as to how many contacts there are."

"I don't know all of them myself. As I said, Mr. DeVarnay deals with them. Most are people who happened onto an antique or two by accident and told Mr. DeVarnay about it because it's widely known that he pays well for such information. We never hear from them again. It takes a special knack to keep finding antiques."

"I would think so," I said. "I wouldn't know how to go about it."

She smiled. "There are two or three dozen people who continue to find something once in a while, and then there are several, like Francis Dassily, who work at it all the time and receive a substantial part of their income from it."

I ran my finger down the page. Then I began turning the pages backward.

"Does this person bring in very much?" I asked, pointing to a name.

"Probably not," Miss Garnett said. "I don't know him at all."

"I wonder if it would be possible to have a list of these names with some indication of how much business Mr. DeVarnay does with them."

"Yes. I can do that for you. Do you want addresses, too?"

"Certainly."

"Some of them may be out-of-date. Many of these people move frequently."

"Just give me the most recent addresses you have."

She asked worriedly, "Do you think one of these people could have done something to Mr. DeVarnay? I know many of them lead dissolute lives and some have criminal records. Of course it's also true that many of them are perfectly upright, hard-working citizens who pick up some extra money this way. Francis Dassily, the man who was in here, has been working for Mr. DeVarnay ever since he founded the business. There are several like that."

"Right now I'm only collecting information. Later I'll see whether it adds up to anything."

As she turned away, I said, "Just a moment. Did Mr. DeVarnay have contacts in other cities?"

"Of course. He had them throughout the south and in many northern cities. He was adding to his list all the time, and he would make quick trips to take advantage of tips that seemed to merit it."

"How about St. Louis, Denver, and Reno?" I asked.

She consulted her ledger. "Two contacts in St. Louis and one in Denver. There aren't any in Reno. I don't think Reno would be a good source for antiques."

"How about San Francisco?"

"Two there. San Francisco should be very good."

"Seattle?"

"One in Seattle."

I took a deep breath, wondering if it were possible that Marc DeVarnay's idiotic excursion made sense after all. Could he have visited those cities to act on tips his contacts had picked up for him? In Reno, where he had no contacts, he might have been looking for one. But why hadn't he mentioned to anyone where he was going, and where had he gone after Seattle?

As I had told Raina Lambert, the search for a missing New Orleans businessman should have begun in New Orleans. Now the out-of-town agents would be her problem.

"Did Mr. DeVarnay say anything about the possibility of following up tips somewhere else after he finished in St. Louis?" I asked.

"Oh, no! He was coming right back. He had some very important transactions pending here in New Orleans that only he could handle. He wouldn't have changed his plans without letting me know, I'm sure."

"What's happened to those transactions?"

She gave me a worried look. "I don't know. I don't know anything about them except that Mr. DeVarnay was about to close them. Probably he has lost out by this time."

"I'm sorry to dump this work onto you," I said, "but I urgently need two lists—one of the out-of-town names and one of the local names. All of those people will have to be contacted to see whether any of them have heard from Mr. DeVarnay."

She promised to type the lists immediately.

As I left the store, I noted that both the beggars were still on duty.

I stopped at the first public telephone I could find to place a call to Sister Merlina, who was the only witch I had ever known with a listing in the Yellow Pages. I had a message for her to pass to Dick Tosche. I wanted to see him. One of the contacts in the store's ledger was Griff Wylan, also known as Little Boy. I had found DeVarnay's street connection.

CHAPTER SIX

With Sister Merlina relaying messages, I made a date to meet Dick Tosche in the plaza in front of the cathedral at noon. When I left the hotel, the same two beggars were stubbornly posted near the entrance despite the lack of business. Turning onto Royal Street, I found the other two still sitting opposite DeVarnay's.

I started early so I could savor the French Quarter in leisurely fashion along the way. Royal Street was crowded, now, and there were lines outside the most popular dining places. The people waiting there were the hardiest known specimens of *genus touristus*—they had already recovered from last night's binge of oysters Rockefeller and beef tournedos at Antoine's, or of trout meunière at Broussard's, or of seafood-stuffed eggplant at Galatoire's, and they were eager to top that off with a popular New Orleans favorite for lunch, perhaps one of the dishes Marc DeVarnay specialized in. Gumbo and jambalaya are in fact commonplace regional dishes, along with red beans and rice, shrimp Creole, and various étouffées and rémoulades. DeVarnay, despite his brilliance with antiques, lacked originality in the kitchen.

I wove my way through the throngs, taking my time because I had plenty of it, and marveling at the stark contrasts between the shops I passed. Exquisite, extremely expensive merchandise and artwork were offered next door to junk. Here was an emporium featuring cheap souvenirs and cheaper T-shirts (direct from the factory, 3 for $9.99 on the rack only); next door, a shop specialized in expensive imported oriental artwork. Then came another souvenir store with more T-shirts, alligator skulls ranging in size from tiny to huge, and feather masks. Just beyond it was a display of beautiful needlework and laces followed by a praline shop—pralines being sugar-and-pecan patties in various flavors, another regional specialty. On the other side were offerings of expensive jewelry, a craft shop, a doll shop, a shop featuring Christmas decorations and ornaments, and then a serious art gallery.

One shop exhibited hand-decorated clothing. Local artists work in iron and brass, as well as glass, wood and ceramics, and their creations were prominent everywhere. Drafty passageways leading to an interior courtyard served as art galleries and were lined with paintings for sale.

Prepared mixes of famous New Orleans dishes filled the windows of several shops, and the displays were ornamented with aprons imprinted with recipes, sweat shirts that said "Bon Appétit," cooking utensils, and items such as hot pants featuring the Tabasco Sauce logo. Musical symbols are also popular on souvenirs and even in the art galleries where there are surrealistic as well as realistic paintings and sculptures of individual musicians or entire orchestras on display.

I was enjoying all of this when a burly, bearded man rudely elbowed me aside. There seemed to be nothing personal about it. It was only a French Quarter resident in a hurry. He pushed his way along the crowded sidewalk, using his elbows freely and chanting, "Idiot alert! Idiot alert! Coming through!" The tourists paid no attention to him.

I had just crossed a side street when I heard a parade coming. New Orleans is famous for its Mardi Gras parades, but the city hosts festivals of various kinds throughout the year: a Jazz Fest, a Festa d'Italie, a Renaissance Festival, a Louisiana Swamp Festival, even a Tomato Festival. In addition, there are various festive days, some of them, such as the ones dedicated to St. Patrick and St. Joseph, lavishly celebrated. Any festival is ample excuse for parades, and local people or business firms are likely to break out in parades on any day at all as though just doing it for practice.

That was what had happened. The little parade I had heard approaching was headed by a group of musicians led by a plump, middle-aged woman. She was performing elaborate gesticulations with a small parasol that was violently striped in red, yellow, and purple. Behind the musicians came an old fire truck loaded with children who were tossing "throws"—candy, beads, cheap plastic do-dads—to the spectators. On either side of the musicians, men were passing out circulars advertising a night club.

A New Orleans parade is always a good show, so I paused to watch it, thinking I might grab a throw or two for myself. A bicyclist riding along Royal Street swung to the curb beside me for the same purpose—to watch the parade go by. As the musicians approached us, blaring lustily, he turned, our eyes met, and we both experienced the shock of recognition.

His reflexes were better than mine. He shot away, looping around the parade and almost knocking down the woman with the parasol. Before I could react, the street was blocked, and I could only glimpse him vanishing down Royal Street at top speed.

It was Little Boy, Griff Wylan. In his frantic flight, he pedaled past the police headquarters of the Vieux Carré District as though totally ignorant of the fact that its detective squad urgently wanted words with him. Police officers come and go constantly in that block and even seem to congregate around the building, but he slipped past it unscathed.

He was out of sight by the time the parade had passed, and the distraction deprived me of my fair share of throws. Only by alertly putting my foot on one was I able to keep a string of cheap beads from being snatched up by my ravenous fellow spectators. I ceremoniously presented it to an elderly woman who had been watching enviously while the more agile spectators scrambled for loot. She was delighted.

The plaza in front of the cathedral, actually a pedestrian

mall, is called Place Jean Paul Deux in honor of Pope John Paul II, who held a prayer service there during his 1987 visit. Beyond it is a park enclosed by an iron fence that features the famous equestrian statue of General Andrew Jackson, whose defeat of the British at the Battle of New Orleans in 1815 gave him an eventual leg up on the presidency. Streets on either side of the park have also been made into pedestrian malls. On the fourth side, the one toward the Mississippi River, is busy Decatur Street, lined with vendors and jammed with traffic, touring coaches, waiting donkey carriages, and death-defying pedestrians. Beyond that are the high levee, the Riverfront Streetcar line, a walkway along the Mississippi, and docks for cruise ships.

The pedestrian malls are the sites of a small-scale, year-around carnival during daylight hours. Mobs of tourists wander about trying to pick their ways through the crush. Artists display paintings and drawings for sale on the park's iron fence. Portrait artists, with their subjects posing nervously, labor to preserve honest, forthright, touristy features for posterity in pencil, water color, or oil with graduated prices to match. Tarot readers, each with his or her own small table, dramatically lay out one card after another, invoking fate for curious customers. White-faced mimes, with hats lying hopefully on the ground in front of them for charitable donations, strike one commonplace pose after another. Balloon sculptors and street vendors try to catch the attention of passersby with banter and antics. Lucky Dog vendors in red striped, short-sleeved coats, wait for customers in stoic silence, their hot-dog-shaped carts being all the advertisement they need. Street musicians warble or twitter or blast. Panhandlers watch hopefully for victims, and passersby quickly learn to avoid eye-contact with them.

I had suggested meeting Dick Tosche there because it was easy to find, but I had forgotten the turmoil. I was a bit early, so I seated myself on a bench directly in front of the cathedral where I could watch the crowd and enjoy the antics of the vendors.

A good-looking, neatly dressed black man sat down beside me. He greeted me with an engaging smile, told me hello, took a careful look at me, and then inquired politely, "Are you a tourist?"

"Yes," I said with great warmth. "Seeing New Orleans for the first time."

"How do you like it?"

"I'm absolutely in love with it," I said. "Are you a tourist?"

"I'm homeless," he said. "I'm stranded here."

"How are you making out?" I asked.

"Not bad. The people are very nice. It gets a little cold at night, though, and I really would like to get home to Cleveland."

I nodded understandingly.

"You know, I think Jesus intended for us to meet like this," he said. "I've been praying that He would send someone to help me. All I need is—" He paused a moment to calculate the size of the bite he might successfully put on me. "—forty dollars for the bus."

"Really?" I said. "Can you get all the way to Cleveland on forty dollars?"

"I already got some of it. Forty dollars more is all I need. I know how to travel cheap." He grinned. "I have to know how to travel cheap."

I might have strung him out a little, but at that moment Dick Tosche arrived and looked down at us angrily. "Ricardo, are you trying that worn-out pitch on my friend Jay?"

The homeless man suddenly lost his loquaciousness.

"This character has been hanging around here for months, making a sort of living with his story about wanting to get home," Dick said. "Where is he trying to get to this time?"

"Cleveland," I said.

"Last week it was Toledo. At least he's consistent. He pretty much sticks to the state of Ohio. Maybe he actually comes from there. If you ask him, he'll even give you his parents' address. He has a parents' address for every town in Ohio—none of them known to the Postal Service, of course. Once out of curiosity I checked one of them. The letter came back—no such address. How much did he say he needed?"

"Forty dollars."

"You ought to feel insulted. You look a lot more prosperous than that."

Ricardo had started to slink away glumly. I called him back. "Ever hear of a man named Marc DeVarnay?" I asked.

He shook his head.

"He's missing, and I'm trying to find him. If you can dig up information about him, you can earn some honest money."

The possibility of actually earning money impressed him so unfavorably that he almost fell over a tarot table in his hurry to get away.

"You shouldn't have said 'dig up,'" Tosche said. "You made it sound like work. These people are actors, you know. There's no more truth in the lines they feed you than in lines spoken on the stage. If they have a good act, people will give them money. If they don't, they keep discarding the bits that don't work and trying to develop new material the same way night club comedians drop jokes that don't work and add new ones. If Ricardo's line about trying to get home ever fails completely, he'll try something else."

"Some of them use signs," I said. "I suppose a clever person might pick up a bit of money thinking up cute signs for beggars."

"The problem with a sign is that if it works, someone else will copy it."

"Ricardo is a fine-appearing person," I said. "He seems bright enough. One would think he could find regular employment if he wanted it."

"That's it. He doesn't want it. He prefers the life style of lounging around and spending a little time each day begging. But don't feel sorry for him. He likes New Orleans, and this is the way he's happy. A lot of people are sorry for me because I spend my time scrounging for things to sell, but I'm happy. I call the beggars '*poux*,' which means 'lice.'" He added almost apologetically, "They are parasites, you know."

He worked hard for a living, and he had an honest indignation toward those who didn't, but he was trying to be fair about it. "I suppose most of them don't do any harm, and some people think they may even serve a purpose. The tourists who support them can afford it, and the *poux* give them some entertainment and the warm feeling of having helped unfortunate people who are down on their luck, so who's to say they don't get their money's worth? If the pitches the *poux* hand out are mostly fraudulent, the tourists never know it." He paused and added, "I got your message. Obviously."

"Have you had lunch?"

He hadn't. We went to a small restaurant and ate gumbo, and a man at a neighboring table almost spoiled it for me by ordering andouille jambalaya, andouille being Cajun sausage. It reminded me again of the shiny new pan on the camp stove in Old Jake's *cabon*.

I described my encounter with Little Boy. Tosche hadn't seen him since he pursued him out of my hotel. He had been making discreet inquiries to find out how well Marc DeVarnay was known to the street people of his acquaintance.

"I haven't found anyone who's done business with him, but everyone knows who he is because he pays good money for tips on antiques."

I told him about DeVarnay's "contacts."

"I haven't encountered any of them," he said. "When you get the list, we can check it out, if you want to do that."

It sounded as promising as any other way I could have spent the afternoon, so we headed for DeVarnay's. Along the way, I described the beggars I had seen across from the store and near my hotel. I asked him about the likelihood of a bonafide street person taking up a position on an empty side street at seven in the morning or even on a lightly trafficked Royal Street at twenty minutes to ten.

"They do some screwy things," he said, "but I'd have to see that to believe it."

The two were still sitting across from the store. Dick took

one glance at them and then followed me inside.

"I've seen both of them around for years," he said. "The musician is called Horowitz, but I don't know if that's his name. The things people are called often aren't."

"Horowitz was a famous musician," I told him. "A great piano player. Someone called the beggar that as a joke. Does he have facetious friends?"

"These people move in their own little cliques. They know each other well, and very few outsiders know much about them. I can't tell you anything about Horowitz, but the old man is called 'Shoeless Sharley.' Did you notice his overshoes? He has unusually large feet, and it isn't easy for him to find cast-off shoes that fit him, but he docs sometimes get hold of large-sized overshoes, so that's what he wears—without shoes, of course. A long time ago, an artist pal painted bare human feet on his over-shoes. Made it look as though he were going about barefoot, which got him the name 'Shoeless.' By the time those overshoes wore out, he'd had a tiff with the artist, so his present overshoes have feet on the inside only."

I found the vision of an illustrated Shoeless Sharley far more appealing than the slovenly, unillustrated one I had seen.

"Do you want me to find out more about those two?" Dick asked.

"Yes," I said. "But first, we'll tackle the names on the list."

Miss Garnett had both lists typed. I folded the pages of out-of-town names, added a note of explanation, and borrowed an envelope to send them to our Los Angeles office. Tosche and I studied the local names.

"Some of these characters hang out around the flea market," he observed.

It sounded like a good place to start. Before we headed in that direction, we circled past my hotel to see if the beggars were still working there. They were.

Dick didn't look directly at either of them, but when we had rounded a corner, he announced, "The woman is Hattie the Hat Lady. I don't know if Hattie is really her name. The only thing

I know about her is that she's considered one tough cookie. A couple of guys tried to mug her one night and grab her day's take, and she beat them up. She's been around for a while, too. The man is a surprise. His name is Cal Dreslow, and I've never seen him begging before. He has a part-time job somewhere outside the Quarter, and he fills in with whatever work he can get. He's a good worker, and people like him. Begging makes no sense at all for him."

"Find out what you can about both of them," I said.

The French Market offers piles of fruit and vegetables of every kind and description, festoons of garlic, and exotic snacks such as alligator sausage on a stick, which is something you don't often seen in a market in Chicago or even San Francisco. Beyond it is the flea market, which defies description. It contains a bit of everything and an overly generous measure of some things. There are typical New Orleans souvenirs such as Mardi Gras masks—ceramic, feathered, or leather ranging from adult sizes to tiny replicas—along with the ubiquitous T shirts and hats with cutesy slogans. There are alligator souvenirs ranging from preserved heads to skulls, not to mention claws and teeth. There are handbags, luggage, belts, jewelry of all kinds, colorful stones, minerals, fossils, clothing, secondhand books, knick-knacks of every description, ceramics, paintings, prints, handi-crafts, reproductions of old-time advertisements—anything likely to catch a tourist's eye.

The first person we encountered from our list was Francis Dassily. He was presiding over a table heaped with cheap jewelry, your choice two dollars each. Behind him was a canvas panel with a group of quite competent oil paintings displayed on it—souvenir scenes from tourist New Orleans. Working with him was a small, dark-haired girl with fine features and notably sloppy clothing. Both her jeans and her baggy shirt were faded and patched—not that there was anything unusual about that. The dress of the other vendors varied from the almost formal to the slovenly. Dassily stood out among them. Except for his long hair, he looked like a bank teller on his day off. I introduced myself as a detective looking into the disappearance of Marc DeVarnay, and he was astonished.

"Disappearance? You mean—nobody knows where he is?"

"We're hoping someone does," I said. "I'm trying to find out who that is."

"I'll be—" He stared from one of us to the other. "Marc is really—I mean, I was in the store this morning, and Selma didn't say a thing. When did he disappear?"

"It's been a couple of weeks," I said. "He went to St. Louis and assorted other places and then vanished. We're wondering whether he's been seen here recently."

Dassily took a step backward and dropped onto a chair. "No wonder Selma has acted odd when I ask about him. The last time I saw him was just before he left for St. Louis."

"Tell us about it," I suggested.

"There isn't much to tell. I had a good tip on an antique table and chairs. I gave him a call at home, and he met me at the address, looked the pieces over, wrote up a sales contract, bought 'em on the spot, and phoned someone to come and get them. When I left him, he was waiting for the truck to arrive. After that, he was going back to the store to take care of the paperwork. Normally he would have left that until the next morning, but because he was going to St. Louis, he did it that night. He said he had plenty of time, he was all packed for his trip. That was the last time I saw him."

"Did he actually do the paperwork?" I asked.

"Sure. I have proof that he did. I collected my commission this morning. If he hadn't recorded the purchase, my account wouldn't have had money in it. I was in the store a couple of times after that, but he hadn't got back yet. Do you mean to say no one has seen him since then?"

"No one has seen him for a couple of weeks," I said. "If you hear anything about him, please let us know at once."

"I sure will." He turned to the girl. "My God! If anything happens to Marc, I'm out of work. I get more than half my income from him!"

I gave him one of my cards—they carry the addresses and phone numbers of the firm's Los Angeles and New York offices, but I had penned in the name of my hotel and its telephone number. He scrutinized it with a scowl.

"Investigative Consultants?" Then he turned the scowl on me. "'*J*.' Pletcher?"

"It stands for 'Januarius,' which is the month I was born in. Somehow I've never been able to get used to it, so I just call myself 'J.'"

"I don't blame you," he said sympathetically. "That's even worse than my name. 'Francis' isn't all that uncommon, but I've never liked it. I have no idea where my parents got it—I suspect I was named after a woman."

All the time we were talking, the girl had listened with interest but hadn't volunteered a word. Now she asked doubtfully, "Is that really true? About Marc, I mean."

I assured her that it was. "Do you know anything about him?" I asked.

"No," she said. "But I met him a few times. He paid me for information about antiques."

I asked her what her name was. She was Cele Rundley, and she was on the list.

Customers were waiting, so we moved on.

"Know much about Dassily?" I asked Dick.

He shook his head. "He's always seemed like a respectable type, and he isn't afraid of work—even heavy work. Whenever anyone needs help unloading and setting up, he's available. He'll do favors when he's asked as long as they don't involve money, but all that means is that he doesn't have much money."

There were more than a hundred names on the list Selma Garnett had typed up. She had ticked off thirty people who brought in business occasionally and another ten who actually worked at it. Dassily was the only one of this last group we found at the flea market, but we tracked down a dozen people who'd had an occasional tip for DeVarnay. All of them said they hadn't seen him for weeks.

The next step was to try to find people at home. An artist named Aaron Vidler was at work in his living room surrounded by seven children and three wives, or ex-wives, or mistresses. I know from bitter experience that trying to make sense of a situation like that is a waste of time so I didn't bother.

He wasn't a bad artist, but he had an unhealthy preference for dirty purples and blacks, and the results were depressing. He hadn't seen Marc DeVarnay since January when DeVarnay refused to sponsor a mini-show for him.

"Marc's got his own pet artist, Frederick whoever he is, and he won't give anyone else a look-in," Vidler grumbled.

It suggested a motive for foul play, but there was a slight disadvantage. All of the thousands of artists in New Orleans would be suspects except those who chanced to be named Frederick. I decided to leave it as a last resort. We thanked him and left.

A black saxophone player named Cecil Johns lived in a cramped apartment over a nightclub on Bourbon Street. I wondered how a musician was able to practice under those circumstances, but Johns quickly set my mind at rest. "I never practice," he said. "I'm not that kind of musician." It turned out that he worked as a mime, doing poses while holding his saxophone and occasionally blowing a honk on it to attract the attention of passersby. He had turned up very few tips for DeVarnay.

"I don't know the right kind of people," he said. "The old junk my friends own always turns out to be nothin' but old junk."

He thought Mr. DeVarnay was a very nice man, always polite even though he never gave handouts. "He pays well, but you've got to earn it," Johns said. He couldn't remember the last time he saw him.

Connie Dey was a Gypsy. "A lot of scum washes up in New Orleans," she said brightly. "I'm part of it." Her name was actually Konstanze, with a 'K,' but it was easier to have people call her Connie.

She was an elderly woman who lived in a lovely third-floor apartment with a view of a pretty courtyard through her rear windows, but she couldn't open them, she said, because the first floor tenant was a restaurant, and its kitchen was directly below her. If she opened her windows, the delicious smells would keep her hungry all day long.

She wore a long dress and a headscarf, and professionally she called herself Madame Dey. She was a fortuneteller, reading palms or cards. She frequently performed for the tourists in Jackson Square. If you missed her there and didn't want to climb to the third floor, she made house calls and brought your fate to you.

"That's how I've picked up so many tips for Marc," she said. "I'm admitted to people's homes, you see. It's easy to get people talking about antiques if they have anything old, and from the questions they ask when I'm telling their fortunes, I usually know whether they need money. Marc says I find more things for him than anyone else."

She made calls all over the city, even among the wealthy in the Garden District. Her clients there owned more antiques than those in any other part of the city, but she earned very few commissions from them. "They can afford to hang onto their stuff," she said. She had last seen Marc the day before he went to St. Louis. She knew he was going away, but she hadn't known he intended to be gone so long. She had telephoned the store twice since then, with information for him, but he wasn't back yet. She was as astonished and alarmed as Dassily had been to learn that he had disappeared.

As we were preparing to leave, I asked her whether she would like to read my palm. She took my hand, exclaimed, "What a lovely lifeline!" and then thrust it away from her. "There are too many dark things in your life."

That was the way it went. Certainly we turned up nothing bright about Marc DeVarnay that afternoon and evening. We tracked down more than thirty of the people on Selma Garnett's list—tribute to the ingenuity and persistence of Dick Tosche. Some pursued perfectly legitimate occupations—there was a cab driver, a cook, and two waiters. There were two women clothing store clerks who located antiques through conversations with customers. There was one secretary to an attorney who sometimes discreetly picked up hints about antiques owned by his clients. There were several people, both male and female, who had no visible means of support. DeVarnay seemed to have dealt fairly with all of them and paid generous commissions whenever their tips proved profitable to him. All of the people respected him, but none of them had anything concrete to offer concerning his whereabouts.

We even made a tongue-in-cheek call at Griff Wylan's residence. He rented a room from a mustached woman who seemed uniquely qualified to work as bouncer in a crack house. As far as she was concerned, Little Boy's whereabouts were none of our business.

It was after dark when we finally retraced our steps. The beggars on Royal Street opposite DeVarnay's seemed to be doing a trickle of business. Those near my hotel weren't having any better luck than they'd had at seven that morning.

I invited Dick up to my room, and he waited while I made a list for him of the people we hadn't been able to find. He promised to track them down. He had been watching me work all afternoon, so he didn't need any suggestions about how to question them.

I had another job for him. I wanted to know whom the beggars watching my hotel and the antique store were reporting to. I needed someone to watch the watchers. Dick promised to recruit a few reliable street people for me.

"They'll keep an eye on them and see what can be found out," he promised.

After he left, I got out the dossier on Marc DeVarnay. There was nothing in it to account for the beggars' surveillance of me and of the store, but there hadn't been anything in his background to account for Pointe Neuve and Old Jake, either. They were inexplicables, and they could have been part of a pattern and connected, or they could have had nothing to do with each other.

What made the puzzle really difficult was the possibility that neither of them was directly connected to DeVarnay. Both Old Jake and the street people could have been remote tentacles of a beast who managed to keep hidden. To smoke him out, I would need an entirely different tack.

From the list of DeVarnay's acquaintances, I picked the name of Jeffrey Minjarus, a member of the law firm that handled the DeVarnay family's legal affairs. I telephoned him and made a date to meet him at Marc DeVarnay's residence the next morning. Minjarus knew all about Marc's disappearance— he had discussed it with Marc's mother, and he had been in touch with the police on her behalf. He promised to have Marc's cleaning woman there to answer questions.

With that taken care of, I went out to dinner. There was seafood jambalaya on the menu. Eating it might have helped me exorcise the food in Old Jake's *cabon*, but my appetite wasn't up to it. I ordered barbecued chicken instead and tried to pretend I was in Savannah.

When I returned to the hotel, Francis Dassily was waiting for me in the lobby. The desk clerk was keeping a wary eye on him. After the hotel's experience with Little Boy, the management was taking no chances, and Dassily's long hair automatically marked him a suspicious character.

He got to his feet when I entered. "Sorry to bother you," he said. "About Marc. I've talked with some of the others at the market. Everyone likes him, and most of us are indebted to him one way or another. Is there anything we can do?"

The desk clerk had lost interest. Dassily was well-mannered and had a softly pleasant, almost cultured voice. Further, he now was now my responsibility.

His question wasn't easily answered. The search hadn't yet reached the point where we needed a battalion of market vendors to beat the swamp and bayou country or drag the Mississippi. When it did, my part in it would be finished.

"At this stage, there isn't much anyone can do except keep eyes and ears open," I said. "For example—has anyone seen

Marc or heard of him being seen in the past two weeks? That sort of information would be invaluable. It also would be helpful if your friends would remain on the lookout for him."

Dassily nodded thoughtfully. "As I told you, I haven't seen him since the night he left for St. Louis. I don't know whether anyone else has. I'll ask."

"If you turn up any information at all, I'd like to know about it immediately."

"I'll see that you do," he promised.

I walked to the door with him. Then I went up to my room, where I retired early and slept well. I still hadn't caught up on the sleep lost during my hectic jaunt from Savannah to Seattle to New Orleans. If I entertained any intruders, I failed to notice.

CHAPTER SEVEN

At seven the next morning, Saturday, Raina Lambert telephoned. She had finished the case in Minneapolis; she was now in New Orleans and intended to stay there until, one way or another, we found Marc DeVarnay.

"I don't have a telephone yet," she said.

"Nice of you to let me know that—I mean, without my dressing, and going downstairs, and finding a public telephone to call you back."

"I want a full report. I'll meet you in Jackson Square Park at eleven."

"Don't you want to know—"

"Nothing now," she said and hung up.

I left the hotel shortly before nine o'clock and found a new pair of beggars outside. They had taken up different positions—one was across the street this time. The one nearest to the hotel entrance had a deformed walk, a speech impediment, and probably a mental disability as well. He tried to buttonhole me with a line taught to him years before: "I'm just a little boy, and I need something to eat." Now he was all of six feet tall and in his twenties, and he badly needed a new script.

The other was a young black man who went into his act, tap dancing, whenever anyone approached. He seemed genuinely talented, but he was ignoring the law of averages by performing at a time and place where there were few passersby.

There was only one watcher at DeVarnay's—if in fact he was a watcher. He was a balloon sculptor made up in whiteface like a mime, but he wore a clown costume and makeup: large red false nose; stringy orange wig; a battered hat reminiscent of Willy the Tramp; huge, floppy shoes; and a bulging stomach padded with a pillow. He had a cheerful patter and his display sculptures were cleverly made, but like the beggars at the hotel, he was working at the wrong time and place. No one paid any attention to him.

Dick Tosche had promised to check both places first thing in the morning, and he would tell me everything he knew about these three the next time we met.

I picked my way around and through the water splashed by employees of firms on Royal Street as they hosed down the sidewalks, a morning ritual in some parts of the New Orleans French Quarter. The water made no sense because the weather was again gray and overcast, and more rain was predicted.

I paused for another look at the window displays in DeVarnay's, and then I walked on, admiring Royal Street's galleries. I continued to meet few pedestrians, but the flow of passing cars was continuous at that time of morning. Despite its narrowness, Royal Street serves as a main one-way connection to Canal Street and the New Orleans business district.

Looking back, I was startled to see Cal Dreslow, the neatly dressed man whose begging had surprised Dick Tosche, adroitly matching my every move. It hadn't occurred to me that street people might be following me. At certain times of the day, these characters are so ubiquitous, and the French Quarter is so crowded, that it would be difficult for me to pick out a tail even if I knew I had one. I hoped someone had been trying to follow me the previous afternoon and evening when Dick Tosche had guided me in and out of the French Quarter in search of DeVarnay's contacts. We would have given them fits and confounded anyone who was trying to figure out what I was up to.

On this morning, however, I was merely calling at the home of the man I was trying to find, and anyone wanting to waste time and effort discovering that was welcome to it. I put Cal

Dreslow out of my mind and carried my gawking around the corner to St. Philip Street, where I saw more of the same—another street of lacy galleries splashed with greenery.

On my left were a café and a bar, typical side street establishments for the French Quarter except that these were exceptionally neat and attractive looking. They were called Heartbreak Café and Heartbreak Bar. I wondered whether the names might have significance for my investigation.

There was very little traffic of any kind on the French Quarter's side streets at that hour. The one pedestrian in sight was walking toward me, an attractive-looking, middle-aged black woman, neatly and conservatively dressed. She might have been a schoolteacher, but I used my superior powers of deduction and identified her as a cleaning woman because Minjarus and I were supposed to meet DeVarnay's housekeeper here.

The only other person I saw in that block was a thin-faced, middle-aged man with a gray mustache. He was wearing a black shirt with an off-color white vest, and he was seated on a stoop on the other side of the street softly strumming on a guitar. The rows of doorbells in the entranceway behind him indicated an apartment building. He gave me a disinterested glance and returned his thoughts to his music. There are times when French Quarter street musicians are pervasive enough to menace both hearing and sanity—like the professionals, they play loud, louder, or loudest—but normally they position themselves where there is enough foot traffic to make the contributions worthwhile. St. Philip Street at that time of morning didn't qualify, but this musician didn't seem to be collecting money. Of course he could have lived nearby and been playing for his own amusement.

I paid no attention to him, but I continued to ponder his presence there as I walked along. Had someone managed to anticipate where I was going?

Midway in the block was a sign that read "St. Philip Place." The black woman and I both turned in, and she asked, "Is you Mr. Pletcher?"

I admitted it. "You must be Millie," I said.

She nodded. She seemed friendly enough, but she had no smile for me. She was wearing the mask of high tragedy, and I met her gaze with what I hoped was an appropriately sympathetic expression.

"It's a terrible thing about Mr. DeVarnay," she said.

Those who knew Marc DeVarnay well seemed not only willing but eager to grimly proclaim his demise without any evidence at all. For the time being, I preferred to think of his disappearance as inexplicable. Whether nor not it was also terrible remained to be seen.

But I made no comment. My bayou adventure, and my brief review of DeVarnay's business and street connections, had confused rather than clarified the situation. I needed to know more about his personal life, and just for a start, I wanted to see his home. I didn't expect the missing man to answer the doorbell, though an oddity like that does happen from time to time, but before I looked further, I wanted a better understanding of what sort of person he was.

I also wanted to talk with someone who had known him personally. There may be better sources of information about a man than his housekeeper and his attorney—that depends on his own individual quirks—but it makes for an excellent beginning. The housekeeper only worked three half days a week for DeVarnay, but she had been with him for years. So here she was, and here I was, and the attorney would be along directly, all of which pleased me.

On the left as we turned in at St. Philip Place was a narrow two-story building. The ground floor was an artist's studio with paintings in the two display windows. New Orleans artists come in all kinds and flavors, and this one offered firmly expressionistic figures on shimmering impressionistic backgrounds. He brought it off deftly, and there was a solid air of prosperity about his establishment. At the inner end of the building were parking spaces for three cars. The one which was occupied was reserved for the artist himself—probably he lived upstairs. The two empty ones were for use by his customers. At the end of the short street was a tall iron fence of a type frequently seen in the French Quarter. Beyond its railings I saw a blur of greenery and, in the distance, a handsome old building. There was an automobile entrance and a pedestrian entrance, both locked.

Millie produced a ring of keys and unlocked the pedestrian gate. We entered, and I paused to admire the setting.

Buildings at the rear of French Quarter homes were once the living quarters of slaves. Some of them have been restored into the city's most choice dwellings. The space between them and the elaborate home the slave owner once occupied is often a magnificent courtyard. In this case, the owner's dwelling had succumbed to fire or decay long before, and only the former slave quarters remained—tastefully restored into three two-story condominiums with a separate second floor gallery for each. The former courtyard was now a beautifully landscaped front garden circled by a driveway. The entire state of Louisiana couldn't have offered a lovelier setting for a home. It resolved one question about Marc DeVarnay. No man would walk off and leave this place without a powerful reason.

The building belonged to the DeVarnay family, one of several French Quarter properties it owned.

At my suggestion, Millie left the gate unlocked for the attorney. As we strolled along companionably, I studied the cars parked in front of the three condominiums. They were, reading from right to left, a Dodge Caravan, a Ford Escort, and a flaming red Toyota Celica. Since the sporty Toyota was parked in front of the end condominium DeVarnay occupied, I presumed it was his—left at home when he traveled because he wouldn't trust it to an airport parking lot. The car, and his babying of it, suggested all kinds of unplumbed depths to his character.

As we approached the building, Millie suddenly shattered the morning quiet with a piercing shriek followed by several loud yells, after which she subsided to whimpering sobs. Her first outburst would have raised the dead if any of New Orleans's famous cemeteries had been located within hearing distance. It also had an electric effect on the living. I turned in alarm, ready to do battle for her if her life was actually threatened. If not, I was willing to summon a medical doctor or a psychiatrist as soon as I could figure out which she needed.

She pointed a trembling finger at the door. "*Gris-gris!*" she moaned. "Oh, my Gawd! *Gris-gris!*"

I could see nothing except a blob of yellow below the doorknob.

"I ain't goin' near that house," she announced. "I ain't never goin' near that house again."

At that moment the attorney made a timely entrance. Jeffrey Minjarus did not come from an old New Orleans family. He was a renegade from New England and certainly a junior member of his law firm, told off to satisfy the snoop from out of town. I didn't mind. He would know Marc DeVarnay far better than any of the senior partners would. He was a tall, slender man with an artfully trimmed black moustache, and whatever his age was, probably in his early thirties, he looked younger.

He had been assigned to keep an eye on the missing man's property, and he also had been present when the police, prodded by Jolitte DeVarnay, had made a superficial search of the house. Millie was well acquainted with him by this time, and she announced to him, firmly, that she wasn't goin' near that place, now or ever, handed him her ring of keys, and flounced away. He looked after her in amazement, plainly wondering how the study of law had managed to land him in a situation like this.

I introduced myself and gave him a Lambert and Associates card with the phone number of my hotel added. He pocketed it without a glance. "What's wrong with Millie?" he asked.

I pointed out the *gris-gris*. Then I went up to the door knob and removed it—a small yellow bag with a draw string. "What's in one of these things?" I asked him.

He shrugged. "Every doctor of voodoo has his own concoctions."

"Would an expert be able to tell us who put it there or why?"

"Probably not," he said. "The standard ingredients are

powdered brick, ochre, cayenne pepper, and maybe powder from dried herbs. Sometimes nail parings, or pieces of personal property, or hair are included. Bits of reptile skin or insects are other possibilities. It depends on the witch and also on what the object is, and only he—or she—will know that. Since it's hanging on the doorknob, I'd guess someone has placed a curse on this house or tried to remove one. What does it smell like?"

I took a sniff and recoiled. "It stinks."

"That suggests a curse. If the intention were beneficial, it probably would smell nice. But not necessarily. Voodoo doctors make their own rules."

"You seem to know all about this."

He grinned. "I once represented a voodoo doctor in court. It was educational. The plaintiff suing him claimed he had put a curse on her. Our defense was—first, there wasn't any such thing; second, even if there had been, the defendant wouldn't have known how; third, the plaintiff couldn't prove she actually had been cursed. We won the case."

"What's an innocent victim supposed to do? Curl up his toes and spout gibberish? Or maybe run off and hide? I'm wondering if this has anything to do with DeVarnay's disappearance. I've never tried to find a person who was fleeing from a voodoo curse."

"If he disappeared because someone was going to hang a *gris-gris* on his door a couple of weeks later—I know this wasn't here two days ago—he has the gift of precognition, and you'll never find him. But even if he'd known about it, he had no reason to hide. He could have hared off to another doctor of voodoo and bought a countercharm."

"I see. Doctors of voodoo collect from both sides. It's an ancient art with thoroughly modern business practices."

Minjarus belatedly remembered my card. He took it out and studied it.

"You're Jay Pletcher?"

"The 'J' stands for 'Jehoshaphat.' I call myself 'J' for short."

"I'd change it to another letter entirely. I don't suppose there's anything 'Jehoshaphat' could be shortened into."

"Nothing that could be repeated in polite society." I pocketed the *gris-gris* and suggested we continue our conversation inside.

The door opened onto an entrance hall with a broad stairway at the rear. Minjarus turned to the right, but I stopped and stared. The living room looked like a display window for DeVarnay's antique store. It was magnificently furnished with beautiful old furniture that was either perfectly restored or perfectly cared for—the rich finishes looked new. The designs were in a fairly heavy style that I later heard called "American Empire." Even the carpet looked antique.

When I commented on the furniture, Minjarus said, "They're Mallards. Nineteenth-century New Orleans furniture maker. Marc is an authority on him. Mallard is both his business and his vice. He sells, and he collects. When an exceptional piece comes along, he keeps it for himself."

"I know," I said. "Some Mallards were being auctioned in St. Louis. That was what took him there."

I had told Minjarus on the phone that I needed personal information about DeVarnay. He arranged himself carefully on an antique sofa as though preparing for a firing squad and asked, "What is it you want to know?"

"Can you spare a few minutes? I'd like to walk through the house first."

He nodded, and I stood in the center of the room taking it in—the superb furniture, the carpet, the lined white drapes, the antique-looking wall paper. The oil paintings were by "Frederick," the artist whose pictures I had admired in DeVarnay's store and the one Aaron Vidler was envious of. These were pastel views of the French Quarter in that same delicately modern impressionistic style, and they looked exquisite.

Minjarus was watching me. Suddenly he chuckled. "Are you going to pull a Sherlock—open a drawer or two, look behind a mirror and under a vase, and then announce, 'The missing man is holed up in a motel in Houston?'"

"I wish it were that easy," I said. "I may be wasting my time—and yours—but one never knows what's to be found until one looks."

I stood for a moment admiring the view from the front window—the lovely garden with galleries of the French Quarter looming beyond the fence. Then I turned to a dining room that also was furnished with splendid antiques. These included a large table with matching chairs, a chiffonier, and a glass-fronted cabinet. The set of dishes in the cabinet looked more valuable than the furniture. There were more paintings by "Frederick," and anyone not suffering from degenerating moroseness would have refused to trade one of them for all of the paintings I had seen in Aaron Vidler's apartment.

Beyond the dining room was a music room with a fantastically carved piano, a so-called baby grand, that must have been a prized antique, but there wasn't a scrap of music in sight or any indication at all that anyone actually lived here and played on this splendid old instrument. Possessing and displaying beautiful things had been more important to DeVarnay than enjoying the use of them.

There was a fireplace with a white mantelpiece, and on the mantelpiece was a strange plant, a mere stalk with an enormous, hauntingly beautiful purplish bloom that looked like a grotesquely large lily. The flower was all of a foot high with a long spike protruding from it. It was so large, and so perfectly formed, that it looked artificial. On each side of the fireplace was a tall painting by "Frederick" of the same or a similar plant, showing views from either side, and the three plants in a row not only caught the attention but kept bringing one's eyes back to them.

I stepped into the room and turned to admire an antique sofa. Then I halted, sniffed quickly, and backed away. There was no mistaking that smell. It was the relentless, cloying, penetrating stench of death, and the memory of it from Old Jake's *cabon* still burned my nostrils.

Minjarus was seated where I had left him, waiting patiently.

"I'm afraid I've found him," I said.

He arched his eyebrows. "Found—Marc? You mean—you found him *here*?"

I nodded. "He won't be a pretty sight. He may have been dead for almost two weeks."

"But he can't be here!" Minjarus protested. "The police searched the house at the end of last week. They didn't find a thing."

"I've smelled corpses before," I said. "I smelled one day before yesterday. My nose doesn't lie. Come and have a whiff yourself."

He followed me to the music room, took the whiff I suggested—and burst into laughter. "That damned Voodoo Lily," he said.

"Voodoo Lily?" I echoed.

He pointed at the mantle piece. "Beautiful flower, but it smells God awful. I never could figure out why Marc is so fond of these stinking things. He cultivates them, both here and at his mother's place, and he's got dozens of them in an air-conditioned greenhouse where he can simulate the seasons. He's excessively proud of the fact that he almost always has one in bloom for his mantelpiece. I've told him it's a morbid hobby."

"Voodoo Lily?" I repeated again.

"It has other names. Sacred Lily of India and Giant Snake Lily are a couple I remember. The scientific name is Hydrosme Rivieri. It's been known to grow flowers more than three feet high. This one looks to be about a foot, which is the best Marc has been able to do.

"Voodoo Lily," I muttered a third time.

It filled the room with stench and could be smelled even in the dining room. I couldn't understand why it had taken me so long to notice it. I must have been concentrating furiously on the antiques. I hadn't realized how much this case was getting on my nerves: Certified witches, *gris-gris*, Voodoo Lilies, with an entire panoply of street *poux* mixed in.

I pulled the *gris-gris* from my pocket and said again, "Voodoo

Lily. Do you suppose—"

"No, no—there couldn't possibly be a connection," Minjarus protested. "Marc has been growing those plants for years. I suppose they're called "voodoo" because the stock produces its bloom after its growing season is over and without either soil or water. The stench has nothing to do with the name." He regarded me with amusement. "Have you discovered anything else?"

I felt chagrined as well as indignant. "This place is not a home," I announced. "It's a museum. I can't believe anyone actually lives here."

"I suppose no one does," Minjarus said. "Marc eats out and does his entertaining in restaurants. He has never socialized much. He spends most of his waking hours at his store. All he does here is sleep."

"And cultivate Voodoo Lilies," I said grimly. "I can understand why he doesn't entertain much. If he keeps his home filled with those things, he'd have to provide gas masks for his guests. The hobby wouldn't appeal to me, but it's him I'm trying to understand. He must enjoy owning the flowers and all these antiques even if he doesn't spend much time here."

"I guess that's about it."

Minjarus returned to the living room, and I walked through the remainder of the house. There were three bedrooms upstairs, all beautifully furnished with antiques—Mallards, I supposed. Mallard must have been at his best with bedroom furniture. None of the bedrooms, not even DeVarnay's, looked as though it had ever been occupied.

I inventoried the closet and decided DeVarnay's sartorial taste had been influenced by his expertise with antiques. A fashion expert would have called him old-fashioned. There were two tuxedos, which seemed odd considering how little he socialized, but only three suits. Of course two or three suits were missing—the one he was wearing when he disappeared and one or two he had taken with him in the leather suitcase. There was no informal clothing at all, but he would have kept something at his store or warehouse to change into if he did any work on the antiques himself. No doubt he employed a gardener to look after the garden, along with Millie to keep his house up. He was an ideal employer—nothing out of place, ever; no mess to clean; no dishes to wash; no entertaining. Millie must have been terrified of voodoo to quit such a soft job over one *gris-gris*.

I confirmed that his toilet articles and razor were missing. I had caught a glimpse of a set, supposedly his, in his open suitcase in Old Jake's *cabon*. Finally I went back downstairs, seated myself on an antique chair, and—before asking any questions—assured Minjarus that a detective treated confidences at least as sacrosanctly as an attorney did.

He grinned. "It will all be hearsay anyway and therefore inadmissible."

I told him hearsay evidence is the best possible kind for a detective. Usually, that's all he gets. On that bright note, we talked about DeVarnay.

Minjarus had known him socially and professionally for at least ten years as a brilliant, hard-working, immensely capable man. He had been an honor student in fine arts at Tulane University, worked in several antique stores after graduation, and then founded his own business.

"Of course having a rich mother helped," Minjarus said. "Marc wouldn't have made it so quickly without Jolitte's money, but he certainly would have got there eventually. He has everything it takes to succeed and no qualities at all on the debit side. He doesn't even have any bad habits. He doesn't smoke. He'll accept a social drink, but I've never seen him take two."

"Girl friends?" I asked.

"For a long time he was engaged to the daughter of one of his mother's oldest friends. A lovely girl—she's a lovely woman, now. It would have been a union of two old families, and everyone was enthused about it. They 'went together' for years but never got around to setting a date. Finally they called the whole thing off."

"Engagements rarely get terminated from mutual lack of

interest," I said. "One or the other called it off. Which one?"

"I guess she did, but neither of them seemed to feel very strongly about it. I think it was a case of two highly self-sufficient people wanting to keep their independence. Probably there had been family pressure on them to get engaged, and it was useful for awhile to have someone to attend formal functions with, but eventually it got to be a bore."

"He hasn't been carrying a torch?"

"Heavens, no. And they're still good friends. I still see them together—not often, but once in a great while."

"Then he didn't suddenly go to pieces over it."

"Certainly not. They broke up three or four years ago."

He continued with more of the same. Marc DeVarnay was a paragon. Got on splendidly with his mother, remained friendly with his ex-*fiancée*, was liked by everyone. Was spectacularly successful in his work. Was going to inherit a lot of money— Minjarus thought the exact figure would be about nine point eight million. DeVarnay had a fine sense of community and invested time, effort, and money in local charities. He belonged to the Krewe of Cadoc, an old New Orleans carnival organization, and he was working up in its hierarchy to the point where he would be running it and its Mardi Gras parade before many years passed. Only a man from an old New Orleans family could achieve that, and he had all the credentials. Years before, his mother had been a sensationally beautiful Mardi Gras "Maid of the Court" and, much later, queen. His father served as krewe captain for more than a decade. Marc seemed destined for the same role. As far as Minjarus knew, he was looking forward to it. There was no scandal in his life. He had no enemies. "Of all the people I know in New Orleans," Minjarus said, "Marc is the last one I would have expected to disappear."

I told him I would like to come back when I had more time and go over the house like a detective. He telephoned Jolitte DeVarnay, Marc's mother, and got permission to turn Millie's keys over to me. I gave him a receipt for them, and we left together, locking the house and then the gate behind us. We parted on St. Philip Street. He headed for his parked car, and I turned in the opposite direction, away from the Heartbreak Café and Heartbreak Bar. I wondered again whether the names were trying to tell me something.

The guitar player on the stoop across St. Philip Street was still strumming. My mind was on more important matters, and I ignored him. I now had seen the places where DeVarnay was spending most of his life: His business and his home. I had a firm notion of what kind of person he was, and I didn't believe it.

CHAPTER EIGHT

One of the most important streets in the New Orleans French Quarter is Chartres Street, which—because the St. Louis Cathedral is located on it—one might think was named in honor of the French city of Chartres and its renown cathedral. Actually, Chartres—and several other French Quarter streets, Bourbon, Orléans, Burgundy, Conti, and Condé among them—were named for important families of the French nobility by the early eighteenth century promoters of New Orleans. From time to time during the years and decades and centuries that have followed, one or another of those streets has managed to live up to—or down to—its disreputable origin.

When Chartres Street passes in front of St. Louis Cathedral, it becomes the pedestrian mall Place Jean Paul Deux. On either side of the pedestrian mall, Chartres Street resumes.

The name 'Chartres' is pronounced SHAR-tra by the French. The residents of the French Quarter of this grand old French city of La Nouvelle Orleans, which prides itself on its French heritage and the preservation of its noble French traditions, pronounce it "Charters." This is not surprising in a city where the euphonious Terphsichore Street is now pronounced "Texico," a transformation explained to me by a local citizen interested in such matters as a perfectly natural process of word shortening by which Terph-SICH-or-e became TerphSIchor, which became TERPsico, which became Texico. In an even more intriguing twist, Coio Street is pronounced "C-O-Ten." Such local mutilations are clear enough to everyone concerned except the unfortunate stranger who has to ask for directions.

Shortly after I turned the corner from St. Philip Street onto Chartres, I had the feeling, probably influenced by my earlier glimpse of that unlikely beggar, Cal Dreslow, that I was being followed. I was not surprised. In fact, I was expecting it. I hadn't seen Dreslow when I left St. Philip Place, but he could have been waiting down the street and around the corner.

I resisted the impulse to turn and look for him, that being the worst thing one can do under such circumstances. If you practice patience, sooner or later you can catch a glimpse without the guilty party knowing he is spotted.

A few minutes later I paused to glance into a shop window, and to my immense surprise I discovered that my tail was neither Dreslow, as I expected, nor the guitar player whose presence had puzzled me. It was a she. She had turned the corner onto Chartres shortly after I did, and she walked on my heels all the way to Jackson Square, but whether she was following me in the detective sense was an open question since the square was only two blocks away and a common destination in the French Quarter. At that point, my speculation concerning her motives could have been nothing more than an indication of a nasty, suspicious mind, which of course I have.

At Jackson Square, where the pedestrian malls are always more crowded on weekends and holidays, I cheerfully plunged into the turmoil, threading my way through clusters of tourists and around portrait artists, tarot tables, mimes, and blaring musicians.

The uniquely varied shops in the Pontalba Buildings on either side of the square were being heavily patronized by the Saturday crowds of tourists. Even the eating places were enjoying a surge of business from those who had missed breakfast and couldn't wait for lunch. Street characters, some of them offering worthless trinkets for sale, angled for handouts. I avoided all of that and eventually found my way to one of the park gates. Despite my dodges and frequent changes of direction, the woman following me kept resolutely on my heels.

The beautiful fenced park in the center of the square offers a refreshingly tranquil refuge in the midst of the tumult surrounding it. It seemed strange that so few people were taking the time to enjoy it. The grass was green and inviting; the variety of trees and shrubs even included tree-like banana plants on which a few green bunches had survived into November. The landscaping seemed sculptured to provide a frame for the cathedral at the head of the square with the statue of Andrew Jackson at its center. The triple-spired cathedral has a beautiful simplicity of design that makes most foreign cathedrals seem cluttered by comparison.

Unfortunately, quiet loveliness never has been much of a tourist draw. Noise, bright lights, and action attract the crowds, and visitors to New Orleans are far more interested in what goes on outside the park. Those with an urge to meditate can cross Decatur Street and climb the steps to the walk atop the levee, where there are spectacular, sweeping views of the Mississippi, its bridges, the West Bank (over which the sun rises in the east each morning), river traffic that includes ships from everywhere visiting the world's second largest port (or first largest, depending on who is counting), and also the New Orleans skyline.

Even the birds had deserted the park. Because signs there forbade anyone to feed them, I suspected New Orleans of fostering its own special breed of literate pigeons—well-mannered creatures with the intelligence to avoid places displaying such discourteous proclamations. Later I discovered a more mundane reason. There are no strictures on feeding birds in the streets just outside the park, and these are littered with snacks spilled accidentally or on purpose. The birds go where the food is.

My tail—if tail she was—followed me into the park and along the walk, and when I seated myself on a bench, she sat down nearby, took a Guinea pig from a bag she was carrying, and gently placed it on the grass. It wore a harness to which a leash was attached. It was a novel kind of pet to take for a stroll, but novelty is commonplace in New Orleans.

The grass was lush in the park, even in November, and the Guinea pig began to munch happily. I wondered whether its owner was really tailing me or whether she merely belonged to the long line of New Orleans street characters who have contributed their small bits to the obscure history of that craft. A Guinea pig definitely was bizarre equipment for a tailing job but natural enough for a street character, "street character" being just another way of making a living in New Orleans. A "Guinea Pig Lady" fit in nicely with the Bead Lady, and Ruthie the Duck Girl, and a host of others—including Hattie the Hat Lady, whom I had met the day before. Occasionally one of them gains renown outside the French Quarter and even as far away as Baton Rouge. Ruthie the Duck Girl once ran—in a strictly local way—for President of the United States, brandishing the motto "Kiss My Ass," which her supporters thought as good as those of the major candidates and far more apt.

The Guinea Pig Lady seemed of a different sort, but that could have been because she was so obviously pregnant. Perhaps her impending motherhood had had a mellowing effect on her. She was of medium height with long, black hair, and in spite of possessing the gloomiest, most unhappy face I had seen that morning, she was highly attractive. She definitely was not dressed like a street person, which heightened the mystery. She wore a tasteful maternity gown, and it, along with her sweater and shoes, had not come from one of the French Quarter's ubiquitous souvenir stores or even from Wal-Mart. Her clothes were expensive.

I wasted several minutes wondering why anyone as blatantly conspicuous as an attractive, heavily pregnant woman would try to tail me. She might count on being overlooked for that very reason—at first glance, few people would suspect her of a gumshoe act. On the other hand, any subject with a normally functioning mentality would be bound to turn on his curiosity if the same pregnant woman turned up on his heels everywhere he went.

At least she hadn't walked all the way from St. Philip Street with her Guinea pig on its leash in the manner that Ruthie the Duck Girl once paraded about the French Quarter with her pet. Also, she was fond of the little animal. She kept a careful eye on it in case anyone failed to obey the posted strictures on dogs—the sign forbade dogs, bicycles, littering, and soliciting as well as feeding birds—or in case a dog happened along that couldn't read.

She was very pleasant to look at. The sign said nothing about ogling, but I avoided that charge anyway by sending no more than an occasional glance her way while enviously watching the guinea pig. I was wishing my mind had something nourishing to chew on. I would much prefer shoveling manure to looking for a missing person—which is what one frequently ends up doing anyway right after the family's dirty laundry has been sorted.

Police, who have considerable experience in such matters, don't care much for missing person cases, either. Jolitte DeVarnay had called them idiots, but I credited them with being bright enough to figure out that a son who is past thirty and still under his mother's thumb could have had, or thought he had, ample reason for disappearing.

There was one intriguing fact about the case that no one was bothering to explain: The night DeVarnay flew to St. Louis, he ordered a cab and then cancelled it. I had spent considerable time constructing plausible scenarios for that and trying to make one of them fit the subsequent events.

Whatever his original motive had been, DeVarnay now had a reason for dropping out of sight that even the police would consider adequate. He surely knew his name would appear on everyone's wanted list the moment Old Jake's body was found. Where would he hide?

In these days of transportation marvels, a missing or wanted person can be two continents away the morning after his disappearance. DeVarnay hadn't taken his passport, but that might have been left behind as a blind. He easily could have acquired another under an assumed name, paid for out of the missing forty-five grand, and he could have taken as much money with him as he wanted. Not only did he own a thriving business, but he had independent sources of wealth.

By now he might be anywhere—even in New Orleans. The fact that he had been seen in Pointe Neuve shortly after he left Seattle seemed significant. The more I thought it, the more the possibility that a native of New Orleans might decide to disappear by remaining at home appealed to me. Many people are far more comfortable and feel more secure in the place they know best. DeVarnay could put on a T-shirt with the logo of the Hog's Breath Saloon & Café, a silly hat labeled "Texas Alligator Wrestling Team" with simulated blood stains, let his beard grow, and lose himself in the crowds of tourists. Or he could don old clothes, a wig, and a false beard, carry a guitar, and join a crowd of similarly-arrayed street people. It would be a form of invisibility, but a person would have to have the right mental attitude to bring it off. The question was whether DeVarnay had enough savvy to realize no one would be likely to look for him on Bourbon Street or in Jackson Square.

If he did try to hide by remaining in plain sight, street people or market vendors would be more likely to spot him than anyone else. Asking Francis Dassily and his friends to keep their eyes and ears open could have been the best move I had made in the case.

A stunningly beautiful redhead strolled past and winked at me. Fortunately the Guinea Pig Lady, who regarded her suspiciously, hadn't seen the wink, or she might have accused the newcomer of violating the rule against soliciting.

She had, but her morals were above reproach. She was Raina Lambert. I allowed a decent amount of time to elapse, and then I followed her to a remote corner of the park, walked past her to a gate as though I were about to leave, and then changed my mind and found a bench near hers. Raina had got out a couple of books and a notebook, and she was pretending to read and take notes.

The Guinea Pig Lady had started to comb her pig's hair,

which was of the curly variety, and she seemed to be ignoring us. Even so, Raina and I pretended not to know each other. We faced in different directions and talked guardedly.

"I hope I didn't interrupt anything," Raina said.

I told her about the Guinea Pig Lady. "I don't know whether she tailed me to the park or whether she followed me by accident. She could have been coming here anyway. There probably aren't many Guinea pig pastures with public access in the French Quarter."

We had been on the case for more than a week, and we had plenty to talk about, but it added up to a very large nothing.

"Those sheriff's deputies down in the swamp are an unusually suspicious bunch," I said. "The only information I got was what I managed to overhear. Have you been able to pick up anything from Lieutenant Keig?"

"Everything I wanted."

"I suppose DeVarnay left fingerprints all over the *cabon*."

"No, he didn't. They didn't find his prints anywhere except on his luggage—on the *inside* of his luggage, I should say—and on the jambalaya pan."

I whistled. My aversion to jambalaya had just been reinforced.

"Old Jake's fingerprints were on the suitcase handle," she went on, "but that's easily accounted for. He carried his visitor's luggage. There were prints on the pan other than DeVarnay's, maybe from a clerk in the store it came from, since it was new. The police are still looking into that. But none from Old Jake."

"Are the police still taking DeVarnay's disappearance casually?"

"Actually, they never did. They couldn't do much about it before because they almost literally didn't have a clue, and his mother insisted there be no publicity. Now they'll really go after him. He's a murder suspect."

"Which is nonsense," I said.

"Not from their viewpoint. The witnesses you found, plus DeVarnay's fingerprints in the *cabon*, are as much evidence as they need at this stage. As far as they're concerned, DeVarnay is a murder suspect trying to escape. They have it worked out like this: DeVarnay returned from Seattle under an assumed name. Probably he already knew Old Jake and arranged in advance to hide out in his *cabon*. He had been with Old Jake for a day or two before the two of them went to Pointe Neuve to buy supplies. Why are you shaking your head?"

"First, if he'd been with Old Jake that long, there should be a lot more evidence of his presence there. How many days can a man live in a place without touching anything except one pan? What about the spoon? He must have stirred the jambalaya with something. Second, if he really was hiding out, why would he go to the village? He could have sent Old Jake after the supplies. Third, once he got to Pointe Neuve, why would he go out of his way to draw attention to himself by meeting people and making inquiries about real estate? Surely the police can do better than that."

"They figure they can get that kind of information from DeVarnay after they catch him. The police version has it that DeVarnay was in Pointe Neuve with Old Jake—something a defense attorney would have a hard time refuting because of the witnesses—after which the two of them went back to the *cabon* together. That evening DeVarnay started to fix dinner. You can bet the police already know he occasionally cooked up a gumbo or a jambalaya for friends. If they're really astute, they've had the jambalaya in the cabin analyzed for comparison with his favorite recipe. While DeVarnay was cooking, he and Old Jake quarreled about something, and he bashed Old Jake in the head. He lost his own at the same instant and fled without thinking to take his suitcase with him."

"Either the report about his not drinking was wrong, or insanity runs in his family," I said.

"He was under great stress at the time. Or so the police reason."

"Drunkenness or insanity are the only ways I can account for this. If he took the missing forty-five grand with him, and he wanted to disappear, why would he travel as far as Seattle under his own name and draw attention to himself by cashing small traveler's checks when he certainly didn't need money? None of it makes any sense."

"The police think it does. What do you think?"

"I think this is a jambalaya mess. Everyone likes and admires DeVarnay. Huge numbers of people are dependent on him. Therefore no one wanted him missing, and he had no personal, or business, or social reason for disappearing. *Ergo*, he hasn't disappeared, so what are we doing here?" I waited for her to comment. When she didn't, I went on, "It might help if we understood DeVarnay better. I've been trying to figure him out, but any man who lives in a museum is beyond figuring. I haven't the faintest notion of what's going on unless he's pulled an Edgar on us."

She turned and blinked at me. "Pulled a what?"

"An Edgar. From Edgar Allan Poe. *The Purloined Letter.* Hiding something by keeping it in plain sight." I told her my theory about DeVarnay disappearing among the New Orleans tourists or street people. "He turned police attention away from New Orleans by his jaunt to Seattle, and then he came back here."

"How do you fit Pointe Neuve into that?"

"The question is how DeVarnay intended to fit Pointe Neuve into it. Obviously something went wrong there. But New Orleans is still a good place for him to hide."

She didn't think much of it. "How will you look for him? By sitting here in Jackson Square and hoping he'll eventually walk by and fall over you? Even if what you say is true, there's no guarantee you would recognize him if you did see him. There's a barbershop down the street that advertises all kinds of weird haircuts: Warlocks, Dreadlocks, Spindlelocks, Bobtails, Ragtails, Monotails, Sticks, Stubs, Cablecurls, Frizzettes...."

"I've never heard of most of them."

"Neither have I. They'll also install nose and earrings and studs while you wait. I'm willing to pay for a nose ring for you.

Or rings—get as many as you like and put them on your expense account. The point is that DeVarnay may be looking nothing like his picture by this time, whether he's here or in Timbuktu."

"Not Timbuktu. He didn't take his passport—unless he acquired one in another name with a photo none of his friends can identify. Will his mother accept him back if she doesn't recognize him?"

"I've never seen you so contrary. What's bothering you?" she demanded.

"All I've done is run in circles. I don't know how to go about finding a missing man among hordes of tourists in a strange city. I thought I was onto something with his use of disreputable characters to find antiques for him, but a lot of his contacts are highly respectable, and all of them would lose a source of income if anything happened to him. I need new leads and a new approach."

"You're groused because you had to leave Savannah. Turn that off and start thinking. Mrs. DeVarnay will supply all the leads you need. She wants to see you. One o'clock this afternoon. Be cautiously optimistic without promising anything."

"There's no way I could promise her anything. I left my imagination in Savannah. Or maybe it was Reno."

"Seriously—can you give this case any kind of a plausible scenario?"

"I've turned up one suspect, a rival antique dealer named Harold Nusiner. He has a store on Magazine Street. DeVarnay grabbed some antiques Nusiner thought he was entitled to. Maybe DeVarnay engaged in some slick dealing, or maybe he simply got there first. When Nusiner complained, DeVarnay snubbed him. When Nusiner asked DeVarnay to go halves with him on a pet project, DeVarnay refused to discuss it. Nusiner's feelings were hurt. He bought a voodoo charm and made DeVarnay disappear."

"How much of that is true?"

"All of it, even including the voodoo charm, which I have in my pocket. The only thing I can't prove is that Nusiner hung it on DeVarnay's door himself. I supplied that by logical deduction."

"Then Nusiner deserves a look even though that kind of feud rarely amounts to anything. People who make a living dealing in antiques have to expect good luck and bad luck, dry spells along with wet spells. They don't try to do away with a competitor who's having a run of luck. They know their turn will come. See what sort of person Nusiner is. What else do you have?"

"I'm intrigued by the cancelled taxicab. That can only mean one thing—someone offered DeVarnay a ride to the airport, or he asked someone to take him. Remember—he had just talked with his mother. He said nothing to her about changed plans. I'm wondering whether he suddenly found out something between the two calls to the cab company. Or whether someone had urgent information for him and offered him a ride to the airport so he could deliver it. If it was bad news, it could account for his odd behavior at the auction. He decided to disappear, and he tried to cover his trail by disappearing from Seattle. He returned here under an assumed name and hid out with Old Jake."

"Why return here?"

"Because the problem is here, and this is where he has to be if he's going to deal with it."

"And the problem?"

"Blank check. Maybe he decided to magnify his millions by smuggling drugs, like the businessmen the customs agent mentioned, and he got in beyond his depth. Maybe it's a personal problem. We don't know enough about him to say."

"Then let's get on with it and find out."

She finally had acquired a private phone. When she got to her feet and began to gather up her belongings, she left a slip of paper on the bench with her new phone number and also Jolitte DeVarnay's address. I watched her departure out of the corner of my eye and made another discovery. The Guinea Pig Lady had abandoned me. Now she was following Raina Lambert. She picked up her pig and tucked it into her bag when she saw Raina getting ready to leave. By the time Raina reached the park gate, the Guinea Pig Lady was right behind her. The two of them turned onto Decatur Street.

When I started back to my charming French Quarter hotel, I still had the odd feeling I was being followed. I walked a block before I was able to manage a glance behind me. This time it was the character with the black shirt and off-white vest I had seen strumming a guitar on a stoop opposite St. Philip Place. He was carrying his guitar with a strap around his shoulder, and he couldn't have been more conspicuous if he had been pregnant.

When I reached my hotel, I paused at the door to make certain the same beggars were still on the job. Then I entered, leaving the guitar player in the street.

I now felt positive that this wasn't a simple disappearance case—not that I had ever had the slightest doubt. With such a rudimentary problem, the detective is not tailed, no one gets curious enough about him to order a bungled search of his room, and watches are not placed on his hotel and on the missing man's business establishment.

It definitely was not a simple disappearance case. What kind of case it was I still had no idea.

CHAPTER NINE

If Marc DeVarnay's disappearance was triggered by some
incident in his recent past, as I suspected, his mother almost
certainly would be the last person to know anything about it.
Friends his own age, as well as business associates, would be
far more familiar with his day to day activities. They also would
talk about him more candidly. At a later stage of the investigation, Jolitte DeVarnay might be able to fill in a few blanks, but
right now I simply wasn't ready for her.

She was the client, however, and she was ready for me.

First I took time for a quick lunch. McDonald's and others
of its ilk have firm beachheads in New Orleans, like everywhere else, but these upstarts will never displace the hefty
fast food sandwiches indigenous to the city: the Po-Boy, and,
out of the New Orleans's Italian heritage, the muffuletta. The
French Quarter McDonald's has tried to join them with a Cajun
McChicken, which tastes like a regular McChicken generously
peppered. Firms specializing in Po-Boys and muffulettas aren't
likely to lose sleep over it.

Unfortunately, the only indigenous touch available in my
hotel's coffee shop was a croissant sandwich. I had one, and
then, after making certain the beggars were still in place outside
the hotel, I took a cab to the Garden District. I routinely checked
for a tail en route but saw nothing suspicious. Thus far the watch
on me had not sprouted wheels.

New Orleans has been called many things, either with affection or with irritation: Crescent City; the Big Easy; Gumboville;

Food—or Jazz, or Sin—City; Carnival Town; the City that Care Forgot; the City of Canals (it has more than a hundred miles of them as compared to Venice's measly twenty-eight); the International City, so-called because it is home to all nationalities.

It also could be called Museum City. The number of institutions dedicated to the past, or to special interests, is remarkable for a community of its size. There is a Museum of Art; a Pharmacy Museum; various museums devoted to aspects of the Mardi Gras; a Railroad Museum; a Wildlife and Fisheries Museum; an American-Italian Museum; a Confederate Museum; a Children's Museum; a Wax Museum; a Historic Voodoo Museum; a Football Hall of Fame Museum; a Naval Museum (on an aircraft carrier); various historical museums; a National Guard Museum; a museum devoted to the history of jazz. This is only the beginning of a list that also includes a number of "open to view" historic homes with period furnishings.

The overwhelming quantity obscures the fact that two large areas of the city are themselves museums. In most places, the saying "hand in hand with a statelier past" would be poetic fantasy. In New Orleans, it is an ever-present aspiration, glimpsed repeatedly in the French Quarter and still a way of life behind many of the imposing facades of the Garden District, the latter being a sixty-four block area of handsome homes a century to a century and a half old.

Many of the Garden District homes have interesting local histories, and several have national or international importance. The author George Washington Cable entertained such celebrities as Mark Twain and Joel Chandler Harris here. One of the homes was built by the uncle of the French artist Degas, and Degas himself was a visitor to the Garden District. A few blocks from Jolitte DeVarnay's home was the house where Jefferson Davis died in 1889.

I paid the cab driver and stood for a moment admiring the DeVarnay mansion's imposing contours before I started up the walk. It was of stately "Greek Revival" architecture, with "double galleries"—broad porches across the front facade on both levels of the house, with double rows of white columns. The building was L-shaped and festooned with balconies, patios, and open porches.

Raina Lambert had described the household to me. Jolitte DeVarnay kept only two live-in servants, an elderly black woman who had been almost a life-long companion, and an elderly black man who had served as her butler for decades and had been in her employ since the year of her marriage. A much younger woman came in during the day to cook and clean. Part-time servants were hired as needed. A middle-aged black man, who also had been with her for years, looked after the garden and outside work. The thought that this immense, magnificent mansion was inhabited by one proud old woman with two elderly servants was saddening.

The front steps had been recently scrubbed; they were still damp. I looked at my watch as I mounted them. When calling on a duchess, one should take pains to be prompt. I rang the bell right on the stroke of one. James, the elderly butler, gray-haired, portly, superbly dignified in a neatly pressed black suit, admitted me, told me Mrs. DeVarnay was expecting me, and led me to a sitting room at the rear of the first floor.

The house's upkeep was immaculate, and the rich antique interiors sparkled. The fabulous, long dining room had a curved bay window at one end and a stunning chandelier of lacy-looking glass suspended from a high, painted ceiling with ornate cornices. The only false note was provided by the books I glimpsed as we passed the library. They had embossed leather bindings, and there was an aura about them like that surrounding an expensive piano in an unmusical household—faithfully dusted and polished but never played.

This house was not a museum, like Marc DeVarnay's residence. With the exception of the books, the lovely old furnishings had the look of cherished possessions that were enjoyed and used. We passed a spectacular spiral staircase, made a turning, and reached the door of the sitting room, where James announced, "The detective, Ma'am," in the same tone of voice he would have used to introduce the plumber.

Anyone laboring under the false impression that there is no royalty in the United States has never met a Jolitte DeVarnay, and on this afternoon she was at her regal best. She looked as though she had dressed to sit for her portrait. Probably in her youth she had been handsome, rather than pretty, and she still was. No gray hair was out of place in her elegant coiffure, which was the more striking for its stylish simplicity. A woman who is a Royal DeVarnay has the poise and self-confidence to grow old gracefully without resorting to cheapening artifices such as color rinses or dyes.

Her gown also was unpretentious, but it still managed to convey the impression it had cost a fortune. Her eyes were steely gray, and she held her slender form ramrod erect and seemed to regard me sternly without actually looking at me, which is a good trick. Whatever burden fate imposed on her would be carried proudly with head unbowed. Like a true duchess, she made no motion to stand and greet me.

The elderly black woman who was her servant and companion sat nearby. There was a small fire in the fireplace to take the damp chill off the day, and the room felt cozy. French doors looked onto a fabulous garden where flowers were still blooming in November.

Jolitte DeVarnay introduced her servant. "This is my life-long friend Dorothy, who shares my joys and also my sorrows."

We murmured pleasantries, and Jolitte DeVarnay said, "Please sit down, Mr. Pletcher."

Up to that point, I could have written the script in advance. Now she surprised me. I was prepared for a barrage of questions, but she said, "Miss Lambert said you would want to know all about Marc," and she proceeded to tell me. All about him, at least from his mother's viewpoint. She talked for an hour. She described Marc as a child—a good child. Marc growing up—a good boy. Marc as a university student—a fine student, a splendid young man. Marc as a successful businessman.

For the first time in her life she had encountered something she couldn't deal with. Her wealth and influence hadn't helped her, and the people she'd had to appeal to were not susceptible either to feminine wiles or her strength of character. Her only remaining recourse was to hire a detective. She had bought the most expensive one available—her money could accomplish that much—but she didn't quite know what to do with him. She thought perhaps if I saw Marc the way she did, I would understand why he had to be found quickly.

Finally she turned and fixed her eyes on me. "I talked with Lieutenant Keig," she said. "He told me the sheriff's deputies actually believe Marc killed that old man. He even hinted it might be better if I didn't go on looking for him. The police will find him eventually, he said. What is your opinion?"

"Police officers rarely say what they think," I said. "If he were my son, I would go on looking for him."

"What makes you so certain?"

"Right now the few facts we have can point in any direction. It's a question of what one wants to believe. The police think they have witnesses who can place Marc in Pointe Neuve, but I haven't been able to find any reason at all for him to go there. Tell me—has he ever been anything of the outdoor type?"

"Never," she said.

"Has he ever gone fishing or hunting?"

"Never."

"Has he ever been to Pointe Neuve before?"

"Not to my knowledge."

"Those are important facts, but the police aren't considering them—yet. Eventually they will have to. Marc's disappearance really started in St. Louis after the auction he attended. Does he do much traveling of that kind?"

"A great deal. He enjoys it. He started when he was still a university student, visiting art institutes whenever he could. He went to Europe several times, and the contacts he made there are still useful to him. Now he travels all over the country and goes to Europe occasionally on buying trips."

She turned again and fixed her eyes on me. "I want you to tell me exactly what you think. The police are hiding something from me. I'm convinced of that, and I won't have it. I insist on knowing what is going on."

"I don't think the police know enough to be hiding anything," I said. "They're just getting started. As for what I think—I'm just getting started, too. I haven't even begun to explore the possibilities."

"What are the possibilities?"

"One is that Marc disappeared because he wanted to."

"But he wouldn't—"

I held up a hand and stopped her. "Mrs. DeVarnay, Marc is a big boy, now. There are many things about his life you have no awareness of—business activities he is involved in, for example, and people he knows through his business connections. He buys and sells antiques, and from time to time he has to use informants that no one would give a character reference to. I've talked with several of them. Everything he is doing may be entirely proper, but something could have gone wrong with one of his contacts, or with a business deal, that made him think it wise to disappear for a time. This is one possibility. We must go over his life as carefully as we can and try to find a reason why he would want to disappear. While we are doing that, we will go on looking for him, because finding out why he disappeared won't necessarily tell us where he is, and his disappearance could have been for a personal rather than for a business reason. So we have to investigate every possibility we can think of."

She nodded. "I can understand that, though I'm sure there was nothing improper about what he was doing. What other possibilities are there?"

"He may have been kidnapped."

"But wouldn't there have been a ransom note?"

"That depends on why he was kidnapped. His assistant told me he had several important transactions pending that can't be closed until he returns. His disappearance may cause the firm to lose out. What if a competitor wanted to keep him from closing those deals?"

"I see. I hadn't thought of that."

"While we are going over his life as thoroughly as we can, we also will investigate the possibility that we have a kidnapping to deal with."

"Are there other possibilities?"

"Yes, but I don't know enough about Marc, yet, to speculate further. I haven't figured out how to fit this Pointe Neuve business into it. If your son wanted to disappear, that little fishing village would be the last place I would expect to find a person with his background."

"The police think he was hiding there," she said and added defiantly, "I refuse to believe he had anything to hide from."

"That's another reason why it's so important to go on investigating. We have to find out where he was and what he was doing at the time Old Jake was killed. Witnesses have been known to be mistaken. If he should be charged with complicity, his best defense would be to prove he was somewhere else. Anything we can turn up may be useful to him."

"Yes," she mused. "Yes, I suppose it may be."

Dorothy spoke for the first time. "He didn't do it. Marc wouldn't do nothin' like that."

"Is there anything more you would like to know?" Jolitte DeVarnay asked.

She had already said Marc had no reason to disappear, but I asked her again if she could think of any.

She shook her head. "Doug Kallenor told me there's money missing from Marc's business, but there would be no reason for him to disappear over that. It's his money. He had a right to take it if he wanted to."

"Mr. Kallenor said you financed Marc's business for him."

"I did it with his money. Under my husband's will, I have usufruct over my son's portion of his inheritance during my lifetime or until I remarry. It would have gone to him eventually anyway, so I invested what he needed to get his business started. I'm legally responsible for that investment because of the usufruct, but my attorneys thought an annual audit would satisfy my responsibility. Doug is an auditor and certified public accountant and my own tax advisor, so I have had him perform the audit. And because he was already familiar with the business, I asked him to check things when Marc disappeared to make certain there were no irregularities. There have never been any problems with the business except that once an employee was caught stealing, but that was a small thing."

"It must be an extremely prosperous business to have that much loose cash on hand."

"It's bringing Marc a wonderful income. About the missing money—Marc has to keep a considerable amount of cash available so he can buy antiques whenever they come on the market. He tells me that some sources will only sell for cash, and some people are reluctant to sell at all until they actually see the money. They would never part with their property for a check. Marc is an excellent businessman. That's surprising—his father wasn't, but Marc understands these things. Is there anything else?"

"Yes," I said. "Tell me about Marc's girlfriends."

Her face suddenly went blank. "There's only one he was ever serious about. Venita Berent. She's a lovely girl, and she comes from a fine family. Marc started going with her when they were in high school, and they went to the university together. I thought they were only waiting until he got his business established to get married, but suddenly Venita broke the engagement."

"Any special reason?" I asked.

"No. There was no quarrel, or bitterness, or anything like that. They went right on being friends, but Marc must have felt dreadfully hurt. I felt hurt. I've known Venita's mother since we were children, and I've known Venita since she was born. She came to me and apologized. She said she was fond of Marc, and always would be, and they got along splendidly on a social basis because they have the same background and know the same people, but he had always been more of a brother to her than a sweetheart." Obviously Jolitte DeVarnay considered that a feeble excuse for breaking an engagement.

"How long ago did this happen?"

"It was several years ago."

"Has she married someone else?"

"No. Like I said, she and Marc are still friends, and they still go out together, though not very often."

It sounded like an odd relationship. I asked her whether she thought it could have had anything to do with Marc's disappearance.

"I simply don't know," she said. "He's never shown the slightest interest in any other girl."

"Then he could be carrying a torch for Venita?"

"He could be."

There was a pause while we both meditated. Finally she said, "I feel so helpless just sitting here. Isn't there anything I can do?"

"You can make a telephone call for me. I would like to talk with Venita myself. Please call her and ask her when she can see me."

She made the call. Venita was at home and willing to see me at once, so I took my leave of Jolitte DeVarnay, telling her I certainly would want to talk with her again. I knew there were vital things about the case I should have asked her, but I still didn't have enough of a grip on it to know what they were.

Dorothy, who walked with a severe limp, accompanied me back to the front door. As I left, she remarked, "I do hope there's good news soon. Everything we hear turns out to be worse than the last time."

I told her I hoped for good news, too. A little optimism is said to be good for the soul, and in a restrained way I always try to keep my clients hopeful, even when I am expecting the worst.

CHAPTER TEN

Venita Berent's address took me down the street and around the corner. I made a leisurely walk of it, still checking for a tail and not seeing one, and enjoying a procession of fine homes along the way. Several of them looked like collector's items.

The Berent mansion was from a different page of the Garden District collection. It was a splendid old home, but those who built it had been less lavish in their expenditures. There was only a single gallery across the facade. There was no curved bay window in the dining room, the chandelier looked less costly, and the sitting room, to which the maid, a young Latino girl, escorted me, had no fireplace.

It was a magnificent home nevertheless. Snoop that I am, I collected one significant fact about the current residents as I strolled through the house on my way to the sitting room. Unlike the books at the DeVarnay mansion, those in the Berent library weren't bound in leather, and they actually looked as though someone had read them.

Venita Berent could have been Jolitte DeVarnay's daughter—slender, regally postured, with dark hair and eyes. She also was handsome rather than pretty. A boyfriend from another social class would have found her intimidating, but that shouldn't have bothered Marc DeVarnay unless, at some point in their long courtship, the discouraging thought occurred to him that his *fiancée* was a carbon copy of his mother. Since Venita had broken the engagement, perhaps she had made a similar discovery and began to see Marc as a distant echo of her father.

She lacked Jolitte DeVarnay's cool poise, and she hadn't yet promoted herself to duchess. She rose to greet me, and then she stood facing me uneasily until the servant left.

As soon as we were alone, she said, "Mrs. DeVarnay asked me to help you. Of course I'll tell you anything I can, but it's been quite some time—years, in fact—since I saw much of Marc. What do you want to know?"

"I want to know what sort of a person he is."

She asked anxiously, "You are trying to help him, aren't you? I mean, you're not working for the police, or anything like that?"

"I'm working for his mother and no one else," I said. "She wants him found. If it turns out that he needs help, I'll certainly do anything I can for him, but I'll have to find him first. If you want him found, then I'm working for you, too."

"I don't know what to do. I suppose I've got to trust you. You see, I promised Marc I would never tell anyone. He made me swear to it. But it might have something to do with his disappearance, even I can see that, and since you're trying to find him, I suppose you should know. Would *you* swear never to tell anyone?"

"I wouldn't raise my right hand and say 'never,' because if it's something really important, I may have to use it in order to find him. Detectives don't blab secrets for the fun of it—we aren't gossip columnists. I'll guarantee not to tell anyone—except my boss, who's also working on the case—unless it becomes absolutely necessary. I dig up all kinds of confidential information in the course of an investigation, and most of it remains confidential. Why don't we sit down?"

We did, but she perched on the edge of a chair and continued to regard me anxiously. "I don't know what to do," she confessed again.

"Is it about you and Marc?"

She nodded.

"And you think it could have something to do with his disappearance?"

She nodded. "It could. I just don't know."

"Why don't you start at the beginning. Mrs. DeVarnay said you and Marc went together from the time you were in high school."

"We didn't go to the same school, of course. I went to the Academy of Sacred Heart, which is a girl's school, and he went to the Jesuit High School, which is for boys, but our parents were close friends and we knew each other from childhood. We were each other's first dates. We just kept going together, and then we went to Tulane University together, and when we were sophomores we got engaged."

She paused for a moment. Then she said brokenly, "I always loved him. I love him now, and I couldn't stand the thought that something has happened to him."

"I understood that you broke the engagement."

"I did it for him. Because he asked me to. He was deathly afraid of his mother, you see. She was anxious to see us married, and she was putting pressure on both of us. I suppose she had grandmother urges. She was already far behind her friends in that department, and she thought it was time Marc did something about it. Marc's two brothers died when they were children, which left it up to him to keep the family going."

"I didn't know about Marc's brothers," I said. It gave me a better understanding of Jolitte DeVarnay's tragic mien. Two sons dead, one missing, and she was all alone. "Was your family pressuring you to get married?"

"Not really—not in that way. I have two sisters and two brothers. They've already produced ten grandchildren. I'm the youngest, and my mother thought it wise of me not to rush things. She was enthused about my marrying Marc, though. So was my father. Marc's parents were old friends, and our social positions were about the same, and then—I would have been marrying a lot of money, you see, and Marc was making a wonderful success of his business. They were as disappointed as Jolitte was when I called it off."

I waited. She had committed herself to tell me, now, and I didn't want to derail that by trying to hurry her.

"At first Marc said he wanted to get his business established before we were married. That made sense, but I noticed that I was seeing him less and less. And then when it became obvious that his business was really doing well, he still wasn't ready for marriage. Whenever the subject came up, he had some excuse or other, and some of them were pretty flimsy. Finally I decided to have it out with him."

She paused again. Then she buried her face in her hands and sobbed. "He told me he was gay," she said finally.

She broke off, and I was speechless myself. Homosexuality was a role I hadn't imagined for Marc DeVarnay. Probably I should have—he was a solitary sort of person, and he had no girlfriends at all despite his money and good looks—but I hadn't, and having it thrown at me suddenly took my breath away.

"I still can't believe it," she went on brokenly. "I can't understand it. We went together so long, you see, and—" She blushed. "He made love to me—"

"Do you mean you had sexual relations with him?" I asked.

She blushed again and said angrily, "Certainly not. But we made out, as young people going steady do, and—well, he certainly was normal about that. Finally I stopped it because it got harder and harder to draw the line."

"Perhaps he is bisexual," I suggested.

She gazed at me blankly. "What's that?"

I explained bisexuality, and she was astonished. "You mean—he could be both? I didn't know men were like that."

"Some men are. So are some women."

"Then maybe he really is gay," she said dully. "I was afraid he just said that to get out of marrying me."

"He must have been genuinely fond of you. It would have been far easier for him to say nothing and go through with the marriage, since your families and all of your friends expected it, and that would have been a tragedy for both of you. Probably he did you a favor by calling it off."

I said that to make her feel better. It was something she could enjoy believing. As for myself, I didn't know what to believe.

"That's what he said—he thought our getting married wouldn't be fair to me. He was terrified his mother would find out he was gay. He asked me to swear I would never tell anyone, and he also asked me to tell his mother I was the one who broke the engagement. It wasn't easy, but I did it. What else could I do?"

"Nothing," I assured her. "You shouldn't have any doubt at all as to whether you did the right thing. It was the only thing you could have done."

"But where could Marc have gone? What could have happened to him?"

"You must remember I'm just getting started on this, and I never knew Marc. Everything you know about him and take for granted is a discovery for me. It'll take me another day or two to get a proper grip on his background."

The surprise she had just handed me was actually a setback. I would have to wipe out the beginning I already had made and start over. "Has Marc ever shown any interest in hunting or fishing?" I asked.

She shook her head.

"Did he ever mention a fishing village called Pointe Neuve?"

"I had an uncle who used to go fishing down there. That was years ago—when I was a child. No, Marc never mentioned it. All the time I knew him, I don't think he even thought about fishing. He loved to eat fish and all kinds of seafood, but a little swimming was the extent of his outdoor activity. Except for gardening, that is. He was proud of his green thumb, but I don't think he actually used it much except on those odd flowers he raises. Do you know about them?"

"Yes. I saw one of them in his home."

She was silent for a moment. Then she said, "Is there anything I can do?" She wasn't merely making conversation, as people usually are when they say that. Like Jolitte DeVarnay, she really meant it. She had her eyes fixed on my face, and she spoke with a desperate sincerity.

I got to my feet, walked over to the window, and stood looking out at a charming garden. When I turned, she was still looking at me intensely, and she didn't flinch when I met her eyes deliberately and held them.

She had given me an idea. Jolitte DeVarnay would be more than willing to furnish all the contacts I needed, but with a few exceptions, like her phone call to Venita, the people she could introduce me to were the wrong kind. I didn't want to meet the priest who had officiated at Marc's christening. I wanted to talk with the friend his own age who could tell me whether Marc DeVarnay was really as virtuous and temperate as everyone claimed. If he had, just once in his life, gone out and got drunk with someone, I needed to find that person.

I also saw a chance to do my good deed for the decade. It was obvious that Venita Berent's life had come to a dead end when she broke her engagement to Marc. She had been in mourning ever since—the worst kind of mourning, because she had to conceal it and pretend everything was all right. She was like a boat that had run aground. She needed a push to get her back into the current so she could start living again. "Do you have a boyfriend now?" I asked.

She shook her head.

"Have you gone with anyone since you broke up with Marc?"

She shook her head again.

"Tell me something honestly," I said. "This social circle of yours—old New Orleans families, and local high society, and that sort of thing. I may have to ask a lot of those people for information about Marc. Will I fit in? Socially, I mean—do I look and act presentable enough to get by?"

She gave me a puzzled look. Then she realized I was serious, and the look became calculating. "Yes, I think you could. Get by, I mean. With a better tailor, you could get by very nicely."

I remembered Marc DeVarnay's two tuxedos and what I'd heard about New Orleans being the formal dress capital of the nation—more tuxedos are bought there annually than in New York and Washington combined—and I was glad I had come properly equipped.

"This is my everyday work uniform," I said. "I promise to do better for formal occasions. Are you sure I'll be all right?"

"Yes. Of course you will."

"Then I'm going to take you at your word that you really want to help Marc, and I'm going to ask you an unusual kind of favor. I want you to introduce me to your friends and also to Marc's friends as your new *fiancé* from Los Angeles. Could you do that without putting yourself in an embarrassing position? You see—people will be much more willing to talk to me freely if they don't know I'm a detective."

She pondered the question. "I see what you mean. It'll be easier for you to find out things if people think you're a friend of mine. You want me to pretend we really and truly are engaged."

"That'll be the difficult part. Pretending we really and truly are. Putting on a convincing act so people will believe we really and truly are. I don't know what it will accomplish, or whether it will accomplish anything at all, but it seems worth trying. Do you think you're enough of an actress to carry it off?"

"I think so," she said gravely. "I'm willing to try. Anything to help Marc."

"When the case is finished, you'll have the embarrassment of explaining what happened to your engagement."

"If anyone is crude enough to ask, I can always say I changed my mind." She added bitterly, "Marc's friends won't be the least bit surprised. What's another broken engagement when I've already done it once?"

"Then you'll do it?"

She nodded.

"It'll be a thankless job," I warned her. "Even after it's over, you may not want to tell anyone about it. Not even Marc and his mother. Are you still willing?"

She nodded.

"There is one problem. Have you done any traveling lately? We need to invent an occasion when we met. Even the most whirlwind courtship has to start somewhere."

"I was in Salt Lake City last month to visit a friend."

"Splendid. By coincidence, I was there at the same time. We saw each other as much as we could, and we became engaged over roast pheasant at La Fleur de Lys, which is a highly appropriate place for a New Orleans girl to be plighting her troth. You can make it sound as romantic as you like. And now I'm here to meet your family. Can your mother and father keep a secret?"

"Of course!"

"Then you'd better let them know what you're doing. Otherwise, they might be confused and maybe even upset if word got back to them that you were showing off a new *fiancé* without letting them know about him. I have to report to my boss this evening and see whether she has any instructions for me. Then I'll telephone you for a date."

"Your boss is a woman?"

"From high society. She would fit into your social whirl far better than I will, but I don't know what angle of the case she's working on."

Venita called a taxi for me. She walked me to the front door herself, proving again that she hadn't yet promoted herself to duchess or even considered it. While waiting, we chatted a bit about night spots where Marc's crowd hung out. The taxi arrived. I had taken my leave of her and started out the door when I suddenly realized I had been inexcusably remiss.

"I'm sorry," I said. "I've never been engaged before, so I didn't give it a thought. There ought to be a ring."

"I have one my grandmother gave me," she said. "It's rather old-fashioned—a diamond solitaire without any ornamentation at all—but it's highly attractive. I've worn it very little, and I don't think any of my friends will recognize it."

"Excellent. You have all the proper instincts of a detective. Do you mind if I refer to you as an old-fashioned kind of girl?"

"Not at all. Marc always did."

I could see it wasn't going to be an easy relationship, and I would be walking on quicksand all the way. There were things I would have to discuss with her, but this wasn't the moment.

The taxi driver was waiting. I hurried away, promising again to call her later.

The news that Marc DeVarnay was gay had blasted our case into another dimension. I left the Berent mansion with definite symptoms of shell shock, and the taxi was almost to Canal Street before I got them under control and began to consider how my new *fiancée* might be of use to me.

CHAPTER ELEVEN

I consulted the cab driver and had him let me off at a rental car firm instead of driving me to my hotel. I usually rent a car at the airport when I arrive. My swamp mission, with transportation already arranged, scuttled that notion, so I waited to see how much of a parking problem I would encounter in the French Quarter, where space sometimes can't be had at any price.

Fortunately my hotel had convenient arrangements for guests, and I now considered a car essential. I couldn't carry on a believable courtship while fussing with cabs nor could I conveniently expand my investigation beyond the French Quarter.

My first errand with my new car was a call on the firm of Nusiner and Company, Choice Antiques. Magazine Street is actually more of an Antique Row than Royal Street, but the fifty or more antique stores are scattered over many blocks, sometimes occurring singly, sometimes in small clusters. Nusiner and Company occupied a worn brick building in a neighborhood that had seen its best days in the 1920s, but there was nothing shabby about the store's interior. Its displays were far more gaudy and eye-catching than those at DeVarnay's. I wasn't qualified to say how the merchandise compared.

There were several customers in the store. A severe-looking older woman was talking with one of them. The only other clerk was a pretty girl who couldn't have been long out of high school. She was rearranging stock in a jewelry counter.

As I approached, she flashed a warm smile at me, and I returned it. She said, "May I help you with something?"

"Is Mr. Nusiner in?" I asked.

"Yes he is, but he's quite busy today."

"Please tell him Mr. Pletcher is calling. I'm from Savannah. I would like to discuss something of mutual interest."

"I'll tell him," she promised with another smile. She went to a private office at the rear of the store. When she emerged, she smiled again and gestured, waited until I had entered the office, and then closed the door behind me.

Harold Nusiner was a lank, red-headed man in an untidy suit. He would have a violent temper, I thought, and be dangerous if crossed, but he was all hail fellow well met if he thought you had something for him, and that was his attitude now. He greeted me with a handshake, got me seated, took his own chair behind his desk, and beamed at me.

"What can I do for you, Mr. Pletcher?"

Sometimes a frontal attack is the most effective, especially if it comes as a total surprise. I decided to level with him. I slid my card across his desk. He scrutinized it with a frown.

"Mr. *J.* Pletcher?"

"The 'J' stands for 'Justitia,'" I said.

He was still puzzling over my card, and he ignored that. "Investigative Consultants?"

"It's a term for expensive private investigators."

"You said you were from Savannah," he said accusingly.

"I am. My firm's main offices are in New York and Los Angeles."

I'd had a hunch that Savannah might be a good center for antiques. Evidently I was right. Nusiner thought my coming from there was reason enough to give me an audience on a busy day. He decided to remain friendly until he got me figured out. "What can I do for you?" he asked again.

"My firm has been hired by Jolitte DeVarnay to investigate the disappearance of her son, Marc."

I thought I was handing him a surprise, but he had one for me. He nodded his head with a kind of grim satisfaction. "I heard he was missing, but I didn't believe it. I thought it was just another stupid rumor. One hears so many of them these days. What do you want from me?"

"When did you see Marc last?"

He gazed at me blankly. "I really can't remember. He's a snob and also a twerp. I've been trying to get hold of him for several months by telephone. I have a serious business proposition for him that would benefit both of us, but he won't even talk to me about it."

"When did you talk with him last?"

"I can't even tell you that. It's been months."

Suddenly it dawned on him that he was being cross-examined. His face flushed.

Then he grasped the fact that I might actually be suspecting him of some kind of involvement in Marc DeVarnay's disappearance. He jumped to his feet and pointed at the door. "Get out!"

My frontal attack had fizzled, but I tried to salvage what I could. I leaned back and made myself comfortable. "You'll find me much more congenial than the police. Would you rather discuss it with them?"

"Get out!"

I got to my feet leisurely. "Your choice," I told him. "You can discuss Marc with me—or with them. If you change your mind before evening, call me at my hotel—the Maria Theresa—and I'll tell them to lay off."

I gave him a polite nod and left.

In the store, the older woman was now talking with a different customer. She must have had dill pickles for lunch; she gave me a sour look as I walked by. As I passed the jewelry counter, I exchanged one final smile with the younger clerk.

"It's all set," I whispered to her. "I've bought the store, and I'm going to raise everyone's salary."

I left her staring after me in astonishment.

I drove back to my hotel and made my parking arrangements, noting in the process that the beggars I had seen earlier that day were gone. An elderly, shabbily-dressed man with a mouth organ had replaced them.

I returned to the twenty-four-hour sudsomat and called the private number Raina Lambert had given me. She wasn't in, and the bombshell about Marc DeVarnay wasn't something I felt like confiding to her answering machine. I told it I craved human contact and would call again.

I went back to the hotel, ordered a drink in its small bar, and sipped absently while studying a map of New Orleans. In order to drive my new *fiancée* around, I needed a rudimentary idea of where things were. New Orleans is not an easy place to get oriented in. I have already mentioned that the West Bank, the opposite side of the Mississippi, is actually east of the French Quarter because of the river's convoluted loops. The sun appears to rise in the west. In nearby Jefferson Parish, it appears to set in the east. This is only an introduction to the total confusion you can get yourself into if you insist on exploring New Orleans with a compass.

In order to reach the West Bank, you must head southeast and cross two bridges. Once you understand that, you next must cope with the fact that New Orleans's West End is east of its East End. You have made a smidgeon of progress when you understand that "Uptown" and "Downtown" actually refer to "upriver" and "downriver," but you suffer a severe setback when you try to apply compass directions to streets. Those crossing Canal Street, the main thoroughfare in New Orleans, may be called "North" on one side and "South" on the other. These designations have nothing to do with the compass. They actually refer to the "Uptown" (S) or "Downtown" (N) side of Canal. The streets themselves run roughly northeast and south-west—until they change direction to conform to the bends of the Mississippi. This problem is compounded with longer streets. South Clayborne, if followed far enough, can be found running north, south, east, or west.

But not to worry. Most maps of New Orleans don't bother to include the standard north-south arrow anyway, and people who reside there for a time learn to say "Riverside" or "Lakeside" and "Uptown" or "Downtown" instead of using compass directions.

One guidebook remarks that the best way to see New Orleans is to get lost. When you mix a generous sprinkling of one-way streets into the confusion, this becomes extremely easy to do. I could only hope my new *fiancée* knew her native city well.

When I gave up and folded the map, another drinker, seated at the next table, asked, "Enjoying your stay?"

"Just getting started," I confessed. "How do you like New Orleans?"

"You're saying it wrong," he said complainingly.

"How's that?" I wanted to know.

"You said 'New ORleans.' The natives call it 'New OrLEANS.'"

He was slightly drunk, so I decided not to debate the matter. I said, "Really? Where are you from?"

"San Francisco. Been here three months. My firm transferred me."

"How do you like New OrLEANS?" I asked, carefully pronouncing it the way he had specified.

"I don't. There are too damn many tourists here."

"That's interesting. I seem to recall seeing more than a few tourists in San Francisco the last time I was there."

"In San Francisco, tourists don't bother you. They only go where tourists go. Fisherman's Warf, Pier 39—nobody goes there but tourists. China Town—only tourists go there. There are good Chinese restaurants all over San Francisco. The locals never go near China Town. You see tourists in line sometimes, waiting for the cable cars or something like that, but it's easy to avoid them. In this place, there are tourists everywhere you go. Too damn many of them."

"I guess I'll just have to pretend I'm not a tourist," I said.

He shook his head gloomily. "That won't do any good. There are too damn many of you."

I bought a paper and read a short back-page story about a man named Jake Hamler, known locally as Old Jake, who had been found murdered down in the bayou country. The story made no mention of Marc DeVarnay.

When I returned to the lobby, the clerk handed me a message. Dick Tosche wanted me to call him. I first called Raina Lambert; she was still out. Then I called Dick. He wanted to discuss progress, and he thought he had turned up a couple of things that would interest me, so I agreed to meet him at his girlfriend's witchcraft shop.

My rental car was useless for getting around the French Quarter. Once I had worked my way through the traffic and pedestrians to get where I wanted to go, the search for a parking place might take me back where I started. I left the car parked and walked, passing the elderly beggar without giving him a glance. That was a mistake, and my conscience bothered me. I should have sacrificed a quarter or two for the sheer pleasure of seeing a new face. I was getting tired of his predecessors.

Royal Street on a Saturday afternoon could be used for a motion picture mob scene. Skipping through the bumping and weaving crowds of tourists might possibly have been good practice for a ballet dancer, but it was a nuisance for a detective. At DeVarnay's, the balloon sculptor was still on duty and actually doing good business with the heavy afternoon traffic.

The French Quarter's trashy souvenir stores were beginning to look tiresomely familiar to me. If I had to prolong my stay, the striking displays of quality merchandise and art probably would become just as wearisome. Familiarity breeds boredom on the way to contempt.

Looking back, I suddenly caught a glimpse of Shoeless Sharlie. The crowd closed in on him a moment later and rendered him invisible for a time, but I had no doubt he was trying to follow me. I decided to make his job more interesting, so I took a zigzag course, ending up on Decatur. I looked back again just before I turned. He was still behind me and falling over his galoshes in his effort to keep up. He had a Styrofoam cup clutched in one hand. That was his cover. He was ready to go into the begging business any time I paused for a few moments.

I entered a corner shop and went out the side exit for a quick detour back to Chartres Street. When I returned to Decatur again, a block further on, I was no longer being followed.

I passed an impressive array of eating-places in various dialects of Cajun and Creole as well as Italian and Mexican. All of them had menus on display, which I glanced at in passing, and I was ready for dinner long before I reached the small shop called The Witch's Grotto. A sign in the window mentioned psychic readings and private consultations. Among the witch's paraphernalia on display were more kinds of Tarot Cards than I had known existed—including Witch's Tarot Cards, New Orleans Voodoo Tarot Cards, and a deck called Tarot of the Cat People.

There were no customers in the shop when I entered. I was greeted warmly by Sister Merlina, a tall, pretty girl with long, golden blonde hair. She was wearing an ankle-length blue gown and earrings with a single large blue stone in each, and she looked quite capable of putting a spell on any male who came within fifty feet of her—in the nicest possible way, of course.

I have encountered witches before, but they have been of the rural variety, catering to rustic superstitions. An ultra-sophisticated big city witch—certified, no less, with a framed certificate to prove it, and practicing witchcraft as a religion—was entirely outside my experience.

Sister Merlina said Dick would be back in a few minutes. She offered me a chair and a cup of tea while I waited, but I preferred to browse. One doesn't often have an opportunity to buy witches' paraphernalia or even to see what it consists of.

There were shelves displaying powdered or minced herbs for sale by the measure. Each jar was conveniently labeled with the name of the herb and its magical qualities. Chili peppers, for example, were good for hex breaking, fidelity, love, or lust; Solomon's seal brought truth, prosperity, and good luck; eucalyptus brought protection and health; and so on through a long, long display. One could achieve the same things by anointing oneself with special oils, which were also on sale.

I was interested to note that witches weren't above practicing a little voodoo on the side. There were gris-gris for sale, most of them aimed at improving the owner in some way—tuning up his creativity, magnifying his mental agility, or some such thing.

There were shelves of books concerning the powers of magic. There were talismans or charms for sale for various purposes. I thought of buying one for Jeff Minjarus—it promised to produce vibrations that would help control legal situations. There was a charm for sexuality, one for employment, one for love, one to help travelers.

I asked Sister Merlina whether she had a charm for finding a missing person.

"I've never been asked for one," she said with a frown. "A talisman for finding lost articles is much in demand. Perhaps that, combined with charms for luck and success...."

I must have looked skeptical. She flashed a smile. "No charm will work if you aren't willing to believe in it."

"That's my problem," I agreed. "I'd have to see it work before I could believe."

"Dick told me about the man you're looking for. Marc DeVarnay—he paid a friend of mine well for an old armoire she had. She was going to throw it away, and someone suggested she ask him about it. Do you have anything that belonged to him?"

"Nothing except his photo."

"May I see it?"

I handed it to her. She removed it from its plastic sleeve and passed her hand over it. I remembered the sign in the window that advertised psychic readings and remained silent.

She closed her eyes for a long moment. "He's somewhere nearby," she said. "That's all I can tell you."

"How near is nearby?" I asked. "Next door? On the next street?"

She passed her hand over the photo again. "He's in New

Orleans but maybe not in the French Quarter. My impression is a weak one. Is he hiding?"

"He may well be."

"That might account for it. I can't tell you how near 'nearby' is. But he definitely is somewhere in New Orleans."

We had so little to go on in this case that if she had pinpointed a location, I would have gone there to investigate. Unfortunately, the problem of tracking down a fugitive in a large city has much in common with that of finding a needle in a haystack, so Sister Merlina's impression wasn't really helpful. I gave her my sincere thanks regardless.

Dick Tosche arrived and greeted the witch with a kiss. They made a handsome couple. With his long hair, they could have posed as Lancelot and Guinevere if he had covered his jeans and T-shirt with the proper kind of robe.

Dick's watch on the watchers at DeVarnay's and my hotel had turned up nothing. Two or three times a day they left their posts to make phone calls, and he suspected someone might be tossing wadded messages into their cups. Otherwise, they went directly home after their long day's work. He was certain they weren't reporting to anyone in person.

Dick was still in pursuit of several elusive people on the list of DeVarnay's contacts. None of those he had located could offer any worthwhile information. Most hadn't seen DeVarnay for months. He'd had better luck at the French Market. Francis Dassily had put his market friends to work, following my suggestion, and they actually had found a woman who claimed to have seen DeVarnay at least three times in the past two weeks.

"Dassily tried to call you at your hotel, but you weren't in," Dick said. "Do you want to talk with this woman?"

"At this moment, there's no one I'd rather talk with."

"I also found a man you should see," he said.

We told the charming witch goodbye—Dick kissed her again in parting—and strolled over to the French Market, which at this point was a very short block toward the river. In the long shed occupied by the flea market, we found Francis Dassily at his usual table peddling cheap jewelry and paintings. He greeted us and then called to the woman at the next table, "Pam—would you watch my stuff for a moment?"

Pam, who was selling a miscellany of souvenirs—hats with banal slogans; ash trays; toys; jewelry; T shirts showing a couple of alligators tied to a porch railing with the caption, "Louisiana Porch Puppies"—smiled and said, "Sure."

Dassily led us to the other end of the market and introduced us to Ida Gallan, a gaunt, middle-aged woman with a rather large nose, a bad complexion, and a sweet smile. She was presiding over a table of T-shirts ornamented with hand-painted scenes from the French Quarter. They were very well done, and they had prices to match.

"Jay wants to hear about Marc DeVarnay," he told her. Then he hurried back to his own table and left us to do our own interviewing.

"I didn't even know Mr. DeVarnay was supposed to be missing until Francis told me," Ida Gallan said. "My husband and I have an apartment on Esplanade, which is on the edge of the French Quarter. I work for a few hours each morning at Storril's—that's a small antique store just down the street from DeVarnay's. I do cleaning for them, and I dust and polish the antiques. Storril's handles all kinds of things, as do most of the antique stores, but it makes a specialty of brasses and enamel work and also oriental porcelains, which have to be handled very carefully. I go to work at seven and stay as long as I'm needed, but usually I'm through by ten. Coming and going I've often seen Mr. DeVarnay in or around his store. In fact, I got to know him slightly because both of us were walking in that direction about the same time every morning—he often goes to work early. So occasionally he would overtake me, and we would walk up Royal Street together. I'm telling you all this because Francis said you'd want to know whether I know Mr. DeVarnay well enough to recognize him. I really do, you see."

"You certainly do," I agreed.

"There's a little grocery store just off Esplanade on Royal.

There's nothing special about it except that it has fresh baked bread and croissants in the morning. It opens at six, and neighborhood people go there early and buy fresh rolls and croissants for breakfast. We do—my husband goes for them while I'm getting breakfast ready. Then I pass the store on my way to work—usually about a quarter to seven."

She was the ideal witness. She was carefully touching every base, and there was no need for any cross-examination.

"At least three mornings in the past couple of weeks, I've seen Mr. DeVarnay either coming out of that little store or walking away from it carrying a bag of French bread and maybe croissants. The last time I saw him was day before yesterday."

"No doubt at all?" I asked.

"No doubt at all."

"Did he see you?"

"I don't think so. I always pass it on the other side of the street, and he probably doesn't remember my face as well as I remember his."

"Have you said anything to anyone about this?"

She shook her head. "Like I said, I didn't know Mr. DeVarnay was supposed to be missing until Francis came around asking about him. I did think there was something odd about him being there. I know where he lives, and when he left the store he was headed in the wrong direction. But—" She shrugged. "There could have been a simple explanation, and it wasn't any of my business."

"Did anything else seem strange or different about him?" I asked.

"Yes, now that you mention it. He needed a haircut, which wasn't like Mr. DeVarnay at all, and he seemed to be growing a beard. At first I thought maybe he hadn't shaved yet that morning. Then I realized it was just his chin that he hadn't shaved."

"Please don't mention this to anyone," I said. "I'll see that those looking for him are informed. Your information is invaluable—it's the first break we've had on the case. You're an excellent witness, Mrs. Gallan."

She blushed very prettily. I thanked her again and told her I would arrange for a signed statement from her if we needed one.

"What do you make of it?" Dick asked after we left her.

"It sounds as though DeVarnay has gone into hiding and is growing a beard as a disguise."

"That's what I thought."

We had a different kind of interview with a man named Ross Sernold, a short, blubbery, unpleasant man. The word "obese" might have been invented with him in mind. He was selling alligator skulls, collections of minerals, pretty stones, and shells, along with trashy artwork compounded of all of the above. Dick introduced me as the detective who was investigating Marc DeVarnay's business deals, and Sernold went off like a Fourth of July rocket.

Much of what he had to say wasn't printable, but the gist of it was this: He'd had an old desk of the kind antique dealers called an escritoire or secretary. He thought it ought to be valuable, and Marc DeVarnay was supposed to be an honest dealer, so he asked him to come and look at it. DeVarnay said it would have been very valuable if it had been in good condition. Unfortunately, it was a wreck, and it would be expensive to restore it. He wasn't even sure it could be restored. He would take a gamble and pay fifty dollars for it. Sernold thought he was honest, so he took the fifty dollars.

Some time later, passing DeVarnay's, he had seen *his* desk in the window priced at $4,600. When he protested, he was told the desk being displayed wasn't his but another of similar design. As if he didn't know his own desk! Marc DeVarnay was a thief and a crook with a long list of unprintable adjectives, and he hoped I could pin it onto him and send him to jail.

"Have you seen DeVarnay lately?" I asked.

"No," Sernold said, "and it's lucky for him I haven't."

I thanked him and promised to let him know if I needed his testimony in court.

"Have you found any more like that?" I asked Dick Tosche.

Dick shook his head. "But it stands to reason that there must be some around. Maybe quite a few. I thought it was funny the way everyone praised DeVarnay and said how honest he was and how he dealt fairly with people. No one is that perfect."

"You're so right," I agreed. "See if you can find more of them."

On the way out, we stopped to talk with Dassily again. He was in a jovial mood—evidently business was good. "Did you get what you wanted?" he asked.

"Yes," I said. "She seems like an excellent witness. I'm grateful for your help. If you find anyone else who's seen him, please let me know at once."

"It does seem strange," he mused. "Marc disappearing but not disappearing. I hope he decides to surface soon. I've got some good tips for him, and they won't keep forever. I'd hate to have to give them to someone else. Marc always pays best."

I told him about Sernold's desk to see how he would react. He laughed. "I heard all about that from Marc. The desk on display wasn't Sernold's. It maybe had the same general shape, but the details were nothing like his—different maker, different period. Sernold's desk really was a wreck, and Marc wasn't sure it was worth restoring. He planned to use the brass and maybe some of the wood for repairs to furniture that was more salvageable. I wouldn't believe Sernold if a dozen witnesses backed him up. I've dealt with Marc ever since he opened his business, and he's always been absolutely honest with me."

We promised to let him know the moment there was any news about DeVarnay.

Dick returned to his own business of buying and selling, and I headed back to my hotel feeling smugly satisfied with myself. It had been the most profitable day of the investigation. Even my visit to the flea market, in addition to producing a critically important witness, Ida Gallan, and one who was at least highly interesting, Ross Sernold, had given me an entirely unexpected bonus. When we were following Dassily through the market, I had seen, behind a striking display of hand woven goods probably imported from Asia or South America—bags, totes, knapsacks, shawls, and rugs—an unusually attractive sales person, a tiny, very shapely redhead. She was giving tourists an entirely new perspective on pulchritude among New Orleans's market people.

She was Raina Lambert. I wondered whether she had developed a belated interest in my theory about Marc DeVarnay hiding out in the French Quarter or whether she was pursuing some notion of her own. I wanted to tell her what Ida Gallan had seen, but I couldn't risk blowing her cover.

It would be easy to put a watch on the little grocery store and follow DeVarnay the next time he came shopping for bread and croissants. Even if he didn't return there, he certainly was hiding out somewhere in the vicinity, and sooner or later he would be spotted again. The missing person case seemed to be virtually finished but not the Marc DeVarnay case. That was only beginning. There remained perplexing questions concerning DeVarnay's disappearance and his connection with Old Jake, and finding him might not answer any of them.

CHAPTER TWELVE

I now knew why Raina Lambert wasn't answering her phone. She was pursuing her own investigation in the flea market and might be there until late. I telephoned anyway to tell her answering machine I was about to embark on a critically important investigation of my own and would be out all evening. If I finished before midnight, I would telephone again. Otherwise, she would hear from me in the morning. Then I dialed Venita Berent's number. Her parents were having guests for dinner, and she felt obligated to join them, so I arranged to pick her up at nine. We discussed where we ought to go first, and I let her decide.

After a moment's reflection, I next telephoned Jeffrey Minjarus. He was the only one of Marc DeVarnay's friends who already knew I was a detective, and I wanted him to know about my arrangement with Venita. Otherwise, we might meet him accidentally and have him blow the whistle on me before he grasped what was going on.

"Around nine-thirty, I'll be at the Top of the Mart with my new *fiancée*," I said. "I'd like to have you meet her."

"You work fast," he said. He sounded more resentful than admiring. "Is it anyone I know?"

"I can't say. Why don't you stop by?"

"All right, I'll do that," he said.

As for whether I really expected to accomplish anything, I couldn't have answered that myself. To solve a complicated mystery, a detective has to bark up a lot of trees, and it is only to be expected that sometimes he will look silly doing it.

When I called for Venita, her parents left their company long enough to be introduced to their daughter's new *fiancé*. Charles Berent was a recently retired engineer who had built this and that around Southern Louisiana. He looked like a college professor—slender, quiet, scholarly, dignified. Christine Berent, called Tina by her friends, was a plump, motherly type. The two of them exuded a southern hospitality that was almost homespun in its warmth and friendliness. The contrast with the regal Jolitte DeVarnay was startling. The Berents would have been willing and eager to discuss Marc with me, but it was immediately obvious that neither of them knew anything that would be useful.

They were mildly puzzled about the role I had asked Venita to play, but they raised no objections. If Jolitte DeVarnay, a old friend, needed help, they wanted Venita to do whatever she could.

Top of the Mart is a revolving lounge on the top floor of the World Trade Center. It is unlike most prominent night spots in New Orleans in that it offers canned music. Even so, it is an excellent spot for starting or continuing a romance if anyone happens to be in the market for one. The music is restful and subdued, and the bar seems to hang suspended while the lights of the city and the West Bank, divided unequally by the dark, sinuous shape of the Mississippi, slowly circle below. The lines of automobile traffic have a hypnotic quality. All of their lights seem to be converging on the World Trade Center (white head-lights) or leaving it (red tail lights).

Because the lounge is shaped like a doughnut, one can see only the segment of it where one is seated, which is another advantage to trysting there. This is also a disadvantage, because one can't see who is approaching until suddenly there they are. As we were being shown to our table, an abrupt flurry of move-ment occurred several tables further on when a couple suddenly decided to leave. The woman got to her feet and hurried away in the opposite direction. Her companion, far less agile, waddled after her. It was Selma Garnett, Marc DeVarnay's assistant, and Doug Kallenor, the accountant.

I said to Venita, "Look quickly. Do you know those people?"

She stared after them. "I know the woman," she said. "That's Selma Garnett. She works for Marc. I don't know the man."

"Perhaps they left in a hurry because they saw us come in," I said. "Or perhaps they just noticed the time and decided it was getting late. The detective business is like that—full of perhapses."

Venita was wearing an attractive peach colored gown with a simple pearl necklace. She looked stunning, but she acted nervous and unsure of herself, which is not the proper romantic attitude for a girl on the first post-engagement date with her intended. Now that her adventure had actually begun, she seemed more perplexed about it than her parents had been.

"Exactly what *do* you want me to do?" she asked when the waitress had departed with our orders for drinks.

My mind was on Selma Garnett and Doug Kallenor, an unlikely couple if I had ever seen one. I had to think for a moment before I answered. "You have a part to play," I told her. "You can do that best by enjoying yourself—or pretending to. Smile. This is a happy occasion. That's better. Now look around and see whether any of Marc's friends are present."

She couldn't see any in the section of the doughnut that was visible, but as we entered she had seen, around the curve in the other direction, a man who wasn't exactly a friend but could be considered a long-time acquaintance.

"That'll do for a start. You can use him to practice on. I'm a trophy, and you're eager to show me off to him. You've captured the scion of one of the oldest and wealthiest families on the West Coast."

She turned and regarded me with interest. "Are you really?"

"Nope. My father was a bookkeeper who four times was defeated when he ran for dog catcher. At least he was fond of animals, and the S.P.C.A. thought highly of him. But you're acting a part, and the part requires you to think of me as a trophy. Now we'll take a tourist's tour while we're waiting for our drinks. This is my first visit here, and naturally you're eager to show the place to me. When we pass Marc's acquaintance, or anyone else Marc knew, you can stop and introduce me."

On that first run-through, my ingenious scheme fell flat on its face. The acquaintance, who was with a girl, acted as though he'd been caught stepping out on his wife. Probably he was. The conversation was fleeting: Venita introduced me, I fielded a question or two about whether my conscience bothered me for snatching Venita away from the cradle of southern civilization to install her on the barbarous West Coast, and we moved on. There was no opportunity to turn the conversation to DeVarnay, but from the friend's odd behavior, I suspected Marc may have been on his mind. Rumors must have circulated despite Jolitte's efforts to keep the disappearance a secret.

The plan looked like a flop, but Venita was a huge success. As she gradually felt more comfortable with me, she began to relax. We sipped our drinks and waited for Minjarus, who was late.

He arrived, finally, approaching the table from Venita's rear, and he gushed apologies until he turned and saw who my "*fiancée*" was. Then he froze with astonishment. He stammered to me, "You're...engaged...to...." He broke off, suddenly realizing how odd he was sounding, and lapsed into speechlessness.

"He thinks I'm a remarkably fast worker," I explained to Venita.

"But you are," she murmured demurely.

I filled Minjarus in on the betrothal project. His amazement faded as he begin to understand what I was doing.

Finally he turned to Venita. "This is very courageous of you."

I entered a protest. "Come, now. I'm not that bad a catch."

They both laughed, and we talked about Marc DeVarnay. "He comes here occasionally, but he doesn't really like the place," Minjarus said. "I never could figure out why. It's a lovely setting, and they keep the music under control. Usually when Marc doesn't like a place, it's because the music is too loud."

"A music lover could say that about almost every night spot in New Orleans," I observed. "Including the entire length of Bourbon Street."

"It's certainly true of a lot of them," Minjarus agreed, "but this is an excellent place for drink and conversation. Maybe Marc doesn't care for the bother of getting here—finding a parking place, which can be a problem, and then having to change elevators on the way up."

"What sort of night clubs does he like?" I asked.

"He's addicted to piano bars. Especially to one in the French Quarter. He says they're the only night spots where it's possible to talk quietly and enjoy the music."

Venita said absently, "That's odd. He never took me to one."

"Perhaps what we should be doing is touring Marc's favorite piano bars," I suggested.

Minjarus frowned. "But you aren't looking for Marc—or are you?" He sent a questioning glance at Venita, then one at me, and then another at Venita. Obviously he enjoyed looking at Venita. "Not all of his friends agree with him," he went on. "If it's his friends you're looking for—"

"We were just sitting here waiting for someone with a legal background to give us a proper perspective on the problem," I told him. "Why don't you think of some places where we're likely to meet Marc's friends?"

We finished our drinks and left. That is, Minjarus and I finished our drinks. Venita only sampled hers. I had thought of inviting Minjarus to join our investigation, but that proved to be unnecessary. He attached himself to us like a plumed knight escorting unarmed pilgrims across the wastes of the Holy Land. From my conversation with Venita while we were driving from one night spot to another, I gathered that until this evening she had known almost nothing about him except that he existed. From a conversation with Minjarus while Venita went to powder her nose, if girls still do that, it was obvious that he knew all about her. Apparently she never had an inkling that for years she'd had a secret admirer.

But Minjarus made himself useful in a number of ways. He may have been from New England, but he certainly knew New Orleans. He guided us expertly, he knew all of DeVarnay's friends, and, over and over again, he used an attorney's skill to turn the conversation from Venita's engagement, which astonished everyone, to her former *fiancé*, Marc DeVarnay. Thanks to Minjarus, my ingenious scheme got up off the floor and began to look robust.

But none of the friends we talked to admitted to seeing DeVarnay lately. No one seemed to be harboring guilty knowledge about him. None of them were intent on anything at all except having a good time, and DeVarnay's name didn't cause a ripple of diversion from that.

We hit four night spots. Since it was Saturday evening, all of them were crowded and jumping. We heard four bands, ranging in quality from superb to indifferent and in volume from loud to loudest. People think of the French Quarter and Bourbon Street as the center of the popular music universe. There are places elsewhere in New Orleans that are far more famous among locals—including local musicians, who come on their nights off to sit in the audience or take a turn with a really good band. One was so impressive I wouldn't have minded spending the rest of the night listening to it, but I had work to do, so we moved on.

I got to talk with at least two dozen friends and acquaintances of DeVarnay's, and—since each establishment had a mandatory one drink minimum except for one place that required two—we were beginning to feel like old friends by the time Minjarus suggested we wind up the evening at a piano bar.

Even though I turned up nothing of interest about DeVarnay, my evening was not a total flop. The knowledge that twenty-four friends and acquaintances of his, all of them his social equals, not only had no knowledge of his whereabouts but still weren't aware he was missing, was significant. I reminded myself, however, that raising the total to forty eight would not make the result twice as interesting. I reluctantly decided that repeating the experiment would be a waste of time. This bothered my conscience. Venita would be left holding the bag with the burden of another broken engagement on her reputation, but I couldn't invest my time in a series of reruns if there was no information to be obtained.

The wear and tear on my expense account had been much less than I expected because Minjarus insisted on picking up the check in three of the four night spots. As for Venita, she continued to display the sterling qualities of an old-fashioned girl. She was a very capable dancer—a bit stiff in the beginning, but as the night progressed, she brightened, became more relaxed, and began to enjoy herself. Each successive night spot was another way station where she could get her bearings on life and put Marc DeVarnay further behind her.

She drank very little. She stuck with a cocktail called a Cajun Screwdriver, which I found to be mild, like a regular Screwdriver, but with New Orleans refinements. A bartender gave me the recipe later: mix a regular screwdriver with vodka and orange juice, and add half an ounce of fresh lime juice and a drop—or two, or three—of Tabasco Sauce. Venita sipped these in a lady-like manner and left her glass two-thirds full when we moved on. If she was still grieving for Marc DeVarnay, she wasn't about to let it get out of control.

For our final nightclub, Minjarus guided us back to the French Quarter, and when we ran up against the Quarter's parking problem, he again proved his sterling value as a guide. He not only had connections, but he also knew his way around. He led us down a narrow byway to the rear of another attorney's office. Since it wasn't open at that hour, there was plenty of parking there.

Our objective was DeVarnay's favorite piano bar. It was called Club Edie, and it had an out-of-the-way location a block and a half north-east of Bourbon Street—if you insist on using a compass in New Orleans. To reach it, we had to walk for two blocks along Bourbon Street, which at that time of night was throbbing with people and music. The street had been cordoned off between cross streets, and this converted it into a mall crowded with pedestrians. The sidewalks were left to panhandlers, street performers, hawkers touting their wares, and barkers for the various establishments. The latter bustled about flagging down tourists and touting girl shows, or food, or music, or all three. The signs overhead, ablaze with light, seemed to blare their topless bottomless come-ons as loudly as the music.

Almost every restaurant and nightclub had a band that was trying to drown out the band next door, and the cacophony was overwhelming. Sometimes the musicians came out onto the street and assaulted the ears of passersby directly.

One of the genuine oddities about Bourbon Street is its tiny, hole-in-the-wall bars. No space is too small to rent in the French Quarter, and these are located in passageways a few feet wide that lead to a rear courtyard. The bar is located no more than a stride or two inside the entrance. They are fast drink, rather than fast food, establishments, dedicated to the principle that any twitch of thirst should be instantly satisfied. All of their drinks are advertised to go—the available space limits drinking on the premises to what you can gulp as you walk away—but they offer super cut-rates on their cocktails. The famous Hurricane, which will set you back a sawbuck or more in one of the better night spots, can be had for three bucks or even two fifty at one of these quickie bars. Of course the amount of liquor is reduced proportionally, and the resultant impact is more like a soft breeze than a hurricane.

Our party of three arrived at Club Edie unscathed. Several former souvenir stores or praline shops had been combined with ingenious remodeling to form the club's four large rooms. At the corner where they met was a platform with a grand piano. The pianist thus performed in all four rooms simultaneously.

"It used to be called 'Missie's Place,'" Minjarus said. "But Missie was elderly and in poor health, and it was Edie who really made the club go, so she took it over. Edie is the piano player."

Edie was nowhere in sight when we walked in. The piano had

been pushed out of the way, and three young folksingers were performing unobtrusively—a regular feature here, Minjarus said. Edie often gave young musicians a chance to perform. She also gave young artists a chance by exhibiting their paintings in the former shop windows and all through the club. If one was purchased, Club Edie took only a small commission.

The place was tastefully decorated in subdued tones, and it had a restful, restorative quality to it. The quiet music and the unobtrusive decor were in fact a stark contrast with the other night spots we had visited.

I felt revitalized and eager to continue work the moment we walked in because I recognized the bartender. It was the guitar player—now minus his guitar but still in his black shirt and white vest—whom I had seen sitting on the stoop across the street from St. Phillip Place and who had followed me from Jackson Park to my hotel.

Minjarus said DeVarnay liked Club Edie so well that he often came there by himself for an evening to relax. I could believe that. It was only a short stroll down the street and a block or two over from his home.

The place was crowded. We threaded our way among the tables while Minjarus looked around for an empty one. Someone in a corner recognized him and waved an arm. He turned in that direction, and we trailed after him and found him warmly greeting two couples who not only were his own social acquaintances but who also knew Venita and, as it turned out, Marc DeVarnay.

Minjarus, with an adroit conversational maneuver that enhanced my admiration of his legal ability, got us invited to join them. The two of us helped a waitress move a nearby table over to form one large table, and we settled ourselves while Minjarus made the introductions.

Wesley Jervis, a pleasant-looking, dark-haired man in his early thirties, was a Realtor. By coincidence, he was the one who leased Marc DeVarnay's store to him. Mrs. Jervis—Adelle, a pretty blonde woman—seemed both young and immature. I surmised that Jervis had married his office girl.

The other man, John Robler, was about the same age but already balding. He was Dr. John Robler, a staff doctor at Tulane University Medical Center, as was his *fiancée*, Dr. Sylvia Trelling, a small, dark woman.

They registered suitable surprise over Venita's engagement, and I exchanged pleasantries with them. Probably I seemed preoccupied because I was. My mind was grappling with a conundrum involving Marc DeVarnay's favorite night spot, its bartender, the bartender's odd hobby of practicing the guitar on a stoop opposite DeVarnay's home, and the considerable coincidence of his following me. Probably I seemed incoherent for a few minutes. When I came to myself and put the problem aside for later consideration, Venita was looking at me perplexedly, and Minjarus, who always had the air of waiting for me to pull a rabbit out of someone's hat, was watching me expectantly.

I had to restore the situation quickly, so I announced, "There's something I don't understand about this city."

They promised to enlighten me at once if I would describe my problem.

"How do you pronounce it?" I asked. I told them about the uninvited instruction I had received on that point. When they stopped laughing, they took turns, each of them carefully enunciating "New Orleans." The results ranged from "Ne-yew-or-LEANZ" from Jervis and his wife and also Venita, all three of them natives, to "Noo-OR-le-ans" from Minjarus, a long-time resident who in many respects was an unconverted heathen. Dr. Robler, an outlander like myself but a native southerner, favored "NooAHleans; Dr. Trelling, from the Midwest, made it "NORluns," but she confessed a personal preference for the version a patient of hers had used recently, "NAWlins."

Our drinks arrived, with another round for the two couples, and Dr. Trelling told us about something hilarious she had noticed just that evening on Bourbon Street.

"Some of those night places have a cover charge," she said. "Others only require that you buy a couple of drinks, and they advertise it by saying, 'No cover.' Well—some distance down Bourbon Street I saw a large sign that said 'Bottomless Topless Table Top Dancing,' and underneath it said, 'No Cover.'"

Everyone laughed. The conversation turned to Bourbon Street, and I became preoccupied again. Marc DeVarnay hated Bourbon Street—or so he said, frequently and emphatically—but Marc DeVarnay had been seen going into a girlie show the night he left for St. Louis.

Marc DeVarnay was gay. Exactly *what* girlie show Doug Kallenor saw him patronize suddenly became a matter of interest and maybe even importance. Bourbon Street offers a little of everything and entirely too much of some things. Among the attractions I had seen there were several that might have appealed to a gay male—night spots with female impersonators, night spots with both male and female topless and bottomless dancers, bars with a frankly gay slant.

"Here's something else I don't understand," I announced. "In these strip joints, what do the girls—or men—do?" That brought me six blank looks, so I continued, "The sign says 'tabletop dancing,' which sounds like a fairly restricted place to perform. What sort of dancing? Do they also sing? Do they recite? Do they do skits? Do they form a chorus line? What sort of entertainment is it?"

"I've never been to one of them," Minjarus confessed.

"Neither have I," Jervis said. "Locally, they're called 'Strip and Clip Joints.' They're strictly for tourists. The girls strip, and the tourists get clipped. A two-drink minimum might sound reasonable, but they'll charge exorbitantly for the drinks. I mean—*really* exorbitantly. I've heard of joints where a shot of beer goes for five bucks. The music is lousy, the girls are ugly, and since the owners cater to tourists and have no regular clients to worry about, they don't care if everyone goes away mad."

"Do they really dance nude on the tables?" Adelle Jervis asked with wide-eyed naivety.

Minjarus contributed his legal expertise. "According to the law, they can't. They're supposed to wear tassels, at least, but if they haven't been raided for a time, the tassels get shorter and shorter and fewer and fewer. Or so I've heard—fortunately my firm avoids that kind of business."

He did another of his adroit shifts and brought DeVarnay into it. "Marc loves Club Edie, but he hates Bourbon Street." he said.

"We all hate Bourbon Street," Dr. Robler said. "It's an affliction New Orleaneans have to bear."

"That's interesting," I said. "About Marc hating Bourbon Street, I mean. One of his business associates told me he'd recently seen Marc going into one of the girlie shows there."

That brought sudden silence. Then Jervis said, "I don't believe it."

"Neither do I," Dr. Robler said. "If you'd ever heard Marc really get going on the subject—"

The folk singers had finished their stint and retired. The bartender and a waiter pushed the piano back into position, after which, to a burst of applause, Edie appeared. She seated herself and with a sure, deft touch, began a medley of Broadway show tunes.

Conversation halted. We sipped our drinks and listened. I gave Venita a smile and leaned back contentedly. For the first time since I left Savannah, I had a genuine sense of accomplishment.

"Edie" was the highly pregnant Guinea Pig Lady.

CHAPTER THIRTEEN

At seven on Sunday morning, I called Raina Lambert. This time she answered.

First I told her about Marc DeVarnay being gay, and we discussed that. Then I told her about identifying the Guinea Pig Lady and the guitarist. I now knew them as Edie Aronska, who owned Club Edie and played the piano there, and her brother, Karl Aronska, who was Club Edie's bartender. The one critical fact I didn't know was why they had followed us.

"Obviously they have a strong interest in Marc DeVarnay," she said. "It would be interesting to know whether the street people who have been hounding you have any connection with them. What else do you have?"

I told her about Ida Gallan, who had seen DeVarnay in the French Quarter several times since he disappeared, and Ross Sernold, who had a censorable opinion of DeVarnay's character. She clucked her tongue at Sernold's story, but she was frankly skeptical about Ida's powers of observation.

"You wouldn't be if you'd heard her," I said. "Besides, her testimony has been confirmed by a psychic witch."

I had to explain that.

"So you really believe DeVarnay is hiding out in the French Quarter," she mused finally.

"In it or near it. It stopped being a mere theory when it grew a witness. Has it occurred to you that DeVarnay himself might be having me watched?"

"No. Why would he do that?"

"I'm an unknown element. He expected the police to be looking for him, but he wouldn't know his mother had hired private detectives. He would want to know who I was and what I was up to. Hence the watch on me and on the store. He has the street connections. He could have arranged it easily."

"That hadn't occurred to me, but I'm glad you thought of it. Keep on thinking. Your job is to find him—alive or dead."

"I'd much rather find him alive," I said.

"So would we all—if we had our druthers."

"If my job is to find him, what's your job?"

"I'm assuming he's dead. If you find him alive, splendid. I'll rejoice with his mother. If it's his body you find, I want to be able to point my finger at who did it."

"How do you expect to do that by mucking around down in the flea market?"

"I'm covering all of the ground you're covering plus some that you aren't, and of course I'm using a different viewpoint."

"So what have you done?"

"For one thing, I persuaded Jolitte to let me read her will, and after I had done so, I went to see David and Nadine Dolding."

"Who are they?" I asked.

"David is Jolitte's first cousin. If Marc predeceases his mother, all of her money goes to David. So I had a long talk with David and his wife."

"Good thought. Did you learn anything?"

"Yes. If anyone has concocted a plot to benefit from Marc's death, it isn't the Doldings. They're a charming old couple in their mid-eighties. They aren't rich, but they're comfortably well off. They have one of the more modest Garden District homes and enough money for their own needs. Their only son and his wife are dead, and they have no grandchildren. Jolitte is their only surviving relative, and she doesn't need their money, so they've willed all of it to various Catholic charities."

"Dead end," I said.

"It would seem so, but there may be an angle we don't know about, so I've hired three local operatives for this case—one who can impersonate a butler, one who can pass in high society as a social secretary, and one who can make like a gardener and chauffeur. I've already planted them in the DeVarnay mansion. Three times that many would be too few guards in that enormous house, but if they're competent, they can handle it. The secretary—and, of course, the chauffeur—will stick to Jolitte like glue whenever she goes out."

"So you think it's that kind of case."

"I do think it may eventually prove to be that kind of case, and if we wait until it does, we'll be too late."

"What about the fuss down in bayou country?"

"Cloud of dust."

"DeVarnay's fingerprints on the jambalaya pan?"

"There's no proof as to when they got on the pan."

"Maybe so," I mused. "I sort of thought that myself, but I'm not quite ready to bet money on it."

"It won't cost all that much, and Jolitte can afford it. Better safe than. I told Jolitte it was a rule with us. When there's ten million dollars involved, we always make certain the client is protected."

"Even when no one benefits from her death?"

"Even then. There's still a lot more to this case than meets the eye—our eyes, anyway."

"Don't tell me you're entertaining the notion that some ambitious young priest has done away with Marc to get control of the Doldings' charitable donations!"

"No. I'm not entertaining that. You asked what I've been doing. I've also been looking over DeVarnay's associates, friends, rivals, competitors, and hangers-on for a possible murderer. As I said, if you find him dead, I hope to be ready to point. What else do you have?"

I told her about my engagement. Her reaction was caustic. "Can't you handle a case without a romantic entanglement?"

"What's romantic about getting engaged?" I demanded.

We discussed the possibilities, and eventually she conceded it might prove useful. She also wanted to know whether I thought

Venita Berent could be nursing a grudge over her broken engagement. "She certainly had a motive," Raina observed.

"A motive for what? Bashing Old Jake and putting the murder onto her ex-*fiancé*? She's not capable of that, and I don't think she has a grudge. She's never got over the hurt, but she doesn't seem to have blamed Marc for it. She worshipped him and thought he could do no wrong."

"In that case, she has a damn silly attitude toward men," Raina said. "What did you think of Jolitte DeVarnay?"

"I didn't. Royalty is beyond my comprehension."

She snorted. "About your new *fiancée*—take it easy with the night-clubbing. In this town, that quickly gets expensive."

"It quickly gets expensive in any town, but Marc's crowd seems to do its splurging with moderation. His friends are young enough to still be on their way up, even if they have rich parents."

"So you think. I want daily reports. Do you have anything else?"

"You mentioned competitors," I said. "If one of them is capable of murder, I've found him. Harold Nusiner, whom I've already mentioned." I told her about my conversation with him. "I want you to drop a hint to Lieutenant Keig that he might know something. He needs raking over."

"What would that accomplish?"

"It would teach him manners just in case I have to talk with him again."

"All right. At least that won't cost anything. What else."

"Doug Kallenor," I said. "I caught him in a Top of the Mart tryst with Selma Garnett. I have a feeling about him. I wouldn't trust him to audit my collection of lead nickels. Let's have him tailed."

"By Dick Tosche's crew?"

"Nope. They're all right for the French Quarter, but they'd be overly conspicuous anywhere else. This has to be a professional job. Since you've already hired three local operatives, invest in a few more."

"All right. I'll arrange something. I'm considering having someone else perform an audit on DeVarnay's store. I might do it myself."

"Then you've already met Kallenor."

"I have."

"Right. Have him followed for a few days and do the audit over. That should settle him one way or the other."

"At least it should tell us whether we need to know more about him. Anything else?"

"Yes. Since you've already hired local operatives to guard Jolitte DeVarnay, and you'll be hiring more to tail Kallenor, stretch it another notch and put a stakeout on the grocery store that sells fresh bread and croissants."

"According to your witness, DeVarnay only shows up there occasionally. To do the job right, there should be a watch on the neighborhood."

"I agree. The Esplanade and Royal Street area. Jolitte can afford it."

She argued a little, but eventually she gave in.

"How goes the investigation down in the swamp?" I asked.

"It doesn't. They're waiting for Marc DeVarnay to surface somewhere."

"Have they turned up any kind of a smuggling connection?"

"Not involving Old Jake. There was nothing hidden in his *cabon* and no evidence that he had a secret illegal income. The only suspicious-looking items were the new camp cots and sleeping bags and the jambalaya pan, and everyone believes that DeVarnay gave those to Old Jake to butter him up and make him think more lavish gifts were on the way."

"Were Old Jake's boat and pirogue ever found?"

"No. The murderer probably sank them in a good hiding place."

"Another dead end," I said. "Sooner or later one of these leads has got to lead somewhere."

"Unfortunately, that law has never been strictly enforced," she said.

Leaving the laundry, I went to a small restaurant near my hotel for breakfast, noting along the way that Hattie the Hat Lady was on duty again, this time alone. At the restaurant, I encountered the man from San Francisco who had corrected my pronunciation of "New Orleans." He was breakfasting with two other men, and he waved an expansive invitation to join them.

The restaurant's breakfast menu included a jambalaya omelet. I passed it up. The pan in Old Jake's *cabon* had placed gastromic blight on my visit to New Orleans. Fortunately I was eating everything else with good appetite. I gave the waitress a suitably prosaic order and turned my attention to the companions I'd just acquired.

They were talking about tourists, evidently a favorite subject with my friend from San Francisco. "They trash the city," he said. "Then they complain about it being filthy. A rich tourist will drop food wrappers in the street when there's a trash can right under his nose."

"They also complain about the weather," one of the other men said. "As if anyone could control the weather."

I suggested that tourists who mess up New Orleans probably do the same thing at home. My friend from San Francisco countered with the information that tourists arriving in New Orleans lose their inhibitions and do all kinds of things they wouldn't dream of doing at home. "Look at how they throw money away on strip joints," he said.

This was an opening I couldn't ignore. I still was wondering whether to believe what Doug Kallenor said about Marc DeVarnay's inexplicable attendance at one. If it were true, I wanted to know what the attraction had been. I wasn't interested enough to pay money to see for myself, but I am always willing to acquire free information. According to Confucius, or maybe it was Karl Marx, it is better to have useless knowledge than to know nothing at all.

"In these strip shows, what do the girls do?" I asked.

"That's for tourists," the man from San Francisco said disgustedly. "Go have a look for yourself."

"That would take time and money, and I'm not all that curious. I was hoping one of you gentlemen could tell me."

The other two, who confessed to be native New Orleaneans, said they never went near Bourbon Street.

"That's hard to believe," I said. "You've lived here all your lives, and you've never been to a show even once?"

"Actually, I did go once," one of the men said. "That was a long time ago. I couldn't have been more than sixteen."

"Really? Only sixteen, and they let you in?"

"I was a big sixteen, and I had money. They don't card people at girlie shows. I mean—they have to pay lip service to the law, whatever that may be, but there wouldn't be any point in their being fanatical about it."

"So what did the girls do?"

"I don't remember, but for years afterward I had the impression that all naked women were ugly."

"I've also been once," the other native confessed. "A long, long time ago. I was probably twenty-one or two. Once was enough."

"So what did the girls do?"

"Someone played music, and they paraded out and danced. After they danced, they came out into the audience for tips. If you didn't tip them enough, they called you names and even spit at you. They're not supposed to take everything off, but these girls did. It was a cheap place and so were the girls—they would have looked better covered up. Not long after that, the joint was raided."

"What happens in the better quality places?" I asked.

They didn't know. They went back to grousing about tourists, and I ate my breakfast and thought about Marc DeVarnay, who hated Bourbon Street but was seen there going into a girlie show the night he left for St. Louis.

When I finished eating, I thanked my three companions for their enlightening conversation and took my leave of them. DeVarnay's antique store didn't open until eleven on Sunday, and I needed information immediately, so I strolled down to the

French Market's flea market. I found Francis Dassily getting set up for the day. He still had the display of oil paintings behind his jewelry table. I took the time to look them over. Despite the triteness of the subjects, they were quite well done.

I said, "You're a very capable artist."

"They aren't mine," he said. "My girl friend painted them."

"She has a nice touch. She ought to sign them."

He shrugged. "They're just souvenirs. They bring her a little money for rent and groceries so she can take the time to paint seriously."

"I have a question for you," I said. "On the night Marc DeVarnay left for St. Louis, you gave him a tip about some antiques. A table and chairs, wasn't it? He went wherever it was and bought them. Remember?"

"I certainly do," Dassily said with feeling. "That's the last money I earned from him."

"Where did he buy them? What was the address?"

He stroked his goatee thoughtfully. "I remember the street and the apartment number but not the address. Just a moment. Maybe I can find out."

He called to the woman at the next table, "Pam—will you keep an eye on things?"

Pam smiled and nodded.

He dashed away, and I waited. When he came back, he handed me a slip of paper with a name and address on it. "Is anything wrong?" he asked.

"Not as far as I know. This is more of the same thing— talking with people who saw Marc that day."

As I expected, the address was Bourbon Street. On Saturday night the street had throbbed with people and music. On Sunday morning, it might have existed on another planet. Everything looked washed out and dead. There were few people around. Lines of trucks were unloading stocks of food and drink. Service and repair vehicles were parked along the curb, and their workers came and went. Sidewalks were being hosed down. The signs were still there, of course, advertising topless bottomless everything; female impersonators; free drinks for unescorted girls; ten-girl show no cover; burlesque; beautiful girls; Dixieland jazz; home of the best in strip tease; girls! girls! girls! With the prosaic activity going on up and down the street below them, these blatant overhead messages had a surrealistic quality.

Even the hole-in-the-wall bars looked boarded-up and abandoned in the harsh reality of a Bourbon Street morning. The entire street had the air of a resort that had closed for the season. The few regular bars that were open and functioning had a halfway closed look about them. One was left to wonder whether the patrons energetically bending their elbows at that hour were left over from the previous night or getting an early start on the new day.

I found the address Dassily had given to me. Then I crossed the street and backed away, looking at it from several angles and distances and trying to guess where Doug Kallenor had been standing with his out-of-town guests when he saw DeVarnay going into the girlie show. DeVarnay had in fact entered the doorway to a stairway that led up to a third floor apartment—the one where Francis Dassily had found an antique table and chairs for him—but the girlie show entrance was adjacent to it, and from a short distance down the street, especially at dusk, he easily could have appeared to be entering the girlie show.

Having thus established Kallenor's veracity and at the same time restored DeVarnay's reputation to him, I returned to my hotel, giving Hattie the Hat Lady a nod along the way, checked for messages, and then went up to my room to plan my next move.

There was a critically important question I had been neglecting. My job was to find Marc DeVarnay, but where was he? On the basis of Ida Gallan's testimony, confirmed after a fashion by the psychic witch, somewhere in or near the French Quarter. That covered a large area populated by a huge number of people. I badly needed some kind of clue that narrowed this down to a block or two so I could go there and look.

A thorough search of DeVarnay's French Quarter home was long overdue, and I decided to do it immediately. Thanks to Minjarus, I still had the keys.

Then I reminded myself that going over a house is not only hard work but also tedious, and I would be able to do it more efficiently after an early lunch. This is never a difficult decision to make in New Orleans.

I usually avoid the famous restaurants, which too often provide nothing more than a fabulous disappointment. Both their prices and their reputations are overwhelming, and one expects a matching perfection in the food, which rarely happens. The real gastronomic pleasures in New Orleans are those furnished by the small, unknown, reasonably priced restaurants that nevertheless provide excellent food.

Of course there is a good chance that the small restaurant will be no better than mediocre, and occasionally one will be downright bad, but the disappointment is less severe because one is expecting less.

I had a light early lunch, sampling the rémoulade and a crawfish bisque at a side street restaurant. Both dishes were very good. They fell short of being superb, but then, so did the prices. Next I headed for Marc DeVarnay's house, taking a roundabout route to check for tails.

Passing through Jackson Square, I was hailed by a woman sitting at one of the card tables. It was Connie Dey, the Gypsy fortune-teller who also served as a contact for Marc DeVarnay. She invited me to join her for a moment.

"I've been trying to find Marc," she said.

I gave her a sympathetic nod. "So have I."

"I mean—I've been trying with cards. They don't tell me anything that makes sense. I thought maybe if I did a reading for you, we might find out something."

I suspected her of trying to drum up business, but no—she was totally sincere. She wanted to help find Marc. He was an important source of income for her, and she was grateful to him for many kindnesses. She simply felt she had to do something. I told her to go ahead, and she began to deal the cards.

I had never seen a deck like them. I remarked on this, and she said, "An artist I know did them for me. Each card is hand drawn and painted. I made sketches, and the artist followed them. I wouldn't take a thousand dollars for them. They're wonderfully effective. Now—please don't talk. Just answer questions if I have to ask any."

She dealt a row of cards. "This represents Marc's mother," she said, indicating a faceless woman in a filmy party dress.

More cards followed—of buildings, of animals, of social groups with the people all faceless. "There's Marc," she said suddenly. "He's distant from his mother. Probably she has no idea where he is."

"She doesn't," I said.

The Gypsy frowned, so I obediently lapsed into silence. She dealt more cards, and another woman appeared. "Does Marc have a girlfriend?" she asked.

"He did at one time, but the engagement was broken several years ago."

"Then there's another woman who's close to him. She may know something about him."

She finished a row and started another. Midway through it, she laid down a card below the card representing Marc and halted. "There. It's done it again."

"Done what?" I asked.

"The cards say Marc is here. The same thing happened when I dealt them at home. I heard he'd been traveling all around— places like San Francisco and Seattle. So how could he be here?"

"Do you mean here in New Orleans?" I asked.

"Perhaps. New Orleans or somewhere nearby."

"There's a witness who claims to have seen Marc several times recently in the French Quarter," I said.

She stared at me. "Then the cards are right! I feel so much better. I'm so glad you stopped."

"I am, too," I said. If it meant anything, I now had the authority of a Gypsy fortune-teller as well as a psychic witch that Ida Gallan's testimony was the whole truth.

But none of that told me where to start looking. I took my leave of the Gypsy and walked on to St. Philip Street and St. Philip Place, entering through the locked gate. Everything looked the same as it had on my first visit. Even the three cars were parked exactly where they had been before. I entered the house, but this time I paid no attention to its museum qualities. I had spent sufficient time admiring them on my first visit. Now I had to make like a detective, which is work.

I looked under rugs. I checked for loose floorboards. I flipped through the pages of books. I emptied drawers, examined the chest they were in, checked their bottoms and backs, and sifted through their contents. I peeked into all of the costly china bowls and tureens and vases. I even looked under and around the pot containing the Voodoo Lily, which stank as badly as it had before. I looked inside the piano without furthering either my knowledge of music or the investigation. I removed sofa cushions to look under them, and then I carefully felt them for tell-tale lumps.

I gave DeVarnay's home as thorough a search as could be done without actually tearing it apart. I found nothing. I was at it until late afternoon, and for all I accomplished I might as well have sat there and read a book. Neither did my effort produce any fresh insights into Marc DeVarnay's character other than what I had already gleaned from the house's contents.

Upstairs, I took beds apart and then remade them. Again I checked for loose floor boards and looked under rugs. I went through the dressers and bureaus. In DeVarnay's closet, I went through all the pockets of his clothing, but my only discovery there was that he always carried two handkerchiefs—the spare being neatly folded to make it unnoticeable at the bottom of a pocket.

When I finished, I meditated for a time, and then I looked around again. At the back of his closet, an irregularity in the paneling caught my eye. I pried at it. It swung open easily—and I found myself looking into a pair of dark feminine eyes that immediately backed away in panic.

I followed them, stepped through the back of another closet and then through its door into a bedroom.

The eyes faced me with absolute terror.

It was the Guinea Pig Lady.

If she'd had a gun available, she would have emptied it into me, and a jury probably would have found her innocent—after all, I had cornered her in her bedroom, and she obviously thought her life was threatened. I wouldn't have been around to point out that she had followed me on my previous visit and probably had been snooping on me in one way or another ever since I began my search.

Fortunately she wasn't armed. I make no pretense at having a hypnotic effect on females I've never been introduced to, but in strange bedrooms I am always mild and well behaved and my manners are impeccable. Even Venita Berent had said I could get by in New Orleans society with a little attention to my dress. I was careful not to make any movement the Guinea Pig Lady could interpret as aggressive, and I gave her my most sympathetic smile. After a few minutes of that, she began to think maybe it wouldn't be necessary to defend her honor unto the death or even to try to frighten me off by screaming.

"I think it's time we had a quiet, confidential talk," I said. "Are you Marc's mistress?"

"Certainly not!" she said indignantly. "I'm his wife—if that's any business of yours."

"Everything about Marc is my business," I said. "I'm trying to find him. If you want him found—"

She burst into tears.

"I don't know what to do," she sobbed. "He's gone, and I can't tell anyone."

Without my quite knowing how it happened, she was sobbing on my shoulder. I patted both of her shoulders comfortingly. "You can tell me," I said. "I'm working for his mother, but I easily can work for you, too, without her knowing about it. That's the idea, isn't it? To keep her from knowing?"

She nodded, continuing to sob. Eventually we went downstairs to her living room, and I got the whole story.

She and Marc had met at Tulane University, where she was taking courses in painting and music, but they didn't really get acquainted until later when she got a job playing the piano at Missie's Place, the predecessor to Club Edie. Soon Marc was coming every night to hear her play, and they had long talks together between her numbers. They fell very much in love. They both wanted to get married, but his mother would never have allowed it.

I said, "Did Marc ask her?"

"He didn't have to. He *knew*. I knew, too."

I shook my head perplexedly. Certainly the name "Aronska" lacked the snobbish pedigree that "DeVarnay" had. No Aronskas had arrived on the New Orleans equivalent of the Mayflower. Probably they used a garbage scow, like most people's ancestors, but I felt certain they had been worthy people and old families like the DeVarnays are invariably improved by occasional mixed breeding. That is what keeps them virile. Anyway, the moment they married she became a DeVarnay herself, and surely the DeVarnay position was far too secure to be unbalanced by one Aronska daughter-in-law.

She shook her head mournfully. "She never would have allowed it. Never. Never. It wasn't the name, it was my work."

"What's wrong with music?" I asked. "I'm sure Jolitte DeVarnay is fond of it, or pretends to be, and Club Edie is the highest class night spot I've seen here."

She shook her head again. "Before I got the job playing the piano at Missie's, I was a chorus girl. A dancer in a cabaret. That's how I paid for my education. Most people think it's synonymous with being a prostitute. It isn't at all. To me it was just a job dancing, and I badly needed a job. But Marc thought there'd be no point trying to explain that to his mother."

I had to nod gravely and concede that Marc had been right. The topless bottomless tabletop dancing signs along Bourbon Street would have graphically defined Jolitte DeVarnay's concept of a French Quarter chorus girl, no matter what kind of high-class club she worked in, and Edie would never, but never, have been accepted as a daughter-in-law.

"Marc thought maybe after we were married and had a family, his mother might be willing to overlook what I was. So we decided to get married anyway and keep it a secret. He had just finished restoring and remodeling this building. I moved in here, and he pretended to live next door but of course he actually lived here, too. He kept some of his things next door, and he ruffled the bed and dirtied a few dishes before Millie came so the place would look lived in."

The poor kid. The longer I thought about it, the less I cared for Marc DeVarnay. He had been a coward where his mother was concerned and a cad in the lying way he terminated his engagement to Venita Berent. Had he also abandoned his pregnant wife? Whether he had or not, he was totally unworthy of her.

"He bought Missie's Place for me as a wedding present, and we changed the name to Club Edie," she said. "It's doing very well. So are my paintings. Marc sells them in his store."

I stared. "You—are Frederick?"

She nodded. "My middle name is Gwendolen. I wanted a pseudonym to sign my paintings with because I thought they would be accepted better if I put a man's name on them. Gwendolen is sometimes confused with Winnifred, so I chose 'Frederick.' I didn't think anyone would make the connection."

"You certainly were right about that," I assured her.

She was an excellent artist and also an excellent piano player, and that order of talent was just what the DeVarnay family needed. Marc had made an splendid choice of a wife if only he'd had the courage to face the world—and his mother—with her.

She described the evening Marc left for St. Louis. "He had a phone call—a tip on an antique that had to be taken care of at once. His flight wasn't until eleven thirty, so he wasn't rushed at all. He went and bought the antique, and then he came home and got ready to leave. He called a cab, kissed me good by, and went next door for his luggage. Then he had another phone call." She paused. "There's an extension line from the phone in the other condo. I never answer it—it's the white phone, and there's one upstairs in the bedroom and one downstairs in the TV room. It has a different ring from my phones. I heard it ring."

"How many times did it ring?" I asked.

"Just once."

"Then he answered it right away or the other party hung up. You have no idea what it was about?"

She shook her head. Tears came to her eyes. "I was watching for him to leave. He went out the door—the one next door—carrying his suitcase, and he turned, and waved at me, and threw me a kiss. That was the last time I saw him."

"I see. I can add a little to that. After Marc called the cab, he called back and cancelled it. In between, you heard his phone ring, so someone must have called him. Since he did go to the airport, and he did catch his plane, the call could have been an offer by someone to take him to the airport. Who knew he was going to St. Louis?"

"I suppose everyone at his store, and probably some of the other antique dealers and quite a few of his friends. People were always inviting him to things or asking him to do things, and he would have told them he was going to be out-of-town."

"Right. It could have been almost anyone." I paused. "Perhaps it was someone who had something urgent to discuss with him. Otherwise, why call off his cab and impose on a friend or colleague for a ride to the airport? It wouldn't seem to matter, but I'd like to know who it was anyway." Even a hint as to DeVarnay's mental state at that particular moment could have been invaluable.

"It's one more thing to investigate," I said. "Have you heard anything at all from him since he left?"

"Not a word. No phone calls, not even a postcard. He always telephoned or wrote to me every day when he was away. Some days he would write two or three times. I've been so worried. I know something must have happened to him, but I didn't know whom to ask about him or how to find out anything. I followed you the other day because I wondered what you were doing here. Then I tried to follow the woman you met, but she took a cab, and it was out-of-sight before I could find one. Karl followed you to your hotel, and he thought maybe you were a tourist, but that didn't explain what you were doing here with an attorney."

"I had permission to look at Marc's home, and the attorney was here to let me in. Now you know, and if you want to know anything else, you have someone to ask. Unfortunately, I still have very little to tell, but I'm working on it, and so are a lot of other people, including the police. If I find out anything at all, you'll be the first to know. If I think of any way you can help, I'll tell you that, too."

I decided not to mention that her husband was wanted for murder. At this point there was nothing to be gained by that.

She thanked me. I gave her my card with my hotel and phone number written on it. I left through her front door and returned to Marc's condo. I now knew why it had an unlived in air about it. It had never been lived in.

I made certain everything was in order and that the panel at the back of the closet was firmly closed.

Then I left, knowing she would be watching my every step until the gate closed on me and hoping I could do something to end her agony of waiting.

CHAPTER FOURTEEN

I found Karl Aronska strumming his guitar on the stoop on the other side of St. Philip Street. I hoped he had a wardrobe of identical black shirts and white vests. If he hadn't, he was still wearing what he had on the first time I saw him. I walked over to him. "I just had a long talk with Edie," I said.

He raised his eyebrows. He said nothing, but he stopped strumming.

"Marc's mother, Jolitte DeVarnay, hired me to find him," I said. "I can work for Edie at the same time, so that's what I'm going to do. Marc's mother doesn't need to know that unless or until Edie wants her to. I'm an expert at keeping secrets. I don't mind telling you, though, that I have an extremely poor opinion of Marc for not standing up to his mother. Is he afraid of being disinherited?"

"I don't think so," Karl said. "I don't think his mother could—not completely. Marc's father left money to him. Anyway, his store is making him rich. No, he's simply scared of her. He's like a little kid with strict parents who's terrified he'll be caught doing something bad. I was opposed to Edie marrying him. She's been happy, though—happy about her marriage, and about the club, and about how well Marc's business is doing, and about the way he's been selling her paintings, and about the baby. Until this." He met my eyes squarely. "How does it look to you?"

"Confused," I said. "Nothing about it makes sense."

"That's the way I feel. Marc certainly seemed happy with

Edie. So why would he run off?"

"When is the baby due?" I asked.

"Any day, now."

"Tough. Really tough."

He nodded. "A wife likes to have her husband around. Especially with the first baby."

"We can only hope for a good break on this."

He nodded again. "Anything I can do—"

"I don't suppose you saw Marc the evening he left."

He shook his head. "If I'd known what was going to happen, I'd have gone along with him. If it turns out he's just playing around somewhere, I'll rearrange his face."

"That wouldn't help Edie," I said.

"No. I guess it wouldn't."

"I don't suppose you've seen Marc wandering around the French Quarter recently."

He was astonished. "You mean—he might have lost his memory or something like that and not know who he is?"

I hadn't considered the possibility of amnesia. "That's as likely as anything else we've thought of," I said.

"No, I haven't seen him. If I had, I would have grabbed him."

"Where can I get in touch with you?" I asked.

"If I'm not at the club, I'm here—this is where I live."

I stopped at the first pay phone I came to and had the good luck to catch Raina Lambert in. I told her about Marc DeVarnay's double life and what had happened the night he left for the airport.

Unfortunately, none of that offered a hint as to where he was or what had happened to him. Usually each new fact an investigation turns up adds a bit more illumination until the whole picture is revealed. With this case, each new fact seemed to contradict what we already knew.

"Is there any chance that DeVarnay got fed up with living a lie and decided to disappear," Raina asked.

"Everything I've found out suggests he was enjoying both his business and his marriage. He must have felt perfectly happy and completely satisfied with life."

"Except for the looming shadow of his mother."

"Yes. But that's been hanging over him from the moment he decided to marry Edie."

"Surely he knew there'd be a day of reckoning. How were they going to handle the birth notice when the baby was born? It's a matter of public record, you know."

"I never thought to ask. No doubt Marc had something figured out."

"So he wasn't perfectly happy," she said. "He was afraid of his mother, and he got around that by telling lies.

"The lies weren't why he disappeared. They were still working."

"It'd be helpful to know exactly what happened the night he left for St. Louis. I'd also like to know what happened in Seattle and what really happened in Old Jake's *cabon*."

"Maybe the gods will be kind and vouchsafe us another glimpse or two," I said. "In the meantime, or if they don't, we'll have to make do with this."

"Have you been able to make anything of it?"

"No."

She muttered something that definitely was not ladylike. Then she brought me up-to-date on her day's work. Jolitte had arranged with Selma Garnett for her to have access to the books and records at the antique store, and she had performed a quickie audit.

"With what result?" I asked.

"The forty-five grand is still missing," she said. "I've arranged for a complete inventory to make certain no valuable items are unaccounted for—though Selma is certain she would know at once if anything important was missing. There's valuable stock in DeVarnay's warehouse, too, and all of it should be accounted for. Do you have anything else?"

"After my association with the psychic witch and the Gypsy fortune-teller, I'm feeling clairvoyant myself. I have a hunch. Nothing guaranteed, but it definitely is a hunch."

"Let's hear it."

"My hunch says Marc DeVarnay's disappearance has nothing to do with his phony gayness, or with his real marriage, or with his business, or with his street connections. It also has nothing to do with Old Jake. I've looked carefully at all of those things, and thought about them, and I heard no bells ringing."

"Then what does it have to do with?"

"Something we haven't put our finger on yet. Obviously we should take another look at who benefits from his death."

"No one except his mother and his wife."

"Jolitte would fire us for thinking of such a thing, and I'll guarantee that Edie has never given a thought to what she might inherit from Marc. She has her own business—two businesses, music and art—and she's doing very well. She doesn't want money, she wants her husband."

"Then we'd better get moving and find him, but I'll remind you—both marriage and death are for better or for worse."

I had absolutely nothing to add to that. I asked again whether there was anything new with the investigation into Old Jake's death. There wasn't, so I hung up.

By the time I returned to my hotel, it was after five o'clock and I was thinking of dinner. There was a message for me. Dick Tosche wanted to see me. By way of the friendly witch, I arranged to meet him at L'Endroit, the bar where he had taken me to meet the customs officer. I enjoyed talking with him, even when he had little to tell me. Amidst the phony sophistication, the brazen conniving, the cynicism, and the sham culture that are encountered on every hand in the French Quarter, I found him distinctly refreshing. He was surprisingly well educated, and there was an air of innocence about him that one rarely meets with these days. Despite the fact that he worked elbow to elbow with greed and depravity, he was untouched by either.

He had finished the job of checking on Marc DeVarnay's contacts. He ran down the list, telling me a little about each of them. Nothing of interest had turned up. He had continued inquiring about DeVarnay around the market without any further success.

"Are all investigations like this?" he asked. "Lots of nothing?"

"Often they are."

"Then what happens? Everything breaks at once?"

"That's rare. Sometimes one encounters a maybe or two among the nothings, and eventually the maybes add up. With a missing person case, sometimes nothing breaks at all. The answer comes years afterward or never."

"How do you keep sane?" he asked.

"I pursue little investigations of my own as a diversion. The last couple of days, I've been trying to find out what the girls do in a stripper show."

"What they *do*?"

"Yeah. Have you ever seen one?"

"A stripper show? I've seen a few."

"What do the girls do? I've heard that in the cheap shows they're ugly, and so is their behavior. Have you seen one of the better shows?"

"The better shows aren't called stripper shows," he said. "They're—what's the word?—cab something."

"Cabarets?" I suggested.

"That's it. There's one over toward Canal Street. It's a different sort of thing entirely. The regular girlie shows can get pretty trashy."

"Strip and clip joints," I suggested.

"That's right. But the cab—cabaret—has class."

"You mean the girls don't strip?"

"Of course they strip. That's what it's all about."

"Then a cabaret is a high class strip and clip joint?"

"Absolutely not. The men wear tuxedos. The girls don't wear much, of course, they wear as little as they can get away with, but it's a whole different class of girl from what you see in the cheap joints. These girls have bodies. They even have teeth. Some of them are so pretty they'd be good looking with their clothes on. A cabaret gives you something to remember with pleasure, but nobody leaves one of those ordinary joints with a smile. You can't get out of one fast enough."

"So okay," I said. "It's a high-class place, the men dress up, the girls are good-looking. What do the girls do?"

He said, "Huh?"

"Do they sing? Do they dance?"

"I don't remember. I was only there once."

"How long ago was this?"

"It must be almost a year ago."

"That isn't very long," I said disgustedly. "Surely you remember *something* about what the girls did."

He said, "Look. There were all those girls, see, and they were wearing very little, and the mind and eyes can only absorb so much."

I told him to keep his mind and eyes on the DeVarnay problem and try to be a bit more observant than he had been at the cabaret.

"That's what I wanted to talk to you about," he said. "Something funny's going on. Up to now, there've been a few *poux* watching your hotel and DeVarnay's store and once in a while trying to follow you. They acted as though you were less important than their begging. Now that's changed. Late this afternoon, some heavies moved in."

"Heavies?"

"Thugs. Muscle men. *Étrangleurs.*"

"I just left the hotel. I didn't see anything."

"They're keeping out of sight. They wouldn't try anything in broad daylight. Too many witnesses around. They'll wait until it's dark and then follow you until they can catch you away from the main drags."

I looked at him questioningly. He seemed deadly serious.

"They may actually mean to do you in," he said. "Send you to the hospital if not kill you. I know these characters—know of them."

"Are you kidding?" I demanded.

He shook his head slowly. He wasn't kidding.

"The street characters—those watching my hotel and

DeVarnay's store and trying to follow me—have been just plain silly," I said. "This is on a different level entirely. It's idiotic. What could they possibly accomplish by attacking me?"

"Someone thinks you're dangerous," he said.

"Maybe you'd better tell me about this from the beginning."

He explained. He'd had people watching the watchers, as we had agreed. They hadn't learned anything, but late that afternoon they reported to him that some thugs had taken up positions in the neighborhood of the hotel. They weren't merely watching the building entrance. They were placed to intercept me no matter what direction I took when I left the hotel. Dick did his own survey and spotted four of them. Then he called me.

"But I just left my hotel," I protested again. "No one bothered me."

"They wouldn't—not now. There are too many witnesses about, and tourists are unpredictable. Some of them might try to interfere. The *étrangleurs* will wait until they can catch you in a deserted part of the Quarter after dark."

"I suppose we could tell the police—"

He was shaking his head.

"What do you suggest?" I asked.

"Someone has been strong-arming tourists, and I think a couple of these characters are responsible. It gives the Quarter a bad name, and that hurts all of us. So I've got some muscle of my own watching you and more on the way. If you'll do what I tell you, we can lead these *étrangleurs* into a trap."

I pursed my lips for a soundless whistle. He was showing me just how tough a person with an air of innocence could be. I had to think for a moment. Dick and his friends had an object of their own. The question was whether my investigation would be advanced or hindered by this. It certainly would be an inconvenience if I had heavies dogging my footsteps everywhere I went and looking for a chance to commit mayhem.

"All right," I said. "I'll play. But you'd better make certain the trap works."

"It'll work," Dick said grimly.

He promised to be there himself, so I took his word for it.

He saw me back to my hotel, following at a distance. Somewhere among the crowds of tourists that filled the sidewalks behind me were several hulking thugs bent on disassembling me; somewhere behind them were Dick's recruits, equally large and determined to disassemble the thugs. I felt like a piece of bait without any protecting trap. I ate a makeshift supper of sandwiches in the hotel restaurant—promising myself something much better later on—and then I went up to my room and removed my 9 millimeter automatic from a concealed compartment in one of my suitcases. I had seen no reason to carry it while investigating a simple missing person case.

When finally I emerged from the hotel, the French Quarter was shrouded in what the Vieux Carré Commission probably liked to think of as glamorous dimness. Someone across the street lit a match when I came out the door. This was Dick Tosche, signaling that everyone was in place. There was little vehicular traffic—local motorists learn to avoid the French Quarter at night as much as possible—but Sunday night pedestrian traffic between Bourbon and Royal Streets was heavier than on weeknights. I turned toward Bourbon Street, and a moment later the seething crowd, the lights, the blaring music, the cries and chants of barkers, the piping plea of an occasional beggar had enveloped and overwhelmed me.

Steel posts had been inserted to keep automobiles off Bourbon Street. Pedestrians had taken over the street, and although auto traffic continued to cross Bourbon on the side streets, it did so with great difficulty because pedestrians tended to ignore it. I walked down the center of the street, picking my way among the tourists and trying to keep a slow but steady pace. After that first signal, there was no way Dick could let me know if something had gone wrong, and I had to be prepared for anything.

For the moment, safety lay in numbers, and there were plenty of numbers. Every night is a holiday on Bourbon Street, and Sunday night is no exception. Groups of small black boys were tap dancing on the sidewalk. Tourists had gathered in the street to watch, and an older sister was collecting contributions. I walked on. A balloon sculptor—not the one who had been on watch at DeVarnay's—was touting his skill without any takers. I wondered if a natural law was involved, balloons having appeal only in daylight. Bourbon Street certainly was bright enough with all of its topless bottomless signs lit. It also was noisy enough in the vicinity of bars and restaurants featuring live music to blast the balloons into orbit.

A barker ventured into the crowd and selected me as his target. "Ten beautiful girls!" he panted. "No admission, no cover charge. Just sit down and enjoy yourself."

I ignored his hand on my arm, and the moment I passed the invisible boundary between his beat and that of the next barker, he dropped me like yesterday's newspaper and looked around for another target. I moved on, trusting hopefully that the machinery of Dick Tosche's operation was functioning like clockwork and a corps of bodyguards was poised to spring to my protection.

The weakness of the plan was that I had to walk so far before the crowds began to thin. If I had turned in the other direction, I would have quickly reached Canal Street where there was heavy auto traffic and at least moderate foot traffic until the wee hours. Probably the *étrangleurs* would have hesitated to act. I had to take this long walk and hope my guards were keeping up with me.

Finally the press of tourists began to thin. I passed Lafitte's Blacksmith Shop, a venerable, sagging, leaning, brick and timber building with legendary—and probably fictitious—historical associations. It is now a popular bar. Many New Orleans drinking places seem slightly askew when one emerges; this one looks out of plumb to customers on their way in. I stopped for a tourist's glance at the place, which gave me an opportunity to look behind me. I saw no heavies. Neither did I see Dick Tosche. I seemed to be all alone in my wandering. I shrugged and continued out Bourbon Street.

Another block—the street was virtually empty, now, and I

was walking on the sidewalk—and I began to hear footsteps pounding behind me. They were not running footsteps but the heavy tread of someone walking faster than I was. They came closer.

I didn't look back until I sensed that the pursuers were almost upon me. Then, as I turned, I swung. There were two of them, both at least six feet six, but I had the good luck to catch the nearest one squarely in the throat. He sank to his knees, choking, and his cohort paused an instant to draw a knife. By then I had my automatic in my hand, and I was backing away. Two more thugs were closing in from across the street. They caught a glint of light on my automatic and circled warily.

Dick Tosche's reinforcements arrived like galloping cavalry, two or three of them for each *étrangleur*, and with feet and fists they proceeded to stomp and pound their victims into the pavement. It was a highly effective performance but not a pretty one, and I turned away.

Dick was at my elbow. "Let's get out of here before the police come."

We started back up Bourbon Street, keeping to the shadows.

"Sorry," he muttered. "Lost sight of you. We were following them. They must have held back, and suddenly they got way ahead of us."

"That's all right," I said. "I got in one good punch. I've been feeling like punching someone for days."

Some tourists had heard a commotion or caught a shadowy glimpse of something going on, and they were edging in the direction of the fights, now almost over. If the action had lasted longer, they probably would have taken it to be another street entertainment and gathered around and tossed money.

A door opened in a nearby building and someone looked out to see what the fuss was about. A glint of light fell on the gathering onlookers, and I recognized Cal Dreslow, the unlikely beggar, who kept turning up at odd moments like the proverbial bad penny. I took a step toward him, but Dick's hand on my arm stopped me.

"Look!" he said, pointing.

On the outskirts of the crowd was a tall, lank figure. A familiar figure. "Little Boy," Dick breathed.

"The vultures are gathering for the kill," I muttered.

"Let's get him," Dick breathed.

We jumped at him. Little Boy was off in a flash, darting up a side street. I thought we would run him down in short order because both Dick and I were leading far more wholesome lives than he was, but suddenly, in the dim shadow along a building, the darker mass of his shadow seemed to rise into the air and then vanish.

When we reached the place where he disappeared, we found a mere crack between buildings, maybe three feet wide. There are many such in the French Quarter, former passageways to the courtyards at the rear of the buildings. Today they are barred by padlocked gates and sometimes reinforced with barbed wire. This gate was at least seven feet high. I went over it with Dick on my heels, and we pounded down the passageway to the courtyard.

There we found ourselves confronted by a maze—an inde- terminable, shadowy pattern of walls and fences, confused rather then illuminated by patches of light from rear doors and windows.

"Either he knows someone here or he lives here," I told Dick. "He wouldn't bolt into a place like this if he didn't have a way out."

"We can look for him tomorrow," Dick suggested.

"It wouldn't be worth the trouble. There's a whole square block of buildings here, and they face four different streets. They must have hundreds of tenants."

"We can spot him sooner or later by having the four street intersections watched. Do you want me to do it?"

"Nope," I said. "I don't think he's that important."

We turned back and scrambled over the tall gate a second time. From Bourbon Street came the sounds of ambulances. "Are you sure your friends won't get into trouble over this?" I asked.

"They left almost as soon as we did. I planted some witnesses, though. Each one saw something different, which should confuse things nicely. I don't think those *étrangleurs* will be bothering you for awhile, but they aren't the only rowdies in the Quarter. Since someone has decided not to like you, we'll have to keep a lookout. You should be safe enough tonight, though."

I took him with me to a small restaurant where we both ate second, more substantial, dinners. While we ate, we talked about the Quarter's street characters and the market workers.

"There are hustlers," Dick said, "and there are beggars. Hustlers will work. Many of them will work at anything. Beggars simply beg. But hustlers may have days when they can't find any work, so they become beggars."

"Aren't there institutions that look after homeless people?" I asked.

"Of course, but the real street people won't have anything to do with them. They suspect there's a conspiracy to reform them and take away their freedom. That's why they're street people—they want to be completely free. They can't deal with a structured life-style. What they don't realize is that the life-style they've fallen into is just as structured, and just as restrictive. They've got to find a place to stay, or at least shelter themselves, all over again every night. They've got to find food or money all over again every day."

"So they'll take a job beating up a total stranger?"

"The ones that would do that are already into crime—which is something entirely different."

This set me wondering about Ross Sernold, the market character who had been so bitter about Marc DeVarnay cheating him. "Was he capable of hiring heavies to pay DeVarnay back with a beating?" I asked. "Beatings sometimes get out of hand."

"He wasn't capable of paying for it, which is all that matters. Unless your credit is outstandingly good, those *étrangleurs* work for cash in advance."

"What if DeVarnay offended someone with better credit?"

"That jerk Sernold is the only person I found who didn't like him," Dick said.

"Humor me," I said. "Is it possible."

"I suppose so, but except for Sernold, I'm positive DeVarnay didn't have any enemies in the flea market."

"Especially wealthy enemies," I suggested.

Dick nodded. "Especially he didn't have any wealthy enemies in the flea market, because no one there has enough money to qualify."

CHAPTER FIFTEEN

In many cities it would have been considered late when we finished eating but not in the New Orleans French Quarter. After I bade Dick good night, I decided to stroll over to Club Edie. I felt a personal interest in the place now that I had fitted it and the Aronskas into my puzzle. When I entered, Edie was playing the piano, Karl was presiding over the bar, and whom should I see at a front table but my *fiancée*, Venita Berent, who was out on the town with my good friend Jeffrey Minjarus.

I waved the waitress aside, slipped into a vacant chair at the table Venita and Minjarus were occupying, and announced, "Fine state of affairs this is. We've only been engaged one day, and the first time I have to work late at the office, my *fiancée* is already stepping out on me."

I expected them to look startled. Instead, they both burst into laughter. When Venita got herself under control and dried her eyes, she leaned over and spoke into my ear.

"Jeff called to see whether we were continuing our investigation tonight. I hadn't heard anything from you, so we decided to see what we could find out on our own. We've already been to two other night spots. When we arrived here, the first person we ran into was Cora McAult. We met her last night and told her about our engagement, but I don't suppose you remember her."

"I was riding a cloud of happiness, and anyone except you was a mere blur," I said.

She started to laugh again. "Anyway, Cora saw us and almost lost her front teeth. She thought I was stepping out on you."

"You were," I said firmly. "You are."

"She came over to the table and was downright snooty about it, so Jeff said we were meeting you here."

"Tsk," I said. "A lawyer telling lies. I thought there was a natural law against that."

"She's been glowering at us ever since, and now you walk in!"

"My timing has always been excellent."

"It certainly is tonight. You've saved my reputation—for another day, I suppose."

"Tell me," I said. "Has this pretend investigation of yours turned up anything?"

"Actually, it has. Cora's date, a man named Cecil Durent, tried to get a rise out of me about Marc. Word is getting around that Marc is missing, and Cecil wanted to know when he was seen last. He said he saw him himself riding through the French Quarter one night in a beat-up car. I tried to pin him down about the date. It could have been the night Marc left for St. Louis."

"Well done," I said. "Other people would call you a snoop, but to me, you're a natural born investigator. Did Cecil happen to notice who was with him?"

"No. Just that Marc was the passenger. What does it mean?"

"It means," I said, "that Marc called a cab to take him to the airport. Then someone called him and offered him a ride, so he cancelled the cab. I already knew that. Now, thanks to Cora's friend Cecil, we know he actually received the ride—in a beat-up car. I wonder what Cecil's idea of a beat-up car is. I'll have to ask him before we leave."

"But what does it mean?" Venita asked again.

"I have no idea. Marc didn't disappear until several days after that. In the meantime, he went to St. Louis, Denver, Reno, San Francisco, and Seattle. I've verified that myself with witnesses. Also, there's his signature on traveler's checks and hotel registers. From Seattle, I followed him back to the New Orleans area. So I don't know what his ride in a beat-up car on the night he left for St. Louis may signify, but I'm glad to know about it. It's a stray fact that may eventually fit in somewhere."

I spent the next forty minutes enjoying Edie's piano playing with one part of my mind while the other vainly tried to find a place for that stray fact.

It wouldn't have been seemly for me to cross-examine Cecil Durent about my *fiancée*'s former *fiancé*, so I asked Jeff Minjarus to handle it. He did so in his usual deft style. Durent's idea of a beat-up car was a bit vague. A last year's model needing a wash job might qualify, and anyway, it had been night and he caught only a glimpse of it heading out Decatur toward Canal Street, but he was positive he had seen Marc DeVarnay riding in the front seat and talking with the driver. The car was gone before he could take in any more, and on that particular evening there was nothing notable about seeing Marc DeVarnay ride past in a car. If he had known Mark was about to disappear, he might have been more attentive.

I sampled two more piano bars with Venita and Minjarus. The second made the evening a double success. We encountered no more friends of DeVarnay's, but in an out-of-the-way corner, what to my wondering eyes should appear but Selma Garnett, DeVarnay's assistant at the antique store, in intimate conversation with Harold Nusiner, DeVarnay's bitter rival and the man she herself had said was no gentleman. They were so engrossed in their conversation that they never looked around all the time we were there.

Afterward, I generously let Venita and Minjarus drop me off at my hotel, which accomplished the double purpose of avoiding any new *étrangleurs* that may have been watching for me and allowing Jeff to take my *fiancée* home all by himself.

I called Raina and told her answering machine what Cecil Durent had seen and what I had seen and done. Then I went to bed pondering Marc DeVarnay's character. He had the courage—and the confidence in his ability—to launch a business enterprise and make a big success of it, but his mother was standing by with a ten million dollar net to catch him if he flopped. He had the courage to break a long-standing engagement to a woman he no longer loved when he fell in love with someone else, but he did it by lying to her, and then he cravenly involved her in the falsehood by making her pretend to his mother that it was her fault. He had the courage to marry a woman he knew his mother would disapprove of but not the courage to make the act public. Was it possible he really had become sick of himself and taken a cowardly run out on the entire jambalaya mess? What was one more cowardly act after so many?

I still needed to know more about him. The next morning, Monday, I telephoned my *fiancée*. "Doing anything today?" I asked her.

"Nothing important. What did you have in mind?"

"I would like a guided tour of New Orleans. I need to see the city Marc grew up in—from infancy through the university. Where did he play as a kid? What did he do during summer vacations? When he was a teenager growing up did he ever take a summer job, and if so, where? And so on. Of course to a considerable extent it'll be the city you grew up in, too."

"What are you trying to do—give me a nostalgia trip?"

"Not unless you want one. Be as blunt and factual as you like. I can put my own interpretation on it."

"All right. I'll do it. But if you don't mind, it would be better if I drove. You keep trying to make one-way streets run the wrong way, and it doesn't leave you much time for sightseeing."

"Quite all right with me. Your car or mine?"

She decided to take her own; she could act as tour guide more comfortably while driving a car she was accustomed to. I parked in front of the Berent mansion and was met at the door by Venita's mother.

She spoke quietly. "Venita will be right down. I just wanted to tell you you're doing something wonderful. We've been so worried about her. Ever since she broke up with Marc, it was as though her life had no purpose. Her father and I will be forever grateful to you."

"She's been very helpful to my investigation. I'm pleased that she's able to receive something in return."

"What about Marc's disappearance?"

"That's still a puzzle. We keep finding out things and hoping that eventually they'll add up to something."

Venita came hurrying down, kissed her mother good-bye, and introduced me to her Honda, which she handled very neatly indeed while elucidating New Orleans. She began her patter before we got out of the driveway and continued it nonstop.

As we followed the itinerary of growing up rich in the Garden District, the impression I got was of a route as firmly laid out, and as restrictive and unchangeable, as that of New Orleans's famous St. Charles Avenue streetcars.

Both Marc and Venita had been born at Hotel Dieu, a hospital now closed. They'd had well protected Garden District childhoods. Venita attended the Academy of Sacred Heart on St. Charles Avenue through high school. It was a select school for girls from wealthy Catholic families, and she showed it to me—a magnificent, three-storied, U-shaped building with a colonnaded portico around the entire first floor facade. It was set far back from the street behind an iron fence with a pattern of walks and carefully trimmed hedges.

Marc attended regular Catholic schools for boys—Holy Name of Jesus and then the Jesuit High School, a sprawling brick structure that had the prosaic look of an office building.

They sometimes played together, and as they grew older and had their own bikes, they occasionally rode over to St. Charles Avenue to wait for the horse-drawn wagon selling a taffy called Roman Chewing Candy—a New Orleans institution still going strong. The grandson of the founder now carried on the business, making the candy in the wagon while his customers waited. Three generations of New Orleans children remembered it with affection. Or they rode their bikes to Audubon Park.

Later, in high school, they joined the Valencia Club, a popular social club for young people from wealthy families. It sponsored its own social events.

"In a way, we were a bunch of young snobs," Venita said

meditatively. "In another way, we weren't. Being rich didn't mean so much when I was growing up. I mean, class lines weren't as rigid as they are now. Middle-class parents who were willing to make the sacrifice could send their children to expensive schools and there was no segregation according to family income—no showing off of expensive shoes and leather jackets. The kids wore uniforms, and they all mixed together. But members of the Valencia Club must have seemed obnoxiously snobbish toward non-members."

There were retreats and summer camps for young people, always sexually segregated. There was the Audubon Camp, a day camp at Tulane University. And of course all the time they were growing up there was the annual Mardi Gras. The Krewe of Cadoc, which their parents belonged to, had roles for children in the annual Mardi Gras parade and accompanying festivities.

Then there was Canal Street, the backdrop to the most important social and business activity of the city, although its grandeur was already fading when Marc and Venita were growing up. Known locally as "The Great Wide Way," Canal Street was where the action was—where everything happened, parades, political and social events, the most posh stores, the most elaborate Christmas decorations, the wildest celebrations.

On Canal Street were the great department stores—D. H. Holmes, Maison Blanche, and Krauss—where everyone shopped. Each fostered its own traditions. Generations of New Orleaneans met "under the clock" at the entrance of Holmes's.

The D. H. Holmes store closed in 1989, and something of New Orleans died with it. Other fondly remembered businesses, such as the locally owned dime store, Kress and Company, also vanished. With them went a New Orleans institution that had been enormously important to its young people: the lavish soda fountains at the Canal Street drug stores. Some of the drug stores vanished as well.

From Canal Street we drove out St. Charles Avenue to Tulane University, which came immediately after graduation from high school for both Marc and Venita. Venita drove me around the campus. The few buildings glimpsed from St. Charles Avenue have a weathered, medieval look, but the expanding campus is huge, and the more recent structures feature a dazzling variety of architectural styles.

Afterward, she drove me back to the French Quarter and pointed out the antique stores on Royal Street where Marc had worked before deciding to establish his own business. Finally, there was DeVarnay's.

"That's it," she said. "What does it all add up to?"

"Two lives," I said. "For most of that time, you two were moving along pretty much side by side. Then you broke apart. If Marc came to you now and asked you to marry him, would you do it?"

She looked at me quickly. Then she looked away. "No," she said. "I don't believe I would. It seems strange that it's taken me so long to realize it, but looking back, I can see lots of reasons for not marrying him. We had our backgrounds in common but not much else. I think of him as highly as I ever did, but I wouldn't want to be his wife. Does this mean I'm finally growing up?"

"You've been grown up for a long time. It may mean that you're finally aware of that," I said.

"I should have picked you up at your hotel. Now I have to take you all the way back to the Garden District so you can collect your car, after which you'll have to drive back here." Then she exclaimed, "Oh—I forgot something!"

She had shown me their lives. Now she asked, almost apologetically, if I wanted to know something about their deaths, too.

"Death is very much a part of life in New Orleans. Sometimes I think we worship our ancestors as much as the Chinese used to do. All Saints Day, November first, is a legal holiday in Louisiana, and it's a massive celebration of the dead. Whole families turn out to clean and renovate and decorate tombs and pay tribute to the departed. They turn the cemeteries into picnic grounds for family reunions. Musical families even bring their instruments."

"An orgy of mourning?" I suggested.

"No." She shook her head. "It's a day of reverence, really it is. It reminds us that death, and the dead, are a part of life. Anyway, cemeteries are enormously important to us."

I told her I already knew that New Orleans's "Cities of the Dead" rank among the world's most interesting cemeteries.

"'Interesting' isn't the right word," she said. "The family tomb is just as important a piece of property as the family home. Everyone proceeds from one to the other eventually, and everyone will reside a lot longer in the tomb."

"Where is the DeVarnay family tomb?" I asked.

"In Metairie, of course."

"Of course," I agreed.

So we drove to Metairie Cemetery, pronounced "Metrie." It is considered by many to be New Orleans's premier cemetery, which may be arguable, but Metairie certainly is a beautiful place in which to spend eternity. Oddly enough, the land was originally a race track. During the bleak economic period after the Civil War, the track failed and had to be sold, and the race track became a cemetery.

There are several impressive memorials to Civil War armies as well as individual graves of soldiers. Jefferson Davis was buried here for a time before his remains were moved to Richmond, Virginia. But it was civilians, especially wealthy civilians, who made the cemetery their own. Because of the New Orleans practice of burials above the ground—made necessary into this century by the high level of ground water— New Orleans cemeteries are cities of mausoleum-like tombs, rather than graves, and the wealthy take great pains to see that they spend eternity in a resting place that offers the same order of luxuriant dignity they have become accustomed to. There are tombs in every style of architecture from Islamic to Celtic to ancient Roman to Chinese to Gothic to Southern Colonial with marble pillars, each on its own carefully manicured plot of ground. There is even a pyramid inspired by ancient Egypt.

A typical Metairie "street" has rows of massive tombs of marble or granite, each with its own distinctive architecture and ornamentation. Angels in various poses stand watch atop many of the tombs, and crosses are another popular ornament. Some tombs have far more elaborate constructions illustrating themes drawn from the lives of those buried there, such as the tomb of an old riverboat captain that displays the bell of his last steamboat.

Venita first showed me the Berent family tomb, the final resting place of family members back to her great-great-grandparents. It was unpretentious, as tombs went in Metairie, with a massive cross over the entrance. The slab of marble that served as a door had the names and dates of those buried there carved on it.

The Garden District home of the Berents was down the street and around the corner from the DeVarnay home. The tombs of the two families were situated similarly. We strolled down a broad cement walk and then over to the next row of tombs. The DeVarnay tomb was much larger than that of the Berent family, with marble vases—filled with flowers—on either side of the flight of steps leading up to the entrance. A rather active-looking angel was poised over the tomb with wings outspread.

As with the Berent tomb, the marble entrance slab bore the names of the DeVarnays buried there. I counted twenty of them, including Marc's two brothers, both of whom died at tender ages. The last name, Damien DeVarnay, was that of his father.

Venita had a pensive expression on her face. Perhaps the thought had occurred to her that this would have been her own ultimate resting place if Marc hadn't backed out of their marriage. It was a notion better left unspoken, so I said nothing.

Then she exclaimed, "My goodness! Look at that!"

She was pointing at the neighboring tomb, a much smaller structure. Unlike the coldly dignified marble and granite tombs nearby, it was covered with dazzling white stucco, and the angel over the entrance was brilliantly gilded. It was the most striking tomb in the area.

"Look at that!" Venita exclaimed again.

I was looking. "What about it?"

"That used to be the most rundown tomb in Metairie Cemetery!"

"A rundown tomb? In Metairie?" I looked at the lavish stone grandeur surrounding me. "That doesn't seem possible."

"There are a few," she said. "This one was the worst."

"It certainly isn't now."

"No, it isn't. It's beautiful, now. I wonder who did it." She turned to me. "It's the Hormath family tomb, as you can see, and that family is all gone. There was no one left to keep the tomb up, and the estate of the last Hormath was exhausted. So the tomb simply deteriorated. It wasn't very well built in the first place—it's brick with stucco—and its condition was simply disgraceful. Most of the stucco had fallen off, and the bricks were starting to come loose. The way it blighted this section of the cemetery was a scandal. Jolitte was furious about it. She was talking about starting a subscription to pay for the renovation. I wonder whether she did."

"Obviously someone did," I said. "Whoever was responsible did an excellent job."

Once you've seen a family tomb, and walked around it, and read the names carved on it, there isn't much more information to be extracted. I soon had enough and was ready to leave, but Venita insisted on stopping at the cemetery office to ask about the Hormath tomb.

"Everyone has been talking about it," the office girl said with a smile. "A person who prefers to remain anonymous made arrangements for the repairs and paid for them."

I experienced a twitch of curiosity. "When were the repairs done?" I asked.

"Early this month," she said. "I have a copy of the work order somewhere. Do you want me to look it up?"

"Please do," I said.

She did, and I looked it over carefully and made notes. When we left, Venita turned to me curiously. "What was that about?"

"I don't know," I said. "I let my instinct ask questions. Sometimes it asks the right ones."

In this case, probably it hadn't. The Hormath tomb had been renovated about the time Marc DeVarnay was visiting Old Jake down at Pointe Neuve. I couldn't imagine any connection between the two events, but I couldn't help asking.

The DeVarnay ancestors hadn't lost a moment of their eternal rest over the fact that the tomb next door had deteriorated into a slum; but cemeteries, of course, are for the living, whatever the names and dates on the tombs may say, and there was no doubt that the renovation had been a considerable improvement. The dazzling white stucco made the surrounding marble and granite palaces look drab.

"I wonder if Jolitte paid for it," Venita said. "If it wasn't her, she'll be pleased to hear it's been done."

I offered to take Venita to dinner; it turned out that she had a date—with Jeff Minjarus. "But you can come along if you want to," she said generously.

I was beginning to feel like the elderly duenna in a Spanish melodrama. I settled for taking her to the Top of the Mart for a cocktail before we headed home. We nursed our drinks, relaxed, and let the city slowly revolve under us. She seemed unusually quiet, but I didn't offer her a penny. I was feeling pensive myself. Looking down at the sprawling city, buildings row on row, I thought of the elaborately expensive tombs, also row on row.

Before we parted in front of the Berent mansion, I promised to look in on her and Jeff about eleven o'clock at Club Edie, just in case someone else got curious about her stepping out on her new *fiancé* and her reputation needed saving again.

I ate dinner alone at a small restaurant down the street from my hotel. Two male tourists at the next table were grumbling about the time and money they had wasted on a girlie show. I already knew more than enough about that subject, so I didn't question them. Back in my hotel room, my thoughts kept returning to the renovated tomb, which was silly because it couldn't have had anything to do with Marc DeVarnay. It was ten o'clock, and I was about to make myself presentable for New

Orleans high society by changing my clothes, when my telephone rang.

The voice was that of James, Jolitte DeVarnay's butler, and he sounded choked with horror. "I can't get Miz Raina. Miz Jolitte says can you come?"

"I'm on my way," I said and went as I was.

I expected to find the DeVarnay mansion a blaze of light with perhaps police cars and an ambulance in the drive. Instead, there was a single light showing from the entrance hall, and everything was quiet. James was waiting for me at the front door, and he opened it as I came up the walk. He said nothing, but obviously he was in a near panic. So was I.

I almost trod on his heels in my hurry to get where he was taking me. We swept into the sitting room where Jolitte, along with a sedately-dressed middle-aged woman and a man about fifty in a black suit, were gathered around the old servant Dorothy, who was lying on a sofa and seemed to be having a fit. The woman and man were later identified to me as the operatives Raina Lambert had hired as Jolitte's bodyguards. Dorothy was sobbing and moaning, and she threshed her legs and arms and occasionally had to be restrained. I was astonished. Obviously it was a doctor they needed, not another detective. "What happened?" I asked.

Jolitte looked up, a troubled expression on her face, and shook her head. The male detective handed me a page of a newspaper. It was the *New Orleans Times-Picayune*. The column he pointed to contained "Memorials"—tributes to the dead, many including photos. Like the celebration of All Saints Day, this is a uniquely local custom. Death anniversaries, birthdays, wedding anniversaries, or any significant personal date is an occasion to remember a loved one and proclaim to the world that his or her memory is still green. On special days like Mother's Day or Father's Day, there may be pages of them. The detective pointed again; midway down the column, I read, "In Loving Memory of Marc D." As with most of the notices, it contained a few lines of verse:

"He is not dead, this friend; not dead,
But, in the path we mortals tread,
Got some few, trifling steps ahead,
And nearer to the end;
So that you too once past the bend,
Shall meet again, as face to face this friend
You fancy dead."

And a final line, "Missed by his Royal Street friends and all who knew him."

The accompanying picture, obviously reproduced from a snapshot, was of poor quality, but it was, unmistakably, that of Marc DeVarnay.

There are no distinctions of class or race in the Times-Picayune's column of Memorials. Dorothy probably was in the habit of pouring over them daily to see which of her friends were honoring their loved ones, and she had happened onto Marc's photo.

How the notice had got into the paper was a different—and far more perplexing—question.

Jolitte was shaken, but she adopted a pose of anger. "What a dreadful thing to do. Who could have done such a thing?"

"We'll certainly try to find out," I said. "I'll need to use the telephone. First, has anyone called a doctor for Dorothy?"

"She'll be all right," Jolitte said firmly. "She's had these spells before."

"But not with such an unsettling cause," I persisted. "I'd suggest a doctor if you know one who makes house calls. It might be a good idea to have a sedative yourself. We can't do anything tonight. It's important for everyone to be fresh tomorrow."

If pressed, I couldn't have said why it was important for Jolitte to be fresh on the morrow, but I convinced her. She called her doctor. Then I called Raina Lambert and told her answering machine what had happened. I succeeded in getting a hold of Jeff Minjarus at Club Edie—they knew him there. He was incredulous. Then he was angry. "This is a lousy kind of joke," he fumed.

"In the worst possible taste," I agreed. "We'll have to find out who is responsible—if we can. If we can't, it still may be possible to learn something from this."

"What?" he wanted to know.

"Right now, I haven't the faintest idea."

I invited him to go with me to the newspaper office the first thing in the morning. "Sometimes you lawyers have your uses. People are always afraid of being sued. They might snub a detective, but they'll hop to it and cooperate with a lawyer."

He agreed.

I waited until the doctor came, and then I left the household in his capable hands and went back to my hotel.

But I won't pretend I slept. I lay awake wondering how many New Orleaneans made a daily ritual, like Dorothy did, of pouring over the memorials.

The question seemed significant. Person or persons unknown had sent a message. It was critically important to find out whom it was intended for.

CHAPTER SIXTEEN

Raina Lambert telephoned me before I was out of bed the next morning. I had to throw on some clothes and go down to the sudsomat to call her back.

The first thing she said was, "The poem is by Robert Louis Stevenson."

"Great," I said. "It's worth dashing downstairs and across the street at the risk of life and limb when I'm rewarded with a gem like that. Also, it solves no end of problems. I lay awake all night in tortured anxiety wondering why the literary quality of the poem in Marc DeVarnay's memorial was so much better than the doggerel that accompanies all the others. If we had any suspects, we could check to see which one reads Robert Louis Stevenson."

"Which one reads Stevenson and has maybe a hundred bucks to invest in a ghoulish practical joke. Or was it a joke?"

I didn't answer.

"Are you going to the newspaper office?"

"With Minjarus."

"Good idea. You won't find out anything, of course. Was it a nasty prank perpetrated by someone who'd heard DeVarnay was missing, or does someone know something we don't?"

"That's what I've been asking myself. In one way, it makes no more sense than anything else about the case. Why would anyone bother? In another way, it makes too much sense."

She was silent for a moment. Then she said, "What are you going to do after you go to the newspaper office?"

"I'm going to call on Mr. and Mrs. Dolding to see whether my impression matches yours. They sound too good to be true. There's got to be a motive in this case somewhere. With ten million dollars up for grabs, we shouldn't have to waste time worrying about the 'what.' The question should be 'who'?"

"Telephone me after you've talked with them. I may want you with me when I call on Doug Kallenor."

"Ah! I knew if we blundered around long enough, something we tried would work. What did you find out by having him tailed?"

"On his way to work yesterday, he left off a bag of shirts at the Crescent City Qwick Wash. It's out on Tulane Avenue."

"Say that again," I said.

She did.

"He left off a bag of shirts? This is an indictable offense in Louisiana?"

"On his way home from work, he picked up the package of washed and pressed shirts."

"If I were a cynic, I'd call that cause and effect."

"You've heard of silent partners. My highly unofficial private grapevine informs me that the Crescent City Qwick Wash has a silent owner. He is one Harlo Primly, and several times he has been convicted of illegal gambling, which can be freely translated as running betting operations. Which explains why he tries to remain in the background. If you're in the know, and you have a favorite in the fourth race at Belmont, all you have to do is leave a shirt to be laundered—with your bet and the money in the pocket. Primly doesn't do credit business. You can pick your shirt up after the race with your winnings, if any, tucked into the same pocket."

"Very neat," I said. "So that's where the forty-five grand is going. Or went."

"The laundry is legit. Said to be first-rate."

"But customers are losing their shirts there regardless. Very well—after I've seen the Doldings, I'll visit Kallenor with you."

The newspaper presented no problems at all except that no

one on duty remembered anything about the person or persons who had inserted that particular memorial. The copy was made out in a firm, educated hand. Payment had been made in cash. The address given, on Esplanade Avenue, was quickly determined to be fictitious, after which it was an easy assumption that the name, Kelda Wimsinger, would not be found in any edition of the city directory.

The newspaper promised its own thorough investigation, and I was satisfied to leave it that way. Minjarus promised to prod it if any prodding was needed. He went back to his office, and I headed for the Garden District.

David and Nadine Dolding lived in one of more modest mansions on the remote edge of the district. They had an elderly black maid who probably had been with them longer than Dorothy had been with Jolitte DeVarnay. The house was comfortable though not sumptuous. When I arrived, they were eating a late breakfast on an enclosed porch that overlooked a delightful garden.

Their hospitality was charming. They were two lovely old people who would not see eighty-five again, and their affection for each other and fondness for their home was touching. They also had a kind of grateful astonishment that both of them had lived so long. My arrival was a welcome event in a day when they expected nothing to happen. They offered breakfast; I settled for a cup of coffee.

"We simply can't imagine what could have happened to Marc," David Dolding said. He was tall and gaunt, and his voice was soft and rather high pitched, but there was nothing frail about the old man. He had the wiry resilience that bows deeply before the storms of life but never breaks.

"We told the same thing to the detective who was here before," he said. "We really don't know anything at all that would help. Marc is a most considerate young man—he even comes to see us occasionally, and not many young men his age would waste time on elderly relatives. That's what is so bewildering. He really is extremely considerate of others. He never would go off somewhere without letting his mother know about it and keeping in touch with her."

"A most considerate young man," Nadine Dolding murmured. "And so talented. So capable. Jolitte has been fortunate to have such a wonderful son."

"I understand you have no family left," I said.

"That's right," David Dolding said. He sounded sad but resigned. "It's the penalty one pays for living so long. Friends and relatives keep dying, and suddenly there's no one left but you. Though in our case, our only son died young. He and his wife were killed in an airplane crash. We raised our grandson, but then we lost him, too. All of my cousins died long ago except for Jolitte. But we still have our home and garden, and we have each other, which makes us many times blessed. The other detective asked us who will inherit our little money. The answer is still the same—no one.

We have enough to keep us comfortable as long as we do live. After that—well, Jolitte doesn't need our money, so we're leaving everything to various Catholic charities. We had a most enjoyable time deciding which ones to favor. That nice young attorney who looks after Jolitte's affairs drew up our wills for us. What is his name?"

"Jeffrey something," Nadine said.

"Minjarus?" I suggested.

"That's right," David Dolding said. "Do you know him? That was years ago—he had just joined the firm. He's a very nice and competent young man. He made sure our money would go exactly where we want it to go. At our ages, there's no longer much pleasure in receiving. We already have everything we need. We feel fortunate indeed that we have something to give."

They insisted on showing me their garden. Not only was it lovely, but the religious statuary there dramatically symbolized their devoutness. The central feature was a Madonna and Child that was almost life-sized. The statue was surrounded by flowers, and a pond lapped at Mary's feet. Walks radiated out from her, and, except for the one that connected with the patio, each led to another shrine.

Some of the statuary had been imported, and names of the saints were given in foreign languages. Saint François, who was preaching to ceramic birds while real birds perched overhead and talked back, came from France. Italy had contributed Santo Pietro, who carried a huge key on his shoulder—no doubt that of the gates of Heaven. An unidentified saint was blessing a beggar, and I couldn't help thinking there would have been plenty of work for him in the French quarter. Another saint—the faded identification looked like German, Heilige something—was praying. One shrine featured a bas relief of the last supper, and Judas would have been a precinct cop's notion of a perfect villain. A martyred statue of Saint John, with no indication as to which of the numerous St. Johns he was, had lost his head, but this was the result of a latter-day accident, and the moldy head still lay nearby. It gave his little grotto a grotesque touch. In a Garden of Eden scene, the serpent also had lost its head, which could have been why both Adam and Eve had such complacent expressions.

All of the saints seemed to be of the benign variety. There was no St. George robustly slaying a dragon or St. Michael leading the Heavenly Hosts into battle.

As we turned away at the back of the garden, I saw a male figure slip quickly into a shed. I suddenly experienced a tremendous revelation. If my name had been spelled Archimedes, I would have dashed into the street exclaiming, "Eureka!" I had no idea—yet—what I had experienced a tremendous revelation of, but I was certain it was a tremendous revelation.

"Who's that?" I asked.

"That's Joel," Dolding said. "Joel Caramus. A very bright and capable young man. Hard working, too. He comes in three half days a week. We couldn't keep up the garden without him. It took us years to find a gardener we could afford who was willing to work for his money."

"He certainly does excellent work," I observed, looking about me.

"He does," Dolding agreed.

"How long has he been with you?"

"About four years.

The fanfare of assorted trumpets and horns I was listening to added a section of trombones. I had already met Joel Caramus in the French Quarter, where he was an unlikely beggar known as Cal Dreslow. I naturally wondered how many other names and incarnations he had.

Whatever Caramus/Dreslow might have been up to, I agreed with Raina that no one could possibly suspect the Doldings of any kind of foul play. That meant the person with the greatest financial interest in Marc DeVarnay's death was his wife, and anything she might inherit now would be piddling compared with the wealth Marc would receive when Jolitte died.

Just to make certain, I telephoned Venita. As far as she knew, there were no heirs left for the DeVarnay millions after Marc and David Dolding.

"It's a sad story," I observed.

"It certainly is," she agreed. "The Doldings' son was a brilliant young doctor. That was before I was born, but I have no doubt they were terribly proud of him. After he and his wife were killed, the grandparents put all of their hopes on their grandson, and he turned out to be a rotter."

"In what way," I asked.

"I don't remember. I was pretty young, then, and I'm sure a lot of it was hushed up. He was mixed up in one mess after another, and finally he ran away from home—he was still a teen-ager—and got into really serious trouble over in Texas. I think he killed somebody, and either he died or was killed himself. The Doldings never mentioned him again."

"So they have no heirs, and they're leaving their property to charity."

"That's what I've heard."

Caution isn't my middle name, but I sometimes behave as though it were.

I next telephoned Minjarus. "You drew up a will for David

and Nadine Dolding," I said.

"You make it sound like an accusation. Yes, I did. That was years ago."

"Who gets their money?"

"Now, really—"

"I've talked with them. They said they'd left the whole works to Catholic charities. I'm just checking."

"Now why would two lovely old people like that—deeply-religious people, no less—tell you a lie?"

"I have a nasty, suspicious disposition, and the lies I've been told by lovely, deeply-religious people would fill a book larger than the Bible. As I said, I'm just checking. I won't tell on you. Where does their money go? Or was it too long ago for you to remember?"

"This is a conscientious firm. We review our clients' wills periodically. Of course I remember."

"So where does the money go?"

"To Catholic charities," he said. "A long list of them."

"How large will their estate be?"

"It's nothing like Jolitte DeVarnay's. It may run between half and three quarters of a million."

"That's what I needed to know. Thanks."

"What's this all about?"

"I don't even know that myself."

I called Raina Lambert. "All right. I'm ready. Let's take on Kallenor."

I drove her to Kallenor's office in my rental car. Douglas Kallenor and Associates occupied its own wing of a small office plaza. It was a flourishing firm. There were six associates listed on the door in addition to Kallenor. Of course Jolitte DeVarnay, with her ten million dollars, rated personal service from the boss whenever she wanted it. No doubt she paid accordingly.

Her ten million also got us instant attention. Raina had told Kallenor on the telephone that we wanted to discuss an important development concerning Marc DeVarnay's disappearance, and before we were comfortably seated, the receptionist—a somber-looking middle aged woman who had the air of having audited more than a few accounts herself—told us Mr. Kallenor would see us.

He was standing behind his desk, all smiles and hospitality, favors cheerfully granted. I paused to close the door carefully behind us, and then I joined Raina at his desk. She had already declined his invitation to sit down, so all three of us remained standing.

His smile began to fade. "A—development?" he stammered. "About Marc?"

I nodded slowly. "We know what happened to the forty-five grand."

I paused. His face had turned the color of overripe liver. "You took it," I said. "What'd you do with it?"

Kallenor's face suddenly needed mopping. Sweat began to pour off him, but he was too paralyzed to notice.

"Never mind that," Raina said. "We know what you did with it. All of your visits to the Crescent City Qwick Wash have been observed. What we want to know is—what did you do with Marc's body?"

That was when he collapsed into his chair and buried his face in his hands.

"I didn't—I don't know anything about Marc," he gasped.

"But you did take the forty-five grand," I said. It was a statement of fact, not an accusation.

He was silent.

"Would you rather talk with us or with the police?" Raina demanded.

He decided to talk with us. The story came out in gasps. His perspiration ran as though someone had left a faucet turned on. The stains on his suit coat quickly progressed from damp to wet.

He began with a protest. "There wasn't forty-five grand. It was only thirty-five. Marc took ten thousand with him to St. Louis."

"Did you find a memo to that effect in the safe?" Raina asked.

Kallenor nodded.

"Then you destroyed it when you took the thirty-five thousand, and you reported all forty-five thousand missing."

He nodded again.

"You must have been confident Marc wouldn't return."

"I didn't even think about that," he protested. "It's just—I'm a compulsive gambler, you see, and there was all that money, and Marc was missing—"

"And you were so certain he would never return and catch you that you grabbed it."

He blanched. "I didn't think about that at all," he protested again.

"And you don't know where Marc is?"

"I haven't the faintest idea what could have happened to him."

"Did you lose the whole thirty-five thousand?" I asked.

He nodded. "What's going to happen?"

"Do you have a key to the store?"

He shook his head. "I have the combination to both safes. That's all."

"All right. We'll tell Miss Garnett she's not to let you into the office again. How do you expect to repay the money?"

He was silent again. Then he blurted, "What are you going to do?"

"We report to Jolitte DeVarnay," Raina said. "She'll decide what to do. Marc's disappearance is beginning to look like a murder case. The police certainly will want to talk with you about that. Are you sure you don't have anything to tell us?

"I don't know anything about Marc. As for Jolitte—I'm sorry, I did think if my luck changed I could put it back. If she'll give me time—"

"You could start by taking your shirts to another laundry," Raina said. "Jolitte might be more inclined to listen to you if she thinks you're trying to reform."

She touched my arm, and we turned and walked out. Back in the car, she asked me what I thought.

"In my book, a CPA willing to gamble with other people's

money is done for," I said. "I don't think he's capable of reform, and if a whiff of this gets around, he won't have any clients."

"He's also sneaky," she said. "The cocktail date with Selma Garnett at the Top of the Mart was to find out whether she knew anything about our investigation. I asked her. He hinted he had a job for her. After he pumped her, he dropped the subject of the job. She also let Harold Nusiner take her out because he said he wanted to talk with her about a job. He actually made her an offer, not a very good one, but he tried to pump her, too. The way things have been going, we can't blame her for looking out for herself. She has to support her elderly parents and pay their medical bills. She would hang on until hell freezes if there were any chance of Marc returning, but she knows she isn't qualified to run the business herself, and a new owner would probably bring in his own assistant. She's been worried about the missing money, too. To revert to Kallenor, unfortunately there's no evidence that he stole the money."

"He confessed in the presence of two witnesses."

She nodded. "True enough. I'll tell Jolitte she has that to hold over him. She can decide whether she wants to be noble and give him another chance. This doesn't advance our case an iota."

"But it does. It's an essential job of brush clearing, and we now have one less complication to worry about. More than one if Selma Garnett can be believed about the reason for her dates. Unfortunately, for every question answered, two new questions get asked." I told her about the Doldings' gardener.

"What do you think?" she asked.

"Someone started keeping an eye on them long before we arrived here. He's been their gardener for about four years. Part of that time, or maybe all of it, he's also been a spy for someone. But what could possibly be gained by spying on those old people?"

She shook her head.

"The only thing we can do is ask Dick Tosche to have this character watched around the clock. I'll do that right away."

"And then what are you going to do?" she asked.

"I'm going to take the rest of the afternoon off and think. I have the feeling that all the evidence we need is somewhere in the clutter we've already accumulated, but it has to be sorted out."

"Why were you so long getting around to it?" she demanded.

I drove her to her hotel, waited while she changed to her flea-market costume, and then drove her to the market. After I had left a message for Dick Tosche with the psychic witch, I drove straight out Esplanade Avenue to the City Park, where there is ample and very scenic room for thinking. I sat beside a bayou and watched several pairs of lovers try to keep their peddle boats going in a straight line while their minds were on something entirely different, and while I watched, I thought— for an uninterrupted hour and a half. I dissected our case into very small pieces, and then I put the pieces back together in as many surprising shapes as I could think of, and then I threw all of them away and did the dissecting over again.

Finally I drove back to Metairie Cemetery, consulted the young lady in the office, and found the Dolding family tomb. Compared with those of the DeVarnays and the Berents, it was much smaller and much less ornate except for the pensive angel over the door, which was far larger than the angels on nearby tombs. That, of course, was to be expected.

The tomb had an unused air about it—for good reason. The last burials had been those of the son and his wife more then thirty years before. I reflected, and not for the first time, that long life is not always a blessing.

Evidently the Dolding grandson had been buried in Texas or wherever he died. He had disappointed the old couple so cruelly that they hadn't even brought his body back to New Orleans. The grim chore of placing such a complete wastrel in the same tomb with the wasted promise of their brilliant son would have added to the bitterness of their loss.

I went back to my car and thought again, this time pondering the euphemisms of death. Venita had said the Dolding grandson died or was killed in Texas. David Dolding hadn't put it that way. He said they had lost him.

I sat for more than an hour in that utterly peaceful place, surrounded by the worry-free dead, and again I arranged and rearranged all of the things that hadn't made any sense about this case. It was only to be expected that when every likelihood and every possibility had been eliminated, the residue was ridiculously improbable. I persisted with my arranging and rearranging until finally what remained made far too much sense.

Then I drove back to the cemetery office. It took some oblique conversation to make myself understood, but eventually I got to talk with a middle-aged maintenance man who knew a bit more about the renovation of the Hormath tomb than the office girl did. He had driven past several times while the men had been at work, and he was able to describe how they had gone about it. He had never heard of the firm before, but its men were good workers, and they certainly had done an excellent job.

I examined the file. There was a letter from the Hormath family attorney authorizing Ently and Company, Monuments and Cemetery Work, to restore the crypt with the understanding that the estate had no liability for any costs incurred. It was dated a full week before Marc DeVarnay had left for St. Louis. There was the copy of a work order with "Anonymous Donation" listed in lieu of the customer's name. The work to be done was described in detail, even to the gilding of the angel, and obviously it had been performed meticulously.

I borrowed the telephone book's yellow pages; there was no "Ently and Company" listed under "Monuments."

By this time the office girl was watching me strangely, but she made no objection to my use of the telephone. I dialed Ently and Company's number. I got a beep and a sugary recorded voice that announced, "The number you have just dialed has been disconnected." I listened through three repetitions, thinking furiously. The question was whether that particular number had ever been connected to a firm named Ently and Company. It was the sort of question the police can get an answer to far quicker than a private investigator, so I put it aside for Lieutenant Keig.

I drove back to the Hormath and DeVarnay tombs and went through the entire sorting process again. Finally, reluctantly, I accepted a conclusion that had been staring me in the face for the past two hours. I left the cemetery and stopped at the first public telephone I saw. Raina Lambert was out, and what I wanted to say couldn't be discussed with her answering machine.

I called Jeff Minjarus. He listened in silence. Then he said, "Somewhere between the time we parted at the newspaper office this morning and right now, you mislaid your brains. Perhaps if you go back over the same route and search carefully...."

"Answer my question," I said. "How do we go about it."

"We don't."

"We'll have to. The problem is to how do it as discreetly as possible."

"There is absolutely no discreet way to get Jolitte's consent to open the family tomb."

"But there is. The tomb next door was restored. There were men working beside it and all around it. At one point they even had ladders leaning against it and, and tools and materials piled around its entrance and every which way, which certainly constituted trespassing. We suspect they may have caused hidden damage, and we want to open the tomb for a few minutes to check. The fact that the firm doing the work has a disconnected phone adds to the urgency. This should be done now while there's half a chance of locating the workmen and holding them responsible. What's unreasonable about that?"

"I'd like to have you as a permanent witness—one I can call on in all of my court cases. You have a remarkable facility for inventing plausible lies to fit any situation."

"I only lie in an effort to determine the truth, and that isn't even a venial sin. You're Jolitte's attorney. You should be able to manage this without disturbing her at all. Surely you can convince the cemetery authorities to cooperate in such a simple matter. You're not going to disturb anything, or remove anything, or add anything. You just want to look at the tomb's interior and make certain there's no evidence of damage."

"You actually want to open—"

"Right. The sooner the better. One more thing—when you get everything set, tell Lieutenant Keig and invite him to witness the operation if he wants to. Nothing guaranteed, of course."

"You must know something."

"How could I? Get moving. I'll call you back in half an hour and see what you've come up with."

My stomach suddenly reminded me that I hadn't eaten since breakfast. I stopped at a grocery store that displayed a muffuletta sandwich sign and bought half a sandwich—I've never known anyone who could eat a whole muffuletta—and a six-pack of assorted soft drink flavors.

After my improvised lunch, I called Minjarus again. He said wearily, "If it weren't for your giving me a chance to get acquainted with Venita, I'd rue the day you came here."

"Sure. Rue all you like—my feelings are made of vulcanized plastic. What have you arranged?"

"Nine o'clock tomorrow morning."

"I'll be there—sitting in my car and watching. This is your show."

"I don't want it."

"You've got it anyway. Don't they warn you in law school about things like this?"

He hung up.

I telephoned Raina Lambert again. That time she answered, and I told her what I had done.

She said, "You're kidding."

"If Minjarus doesn't let me down, you can come out to Metairie Cemetery tomorrow morning and watch."

"Maybe I will. Do you really think—"

"What would I think with? Minjarus told me I'd mislaid my brains. I couldn't produce a scrap of evidence to justify this, but I'm determined to see it done if I have to sneak out there at midnight and do it myself."

"So you're just playing a hunch."

"It's a carefully reasoned hunch. Come and watch."

"It's an idiotic hunch. I'll be there. Right now I have something for you. Guess who lives in an apartment facing the patio where Little Boy disappeared."

"I've done my quota of guessing for the day."

"Millie, Marc DeVarnay's maid. Guess what Millie keeps in her two bedroom apartment."

"Don't tell me she's living with a Doctor of Voodoo."

"Millie would not live with a male of any persuasion. She was disappointed in love when she was quite young, and she swore off men permanently. The only male she had the slightest regard for was Marc DeVarnay, who paid her well for doing very little. When she moved into her apartment, shortly before DeVarnay disappeared, she was alone. She told the landlord she needed a second bedroom because she had to have a place to work. She makes quilts and sells them in the flea market."

"Does she really make quilts and sell them in the flea market?"

"She does. Quilts and other things. She does beautiful work."

"So what's the mystery?"

"I know Millie's next-door neighbor—it's a woman named Obelia Nexit."

"You're kidding."

"Not at all. She's an Oriental. There are umpteen different nationalities working in the market, and I suspect some of them make up their own names. Why not? What they invent couldn't possibly be any odder than the originals would sound in English. Obelia runs her own table in the flea market, and she sells some of Millie's work for her. That's how Millie got the apartment— Obelia told her it was going to be available. Now Obelia wishes she hadn't."

"Very well. Comes the mystery."

"Despite Millie's reputation for living alone, she has someone living with her. Obelia hears her talking with that person and laughing."

"She's playing her TV too loudly."

"The talking and laughing comes from the spare bedroom, which is supposed to be empty."

"You mean—she has a house guest?"

"That's exactly what I mean. Do you see the implications?"

"I refuse to see them. I have a dim recollection of suggesting this very thing early in the case. I said Marc DeVarnay might have pulled an Edgar on us and hidden himself in the French quarter. You pooh-poohed it. When I found a credible witness who claimed to have seen him there several times, you pooh-poohed that."

"At the time it seemed silly, but now—"

"Now you're trying to tell me we're actually going to find DeVarnay hiding out in the French Quarter with his maid. I don't want any part of it."

"Why not? It was your idea, and from Obelia's description, it does seem like a possibility."

"It was my idea *then*. Now I reject it completely. I spent the entire afternoon tearing it into shreds and tossing the shreds overboard. I now have the case solved—I think—and if it turns out that I haven't, I'm going back to Savannah and start over. You're the one who originally thought DeVarnay was dead. You're supposed to be looking for his murderer. Just incidentally, Millie's apartment is nowhere near the Esplanade-Royal area and that little grocery that sells croissants. What about the watch you put there?

"It hasn't turned up a thing, and I don't think it's going to. DeVarnay got nervous about having to go out and do his own shopping. He moved in with Millie so she could do the shopping."

"Nonsense."

"If it were anyone but Millie, I would agree with you. This contradicts every deduction I've made about the case, but that's no excuse for ignoring it. We've got to know who is living in Millie's spare bedroom."

"If it turns out to be DeVarnay, I'll make you do a pilgrimage to Edgar Allan Poe's grave and light a candle there."

"I'll light a dozen candles, but first we have to find out who's there. That's what I want you to do tonight—find out."

"No way," I said. "Hire Little Boy."

"You went over that gate last night. Surely you can do it again."

"Last night I was chasing someone. I wasn't trying to find a door I've never seen before. You don't know how confusing the place is. Rear doors from four blocks of buildings open onto that courtyard. I wouldn't try to find Millie's apartment at night if you could persuade her to nail a towel over the door and leave an outside light on. On any given night at least twenty people will leave their washings out and their lights on. If I do this, it's got to be by way of the front door."

"How are you going to manage that?"

"I don't know. I'll have to go back to the City Park and meditate."

CHAPTER SEVENTEEN

Eventually I worked out a scenario involving Sister Merlina, the witch; Dick Tosche; and Obelia Nexit, who was not the least like the stereotype inscrutable Oriental. Obelia laughed for a full minute when I explained what I wanted to do.

With myself, Dick, Sister Merlina—impressive in her long robes—and Raina, it added up to a crowd in the small living room of Obelia's apartment. Raina said she was only there to watch the fun, but she was chomping at the bit to find out who Millie's unofficial roomer was.

We couldn't do anything until after ten o'clock when activity in the apartment building would quiet down somewhat. In the meantime, I verified that there was indeed someone in Millie's spare bedroom. It was Millie doing the talking, in a voice that seemed unusually loud for her, but she definitely was talking to someone. Her words were indistinct, even when I used the old trick of a drinking glass against the wall, but I could understand how her talk would bother a light sleeper.

I peeked out the door at ten thirty, saw no one in sight, and performed two maneuvers. First, I hung a *gris-gris*—supplied by Sister Merlina—to Millie's doorknob. The certified witch guaranteed it would bring only good things—like health, wealth, and long life—to the person owning it.

Having done that, I dropped a metal tray, which made a crash. I grabbed the tray, ducked back into Obelia's apartment, and closed the door quietly. After counting to ten, slowly, I nodded to Obelia, who went into the hall, closed the door after her with a bang, paused as though looking around, and then knocked loudly on Millie's door.

Millie's door opened.

"Did you hear something?" Obelia demanded.

"I sure did," Millie said. "Sounded like someone dropped something."

"I don't see anything," Obelia said. She paused. Then—she would have been pointing at the doorknob—she said, "What's that?"

On the basis of what I had seen at Marc DeVarnay's house, I expected a strong reaction. Millie exceeded my expectations by a light year or two. She screamed. Then she went into hysterics. Then—as all of us rushed into the hallway—she brought the alleged beneficial magic of Sister Merlina's *gris-gris* into severe disrepute by fainting. Obelia, a small woman, was barely able to keep her from crashing to the floor until Dick and I took over.

We carried her into the room she used as a bedroom, which had the door open, and placed her on the bed. The door to her spare room was closed. Sister Merlina and Raina took charge at that point. They loosened clothing, and Sister Merlina administered a pungent odor from a bottle of herbs she produced from a pocket.

Millie moaned and seemed to be coming out of it. Then she remembered what she had seen and fainted again.

Dick and I left her to the women. We tiptoed to the door of the spare bedroom, Millie's sewing room, and opened it quietly. I aimed a flashlight inside.

It would have surprised me very much to find myself face-to-face with Marc DeVarnay. What I did see surprised me even more. My flashlight beam came to rest on a sleepy-looking but highly resentful monkey.

I searched the room, directing my flashlight into all of the corners, and I found the darnedest menagerie of pets I'd ever seen outside of a circus. There were two parrots. There was a terrarium with a couple of large lizards. There was a tank of fish. There was another terrarium with a snake. There were a couple of lovebirds. There was a canary. There was a turtle. I couldn't make out what two more terrariums contained, but they were anyway too small for Marc DeVarnay to hide in. Likewise with a couple of cages that were covered.

There also was a clutter of sewing materials with a partly finished quilt on a frame.

I nudged Dick, and we retreated, closing the door quietly. Passing the other bedroom, I looked in. Sister Merlina was applying damp cloths to Millie's face. Raina looked up at me expectantly.

I shook my head firmly, gave her a thumbs down salute, and headed for the outer door. By arrangement, Sister Merlina was to give Millie the full certified witch treatment, thus rendering her immune to *gris-gris* for the rest of her life. Raina Lambert, though disappointed, at least would not have to go shopping for candles.

Dick and I stopped at the first bar—one never has to walk far in the French Quarter to find one—and consumed two bottles each of Blackened Voodoo Lager Beer. Then he went back to Obelia's apartment to wait for Sister Merlina to finish, and I returned to my hotel. I noticed a bulky figure following me at a discreet distance. Since it made no effort to overtake me, I assumed it was one of the bodyguards Dick had assigned to me. I went to bed with a clear conscience and slept well.

At nine o'clock the next morning, Wednesday, I was back in Metairie Cemetery where I parked as close as I could to the DeVarnay tomb. I still lacked a day of having been in New Orleans for a week, but it seemed like an eternity.

I waited. Then, for the want of anything else to do, I waited some more. Nothing at all happened for so long I began to wonder if Minjarus had chickened out on me. But no; I had merely underestimated the time required to do obeisance to the formalities. Suddenly everything happened. Cars began to arrive. There was Minjarus; there was a cemetery official and two workmen; there were two men in plainclothes whose official bearing proclaimed them to be Lieutenant Keig and a henchman. The officers remained in their car, watching. At the last minute Raina Lambert arrived in a rush, parked beside me, and came over to my car to wait.

"Jolitte asked me to stop and see her," she said. "Minjarus had just been there. He thought it wise to let her know what was going on. If he hadn't, she certainly would have heard about it from someone else, and he preferred to have her hear it from him first. An operation like this causes ripples of rumor no matter how discreet everyone pretends to be."

"How did she take it?" I asked.

"She's delighted that the Hormath tomb has finally been restored but disturbed at the idea of damage to the DeVarnay tomb. She wanted to know how that could have happened. I explained about the ladders and tools and things. I even implied that the workmen were walking around on the roof to get ideas about how to make their repairs. She agreed it would be wise to check for damage. By the way—the full impact of this didn't hit me when you told me about it yesterday. I didn't see the light until I took the time to think it over after I left Millie's. It took a remarkable criminal mentality to work this out. I can't remember anything that equals it."

"I would have used the word 'diabolical.' How's Millie?"

"Excellent. In robust good health. Sister Merlina is really very good. She convinced Millie that witchcraft is more powerful than voodoo."

"How does Millie account for the zoo?"

"She loves animals, but there's a clause in her lease about pets. It's that simple. She smuggled every single one of them and all of the apparatus into the building late at night when she first moved there. As for her talking to them occasionally, she says if people can talk to their plants, why shouldn't she talk to her pets?"

"It's a good question, but it would be a much better question if the pets were there legally. Is Obelia going to tell on her?"

"I don't think so. Obelia thought it was a hilarious joke. On us, of course. She'll laugh about it the rest of her life."

"So will I," I said dryly.

"Millie is bound to get caught sooner or later. She can't keep that many animals without the place smelling like a zoo, even if no one notices the noise. I suppose when it happens, out she goes. Of course she can always ask Sister Merlina to put a hex on the landlord."

"Sister Merlina wouldn't do that. She's a good witch. She only deals in nice hexes."

"The next time you see her, ask her if she has a spell to keep Millie from being evicted. About this scheme. As I said, it took a while for the full impact to hit me. Even as detectives we don't often encounter single-minded, totally self-centered ruthlessness, and this is something far worse. It's undiluted evil. What hellish ingenuity!"

"It makes ordinary murder look like mere naughtiness," I agreed.

"How'd you happen to think of it?"

"I had help. First I was treated to a tour of the cemetery by a highly knowledgeable guide. After that, I meditated for an hour and a half on the shore of a bayou where several pairs of lovers kept running into each other in peddle boats."

She gave me a look of disgust. "All right. Keep it to yourself."

The cemetery official seemed to be objecting to something, perhaps the whole project. He may have found my fiction about damage to the DeVarnay tomb difficult to swallow. He talked, pointing to the Hormath tomb and gesticulating energetically. Finally Lieutenant Keig decided to join them. When he introduced himself, the cemetery official suddenly suspected he might be out of his depth and shut up.

The workmen had already gone to work. They removed the bolts and the slab of marble. Inside was a grating that folded out of the way. Another debate followed, and then the workmen entered the tomb. They reappeared a short time later, struggling to carry something heavy that clearly didn't belong there. From where I sat, it looked like a large crate knocked together from the wood of light packing boxes.

There was more discussion and then a pause while Lieutenant Keig motioned his colleague to join them. Finally the workmen pried up the crate's lid, and everyone recoiled.

At that moment, my exercise in logic became a police matter, and the responsibility for it transferred abruptly from Minjarus's hands to those of Lieutenant Keig. Minjarus headed for his car. Then he saw me and made a detour. I rolled down the window.

"How did you know?" he asked.

"I didn't *know*. I surmised. It *is* Marc, I take it."

"God, yes."

"You were able to recognize him?"

Minjarus nodded. There was no point in asking him anything else. He was trying to control his stomach, and he anyway had the wrong expertise to provide the kind of answers I needed. It would take a messy autopsy to determine the cause of death.

"You've found Marc, so I suppose your case is finished," Minjarus said.

"No," I said. "It's just beginning. If I read Jolitte DeVarnay correctly, and I think I do, she won't rest until her son's murderer is convicted."

He sighed. "Now I suppose I've got to tell her Marc is dead."

"I'll tell her," Raina said.

Minjarus thanked her sincerely, went to his own car, and drove off. Raina turned to me. "Want to come along?"

"Nope," I said. "I'm sure Lieutenant Keig will want a chat, and then I have an unpleasant job of my own. I have to tell a brave expectant mother she's a widow."

"Right," Raina said. "Chores like this never get mentioned in those 'How to be a Detective' books."

"There is one interesting point about this," I said. "My psychic witch and the Gypsy fortune-teller were both dead on, if you'll excuse the expression, in saying DeVarnay was somewhere nearby. I never thought to check the exact distance. How far is it from the French Quarter to Metairie?"

"A few miles if you're alive," Raina said. "An eternity if you're dead."

She left, and a little later Lieutenant Keig came over and got into the car beside me. Though we had never met, he didn't bother to introduce himself. He knew who I was, and he knew I would know who he was. He said, "It was a brilliant guess. Or was it? Did you have anything at all to go on?"

He was a large man who probably looked good in a uniform, but his street clothes didn't quite seem to fit him. There was nothing of the intellectual about him. He would follow police procedures like a bloodhound on a scent, but that wouldn't keep him from being a good policeman.

"It was the end product of a long chain of reasoning," I said.

"Tell me."

"I kept thinking of the telephone call Marc received just before he left for St. Louis. It had to be someone offering him a ride to the airport, because he immediately cancelled his order for a taxi. Shortly afterward he was seen riding in a beat-up private car. I asked myself—supposing he never got to the airport?"

Lieutenant Keig frowned. "There were all those witnesses, not to mention hotel registration cards and travelers checks cashed—"

"As for the witnesses, all that took was someone with a strong resemblance to Marc—just enough so a couple of weeks later a total stranger could glance at Marc's photo and think that was who he saw and also enough to look as much like Marc's driver's license photo as most people look like their driver's license photos. As for the signatures, if this was a long-planned crime—and it must have been—there was plenty of time to master Marc's handwriting. Ten million dollars are worth a lot of hours spent in learning to forge a signature."

"You're saying someone murdered Marc and then went off to St. Louis—"

"And attended the auction in Marc's place and then went on to Denver, and Reno, and San Francisco, and Seattle. And then came back here under a different name and made another appearance—as Marc—down in the bayou country, where he committed a second murder."

"Why, for God's sake?"

"Not the question I would ask," I said. "The important question is whether there are any indications of this in the pseudo Marc's conduct. The answer is yes. At the auction, Marc wasn't acting like Marc. The imposter had two problems there. Marc was becoming nationally if not internationally known as a dealer and collector of antiques. There could have been someone there who knew him, so the imposter had to keep a very low profile. His second problem was that Marc was a genuine expert. Obviously the imposter wasn't. He couldn't risk bidding on valuable items because he might give himself away by paying too much for them. Also, the ten thousand dollars Marc had been carrying wouldn't have been enough money if he had bid enthusiastically on several valuable items. That wouldn't have been a problem for the real Marc DeVarnay, but the imposter didn't want to risk signing his name any more than he had to, and the signature on a credit card purchase or a check for a substantial amount was likely to be scrutinized a lot more carefully than the signature on a fifty-dollar traveler's check. So the imposter made a few token bids, keeping in the background, and finally he bought a cheap item for cash—one he couldn't go too far wrong on. Even then, he paid too much for it, the auctioneer said.

"After that, he headed west, where he was seen only by hotel and airport people who have hundreds or thousands of customers pass through their hands every week. Just in case they wouldn't be able to identify him at all, he cashed a few token travelers checks along the way as evidence that he had been there.

"At Pointe Neuve, the murderer had to look enough like Marc so those seeing Marc's picture a couple of weeks later would be able to identify him. Probably he worried about that. He didn't want too much time to lapse before Old Jake's body was found. His whole plot would have been wrecked if his carefully-chosen witnesses had forgotten what he looked like. You can bet he was the one who started the rumor that Marc had been seen at

Pointe Neuve."

"But why go to all that rigmarole?" Lieutenant Keig persisted.

"The trek west was to create the impression Marc was alive but on the run for some reason. Old Jake was murdered so everyone would believe Marc had a sound reason for staying on the run, especially his mother. To make this scheme work, she *had* to believe absolutely that he was still alive and keeping out of sight because the police were looking for him. The rigmarole supplied the basis for that. As long as she believed in it, she would go on looking for her son and spare no expense in trying to find him. If she had known he was dead, she certainly would have changed her will. The murderer definitely didn't want that. There was ten million dollars at stake."

"Why put him in the DeVarnay tomb?" Lieutenant Keig asked.

"Because he had to be put where he would eventually be found, and he had to be found at just the right time. If he had been dumped in a bayou, his body might never have been recovered. Alligators may or may not be Louisiana porch puppies, but they're highly effective scavengers. If Marc had simply disappeared, the DeVarnay millions could have been tied up in the courts for years. The murderer didn't want any problem about proving Marc was dead. On the other hand, he couldn't risk having Marc's body discovered while Jolitte was still alive, because then she would change her will. She wouldn't do that if she thought her son was still alive but hiding."

"Eventually she would have had to face up to the situation," Lieutenant Keig said.

"Ah! But the murderer wasn't thinking in terms of 'eventually.' His next act—after a decent lapse of time so people wouldn't start wondering about coincidences—would have been to murder Jolitte. In a discreet way, of course. He definitely wouldn't want it to look like murder. I wonder what method he intended to use. I'm sure he worked it out at the time he devised Marc's murder. This whole scheme was planned in every detail over a period of years—planned as carefully as drawing a complicated set of blueprints.

"Jolitte, however she was done away with, would have had the typical lavish Garden District funeral, expertly staged by the House of Bultman, and her body would have been consigned to the DeVarnay tomb—at which point the startling discovery would have been made that Marc had predeceased her by weeks or months. Therefore all of her estate would have gone to her cousin, David Dolding."

"You're suggesting that David Dolding—"

"David and his wife are elderly—in their mid-eighties. That's another reason the murderer couldn't wait too long before acting. They won't live forever. Their only son is dead. No one has heard anything for years from their neer-do-well grandson, who had a criminal record. The old people have banished him from their lives and minds and left their money to charities. But if he were to enter their lives again as a totally reformed character, would they refuse to accept him? They're a lonely old couple, and this is the son of their beloved son. Certainly they would give him another chance. Their Bible tells them 'Seventy times seven shalt thou forgive,' and they are deeply religious. After that, he would have every incentive to play the part of an upright, loving grandson: Jolitte's ten million plus whatever the Doldings have would be his prize. Even if they irreligiously banned him a second time, he still had several good chances at all or a chunk of the DeVarnay money. For one, he could contest the Doldings' wills and probably win. The other possibilities are complicated legally, and I'll have to turn my lawyer friend Minjarus loose on them. The point is that the grandson would still have a good chance of raking in a very nice inheritance."

"Assuming that he wasn't convicted of murder first," Lieutenant Keig said firmly. "Where is he now?"

"I have one vital clue. A woman who knows Marc DeVarnay thinks she saw him in the French Quarter three times in the past couple of weeks—always early in the morning when few people were around. As we now know, it couldn't have been DeVarnay that she saw. I mention this just in case you're still doubtful about another person looking enough like DeVarnay to bring this off. They are cousins even though several times removed. They must look much more alike than is usual with remote cousins. Of course the murderer isn't looking anything like DeVarnay right now."

Lieutenant Keig heaved a sigh. "What we need is a suspect or two."

"I'll give you one," I said. "A man who's about the right age and stature has been watching my hotel and trying to follow me. I learned yesterday that for the past four years he has been a part-time gardener with the Doldings. He is known in the French Quarter as Cal Dreslow, but the Doldings think his name is Joel Caramus. Obviously he has been keeping an eye on them. When I arrived in New Orleans, he became one of several people keeping an eye on me."

"Do you think he could be the grandson?"

"I don't know. I asked myself if he could have disguised himself as Marc DeVarnay, and I decided he couldn't. That may have been the wrong question. I should have asked whether someone looking a lot like DeVarnay could have disguised himself as Cal Dreslow. I think maybe he could have."

"I'll look into it," Lieutenant Keig said. As he got out of the car, he added regretfully, "This will take a lot of work."

He had every right to complain. He was the one who would have to do it.

"I can give you the murderer's name," I said. "Frank Dolding. Texas, where he served time, can give you his fingerprints. You know what he did. That makes it practically a complete case."

Lieutenant Keig nodded, but he didn't look grateful.

On my way out of the cemetery, I changed my plans. Before I called on the widow, I decided to fulfill an obligation to the might-have-been-widow. I circled around through the Garden District and stopped at the Berent mansion. Venita saw me drive up, and she came to the door herself. She took one look at my face and asked, "What's happened?"

"We've found Marc."

"Dead?"

I nodded.

She looked away from me. "I was afraid he would be. He wouldn't just disappear." She was taking it far more calmly than I had expected.

"There's something else you should know. He was married. His wife is expecting a baby any day now."

"How sad," she murmured. She gave me a searching look. "Then—he wasn't gay?"

"I don't think so.

"Then he simply lied to me?"

I nodded. "I'm afraid he'll never be written up as one of history's splendid gentlemen. In blunt fact, he was a coward. He lied to break his engagement to you. Then, because he was afraid his mother wouldn't approve of the girl he wanted to marry, he kept the marriage a secret and virtually hid her. On the other hand, I really think he did do you a favor even though he lied doing it."

"I think so, too," she said. "A couple of weeks ago, this might have devastated me, but you opened my eyes to a lot of things, and I'll always be grateful."

"If it's any satisfaction to you, I want you to know your help was what made it possible to find Marc. If you hadn't taken me to Metairie Cemetery, I wouldn't have figured out where his body was."

"Where was it?"

"In the DeVarnay tomb."

She wanted to know how it got there and how I found out it was there. I promised to tell her later. I still had the ordeal of a visit to Marc's widow ahead of me, and I wasn't looking forward to it.

"There's something you should know," she said. "Last night Jeff asked me to marry him, and I said yes."

I congratulated her, and for a moment she thought she was going to reward me with a kiss. Then she switched to a handshake. Even though she hadn't yet promoted herself to duchess, she was already a princess, and it doesn't do for royalty to get too familiar with plumbers or detectives.

"I saw Jeff at the cemetery, but he didn't mention this," I said. "Of course we had just found Marc's body, and it was hardly the occasion for making happy announcements. I'll congratulate him the next time I see him."

"Were you expecting this?" she asked. "About Jeff and me, I mean."

"Detectives spend their lives finding out what has already happened. They make lousy prophets. No, I didn't expect this. When I introduced you, I had no idea Jeff had been your secret admirer for years. I did think you needed to get out more, though."

"Yes," she agreed. "I certainly needed to get out more."

"Jeff doesn't come from an old New Orleans family. His pedigree may be almost as shoddy as mine. What do your parents think about this?"

"They're pleased. Father says every family needs a good attorney in it, and Jeff certainly is a very good attorney."

"You have a wise father," I said.

I returned my rental car to my hotel parking lot and walked over to St. Philip Street. At the apartment house where Karl Aronska lived, I rang his bell. He came to the door and looked at me questioningly.

"Marc is dead," I said. "I'm on my way to tell Edie. I'm thinking it might be wise to have her doctor present."

Karl nodded his head very slowly. "I've been expecting it. I'll tell her myself, but I agree it would be wise to have her doctor there."

"It might be even better if we could wait until after the baby is born, but there'll be a big splash in the newspapers, and she's certain to find out. Better tell her now."

He nodded his agreement.

We went to his apartment, and he called the doctor. He had some difficulty getting through to him, but when he did, he spoke firmly and to the point, and the doctor agreed to come at once. We waited outside for him. He was a tall, thin man with a beard, and he wisely didn't carry his bag, though as it turned out he brought everything he needed in his pockets, and he even had an ambulance standing by a couple of blocks away.

Karl had a key to the pedestrian gate. He let us in, and we walked in a group to Edie's front door. There should have been a better way to handle it, but at the time I couldn't think what it would be, and I still can't. We probably looked like a group of undertakers calling.

Karl had a key to the house, too. He let himself in. We followed. Edie heard us, hurried toward the front door, and froze when she saw the living room full of people.

Karl went to her and took her in his arms. "Be brave, sweetheart. Marc is dead."

Her face went colorless. Then she fainted. Fortunately Karl had a firm hold of her—probably he was thinking of that when he put his arms around her before telling her. He picked her up and carried her to a sofa, and from that point it was the doctor's problem.

But not for long. He made only a cursory examination before he phoned for the ambulance. It arrived in a rush, and Karl and the doctor went to the hospital with Edie, leaving me standing at the entrance to St. Philip Place. From the Heartbreak Bar across the street came the sound of jazzy music.

There are always two sides to a detective's cases. One side concerns crime; the other concerns those people whose lives are shattered by it.

CHAPTER EIGHTEEN

Early the next morning I called Raina Lambert from my favorite pay telephone, and she first gave me the gist of the postmortem report. Marc DeVarnay had been shot in the head.

"How did Jolitte take it?" I asked.

"She's shattered, but of course nothing shows."

"'My head is bloody but unbowed.'"

"Something like that. She's occupying herself with planning the funeral."

"Marc's wife will have ideas of her own about that. You should have told Jolitte her only function will be to attend."

"My God! I didn't even think of it! This case has complications I've never experience before."

"You also could have told her she's a grandmother. Karl Aronska telephoned me at midnight. He thought I couldn't wait to hear, I suppose, or maybe he couldn't wait to tell me. Edie gave birth to a healthy boy. Eight pounds, three ounces. The baby is fine. The mother is still in a state of emotional collapse, but when she comes out of it, I'm sure she'll want to bury her own husband."

"It was enough of a strain telling Jolitte her son was dead. The news about her grandson and daughter-in-law will have to wait. We have a murderer to catch. I want to see you right away. I'll pick you up at your hotel."

"Hold it! I'm summoned to police headquarters. Lieutenant Keig's superiors, I take it. Not only do they have a corpse on their hands named DeVarnay, which is very bad form, but the department has wasted a lot of man hours and even woman hours looking for him as a suspect in a murder committed when he was already dead. That's worse form."

"What are you supposed to do about it?"

"I don't know. I told the Pointe Neuve detectives right at the beginning that DeVarnay didn't kill Old Jake. They were rudely skeptical, but they must have reported what I said, and it got passed along. Telling the police where to find DeVarnay's body made me twice a genius. As soon as they finish questioning me about my brilliant reasoning, I'm going back to my hotel and pack. I've checked the flights to Savannah—"

"Wait a minute! What's this about?"

"My job was to find Marc DeVarnay. Dead or alive. You told me so yourself. If dead, your job was to point a finger at who did it. You also told me that yourself. You were going to be ready to point when I found. So I've found. If you really are ready to point, I'll stick around long enough to watch. Otherwise, you said I could leave, so I'm leaving."

"I'm ready to point, and I want you on hand, but there still are a few things to clear up. This afternoon might be better. Call me at one o'clock."

"Sure—if the police are through putting me through the wringer by then."

She picked me up at my hotel at one-thirty and asked me how my morning had gone. "I've done my quota of talking for the day," I said. "I'm lucky I was in Savannah the night Marc DeVarnay was murdered. Otherwise, I'd be a suspect myself. They can't prove anything, but they strongly suspect I put his body in the tomb myself. I pointed the police at the missing Dolding grandson. I also pointed them at Cal Dreslow, alias Joel Caramus, the Doldings' part-time gardener, who also may be the missing grandson. He must have noticed the gleam of recognition in my eyes when I saw him in the Doldings' garden. He's disappeared."

"I'm sure he isn't the Doldings' grandson," Raina said, "but he certainly was put there to keep an eye on them. Their continued good heath has long been a matter of high concern to their grandson."

"So who are you going to finger? If his name isn't Dolding, my reputation will be ruined."

"Your reputation is safe, but first we have to catch him. We'll start at the Doldings' house."

"Do you think the gardener is hiding out there?"

"No."

"Have the Doldings suddenly remembered something?"

"They won't be home. They're with Jolitte, performing their cousinly duty of consoling her in a time of high tragedy. I got permission to use their garden."

I turned to her. "*Use* their garden? For what?"

"Meditation. It's a lovely place to meditate. You missed the chance when you were there before, so you'll have to do it now."

"So's the City Park a lovely place to meditate. So's Metairie Cemetery. New Orleans is full of lovely places to meditate. We can give it another nickname and call it Meditation City. What am I supposed to meditate in the Doldings' garden?"

"The statues. Did you see them?"

"I did, but they didn't strike me as needing much meditation."

"They should have. Did you notice that several were mutilated—including one saint who's missing his head?"

"I did notice that. I thought it might be evidence of his martyrdom."

"In a way, you're right. The mutilation was perpetrated by the Doldings' grandson, Frank. Childish pranks. It's an interesting reflection on their psychology that after cutting him out of their will and banning him from their lives and, presumably, thoughts, they left the mutilated statues there to constantly remind them of what they suffered from him."

"Sure. What are they supposed to remind us of?"

"Not remind us. Inspire us."

She was about to pull a large rabbit out of a small hat, and I knew I would get nothing more from her until she had the stage set. It was her show, so I shut up and rode along quietly.

We headed out St. Charles Avenue, taking the most direct route, and turned into the Garden District a block from the Doldings' house. The maid had had instructions. She led us through the house to a door that opened onto the garden and told us to go right ahead and enjoy the place. If we wanted coffee, or tea, or soft drinks, she would fix them for us, and we could have them on the patio or, since it was a sunny day, at a table outside.

Raina thanked her and told her we didn't require anything. Our meditations probably wouldn't take long. The maid nodded and left us to them.

We strolled down the walk to the Madonna and Child and then took one radiating path after another while Raina showed me the beheaded statue and the headless snake as well as evidence of several other small acts of vandalism I'd missed.

There was no doubt at all that the grandson had been a terror, but I already knew that. "So what am I supposed to meditate?" I asked finally as we headed down another walk to yet another statue."

"That," she said.

At first I didn't grasp what she was pointing at. Then I stared. "I'll be damned."

"How did you manage to miss anything that obvious?" she asked.

"I don't know. I must have been asleep."

The statue was the one of St. Francis that had been imported from France. The caption on it didn't read "Saint Francis of Assisi," as it would have in English, but "Saint François d'Assisi."

The first time I saw it, I should have read it as Raina did: François d'Assisi, Francis d'Assisi, Francis Dassily. That was why she had taken a job in the flea market—so she could keep an eye on him and be ready to point.

"At least he wasn't completely untouched by his upbringing," I mused. "That statue must have made a deep impression on his subconscious to emerge as an alias so many years afterward. I wonder if he remembers where he got it. But surely you had more to go on than this."

"Of course. He's the only associate of DeVarnay's who wears a wig and has a false beard."

"Really? They look real."

"They're very competently done, but they're still fakes. So I tried Sherlock Holmes's ploy and looked at his face without the wig and goatee."

"And you saw DeVarnay?"

"A very close resemblance. My deduction is that Dassily grew his hair long and added the goatee as a disguise when he returned to New Orleans—and just to be emphatic, he bleached both of them blond. When he planned his crimes, he shaved the goatee and substituted a fake one, and he covered his hair with a blond wig while it grew out in its natural color—which must be very similar to the color of DeVarnay's hair. When the transition was complete, all he had to do to masquerade as DeVarnay was remove the wig and goatee and imitate DeVarnay's hair style. When the masquerade was over, he became himself again by donning the wig and goatee, and he immediately started letting his own hair and beard grow. Given enough time, the blond hair and goatee would be his own again."

"One for you," I said. "That's why Ida Gallan thought Marc DeVarnay needed a shave and a haircut. It was early, and there weren't many people about, so Dassily risked dashing out without his wig and goatee a few times to buy bread and croissants."

She shook her head. "Dassily must have known she occasionally walked to work with DeVarnay. People living in the French Quarter tend to be like a massive, extended family. They know everything about everyone. So Dassily set her up as a witness, and when he was certain she had seen him looking like Marc a few times, he called your attention to her. He was using both of you to prove Marc was still alive but hiding."

"Right again," I said ruefully. "And once we swallowed the bait, he had no reason to make another appearance looking like DeVarnay. We could have watched that area for the next year without catching a glimpse of him. Do you have a case?"

"There will be one when this breaks. I'm sure some of his confederates will talk. The main weakness in his scheme was that he had to rely on too many unreliable people."

"Good. He's twice a murderer, and he's planning a third. Let's go get him."

"I'm having him watched. He should be at the flea market right now, but I'm not sure that's the best place to arrest him."

"Wherever it's done, it'll take more than just the two of us. That character is nothing if not resourceful."

"Police job?" she asked.

I nodded. "Much as I would like to apply the handcuffs myself—placing one of them around his neck—I wouldn't want to bungle the job and have to chase him through the French Quarter's alleys and courtyards like Little Boy."

"I agree. I'll call Lieutenant Keig and let him decide."

Lieutenant Keig wanted to grab him immediately, wherever he was. He moved quickly, and by the time we reached the French Market, its normal afternoon crowd had been augmented by the addition of several plainclothes cops. The lieutenant was surveying the flea market from the end of the shed.

"Is that the character?" he asked, nodding in Dassily's direction.

"The one at the jewelry table with a display of paintings behind him," Raina said. "I'll walk down there and pretend to be a customer. If you'll have one man follow me closely while two others close in from the sides, you should be able to grab him without any trouble.

"Right."

He let Raina choose the officers. I knew she would have preferred types who resembled the tourists thronging the market, but most city detectives need some advance notice in order to bring that off. As a result, she had to make do with three rather obvious cops in plainclothes. The others, who were even more obvious, fanned out in support.

It was a good plan regardless, and it should have worked.

Either Dassily saw the two of us talking with Keig, or he recognized one or more of the cops. Raina was about thirty feet from his table, with a detective on at her heels and the other two detectives maneuvering into position, when Dassily turned and called something to Pam, the woman selling souvenirs and T-shirts at the next table. Pam nodded.

Suddenly he ran for it.

A flight through a crowded flea market has no similarity to running in a track meet. Dassily catapulted through the crowd, knocking men aside, trampling women and children, careening into vendors, and bullying everyone out of his way. He leaped over tables, he smashed into stacks and piles and displays of merchandise, he sent cash registers and cash boxes crashing to the floor. He left in his wake an outpouring of alligator heads, a dusty amalgamation of T-shirts, a confused glitter of jewelry, a jumble of leather goods, an execution of dolls, a shattering of glass and ceramics, a hodgepodge of books, and a smear of oil paintings. He made a clean escape, leaving behind him a considerable uproar.

He burst from the market area with a good twenty foot lead on the pursuit, which in its first rank numbered the two plainclothes officers with the best reflexes and myself. Chuffing along in subsequent ranks were the less physically fit officers plus an eruption of furious market vendors, each of whom was intent upon exacting revenge for damaged merchandise. The vendors were bellowing their outrage in a dozen different languages. If they had caught up with Dassily first, there would have been no necessity for a murder trial.

Sheer surprise had given him a head start. On the land side of the Mississippi levee, there is a flood wall, a concrete barrier that serves as backup flood control. A short distance downriver from the point where Dassily emerged from the market, a vehicle gate through the wall was standing open. Dassily certainly knew about it, but he also knew he wouldn't have time to reach it. Instead, he headed for a stairway that functions like a stile over the flood wall for tourists going to and from the

Esplanade stop on the Riverfront Streetcar Line. He tore up the steps and vanished down the other side.

The first of the two detectives was still some twenty feet behind him. The other detective and I were following closely. By the time we topped the wall, Dassily had gained ten feet. He must have taken a long leap from the stairs.

There were four sets of railway tracks, two of them used by the streetcar, which has a turn-around loop just beyond its Esplanade stop. The only other thing in Dassily's way was a fence consisting of a couple of cables suspended between posts. He took it in stride. I thought he would head upstream—he was very close to the end of the Governor Nicholls Street Wharf, and he might have been able to lose himself among the crowds of tourists, vendors, and beggars that throng the excursion boat wharves. From there he would have had a fair chance of making his way back into the French Quarter. Downstream, the Port of New Orleans took over, with a solid line of wharves lining the river bank for hundreds of yards, their warehouses extending out over the Mississippi on pilings.

Dassily had a different idea. Probably it was a better one. He ran directly toward the Governor Nicholls Street Wharf and vaulted onto the loading dock. At intervals there were large, corrugated metal doors used for loading and unloading. Some of them were raised, as were similar doors on the opposite side of the warehouse where ships docked.

Dassily didn't hesitate. He ran straight through the warehouse to an open door on the other side and jumped. When the detectives and I reached the spot, there was nothing to be seen but the swift-flowing, extremely muddy Mississippi.

It was a fiendishly clever maneuver. The water was low, which meant there was dry land far back under the warehouses on the land side. The warehouses were supported by rows and rows of piles—most of them wood posts but some of cast cement—all the way downstream to Poland Street. In that dim, covered area he could hide behind piles and get underwater whenever the chase came close. If he could hold out until dark, he would have a fair chance of getting away.

"What are the odds on his swimming the river?" I asked one of the officers.

"Not good," he said. "It's been tried. Usually the body is found far downstream. This is Algiers Bend. It's the sharpest bend in the area, and the river is at least half a mile wide here, as you can see. Not only is there a hell of a current to contend with but there are depths up to two hundred and forty feet out there with heavy boat traffic day and night—ocean freighters, excursion and pleasure boats, ferries, even an occasional naval ship. If this character wants to try it, he's welcome."

One of the officers was describing the situation by radio. He wanted to know how long it would take to get a boat there. It was a police problem, and I left them to it. Walking back to the market, I passed the trailing procession of panting police officers and vendors, all of them hopelessly late but still determined.

Raina Lambert was waiting at Dassily's table. "What happened?" she asked.

"Just a moment," I said. I went over to Pam, the woman at the next table. "What did Francis say to you just before he ran for it?" I asked her.

She looked surprised. "He said, 'Watch my stuff for me, will you?'"

"A hustler to the end," I murmured.

"What happened?" Raina asked again.

"He jumped in the river."

"Was that a smart thing to do?"

"It's going to give the police this year's largest headache. They may get him, or they may not. If they don't, he may survive, or he may not."

I described the situation. She said, "Damn. I thought the case was all wrapped up."

"So did I. I'm awfully glad we didn't try to catch him ourselves. With only two of us, he might have tried to gun us down. In the market, no less. This is going to require some thought."

"What are the chances that the police can catch him?"

"He'll have walked—or swum—far downstream before they can get a boat on the scene. When they do, they won't have any idea where to start looking for him, and there's a maze of piling under the warehouses. And he's nothing if not determined, not to mention completely ruthless. Like I said, this is going to require some thought. Let's go somewhere and think."

We climbed the levee to the Moon Walk along the river. It was named after a politician and has nothing to do with the moon. There we found a bench from which we had choice seats to watch the gathering activity around the end of the Governor Nicholls Street Wharf. A streetcar was winding its way along the riverfront tracks headed toward its final stop at Esplanade. The drivers on that line are so extremely considerate that they even stop for pedestrians crossing the tracks. Streetcars headed in the other direction pass the Aquarium of the Americas and make a convenient run all the way to River Walk, a half mile long shopping mall along the river on the other side of Canal Street. I briefly considered whether Dassily might try to escape by catching a streetcar. He was audacious enough, but the street-cars, which moved in leisurely fashion, weren't.

Tourists on the levee, as well as those in Decatur Street and the regular market, had begun to edge toward the wharf, sensing another free entertainment attraction. When they were turned away by the gathering crowd of police, they drifted in our direction, looking back and trying to see what the fuss was about. A swirling buzz of activity like that around a bee hive several minutes after someone has poked a stick into it still enveloped the flea market.

Upriver, where the excursion boats docked, all was still tranquil, but tourists there had caught a glimpse of something going on, and some of them were moving our way.

"*If* they catch him," I said finally, "well and good, but we'd better make some preparations just in case they don't. Does Jolitte still have her bodyguards?"

"Yes. She took a liking to them, and with everything else that's happened, no one has thought to lay them off."

"Take a suite at the most secure downtown hotel you can think of. Do it now, while Dassily is still on the run. We'll keep her there until he's accounted for one way or another."

"Then you think he still might—"

"It's unfinished business for him. He can take his chances on a trial, he'll know there isn't much evidence, but even if he wins he'll have lost if she's still alive and he can't inherit the DeVarnay money."

"She can settle that in a hurry with a new will. Now that she knows Marc is dead, she should make one anyway."

"Dassily won't know she's done it, and she'll still be dead. Also, she has a grandson she doesn't know about, and she shouldn't make a new will until she's thought that situation through carefully. Let's put her in a safe place, and make certain she remains safe, and sort everything out later."

"Do you think she's in danger tonight? Even if Dassily escapes, he would still have to find a change of clothing and somehow get back to the Garden District."

"I think we shouldn't take a chance."

We both continued to watch the flurry of activity at the end of Governor Nicholls Street Wharf. "There doesn't seem to be much headroom below the warehouse, and it must be an ucky mess on the land side," Raina said.

"Ucky messes are nothing to a desperate man, and at this point Dassily certainly is desperate."

She got to her feet. "All right. I'll move Jolitte and her body-guards to a safe place. What are you going to do?"

"Go to work. It suddenly develops that this case is a long way from over. It may be just beginning."

CHAPTER NINETEEN

I got hold of Dick Tosche and, through him, his brother Charlie. They were both solid characters who could be relied on absolutely. Charlie had been impressed with Raina Lambert's wage rates, and he was available for whatever we wanted him to do. Dick hadn't been paid anything yet, but he was available, too. Working with me had been fun and a welcome diversion from his buying and selling activities, and he wasn't worried about wages. He had a lavish paycheck coming, but he didn't know that.

Dick recruited six of the large friends who had waylaid my intended assassins. Charlie brought two Cajuns with him from the swamp and bayou country. As soon as it was dark, all of us converged on the DeVarnay mansion.

Jolitte's gardener was gone for the day. Dorothy, who was far more devastated than her mistress by Marc's death, had accompanied Jolitte into hiding. Only the elderly butler, James, was there to greet us. He had his orders. After politely admitting us, he retired to his room, giving us the run of the mansion.

Dick, Charlie, and I surveyed the place inside and out and made our plans. "Why don't you let us grab him outside?" Dick asked.

"I want him to commit himself. We need proof of what he's up to. Anyway, if we wait for him outside, your friends might have to sit absolutely still for hours."

"If they're paid enough, they'll not only sit still, they'll hold their breaths, too," Dick said.

I shook my head. "Absolutely not. This is likely to be an all-night job, and we might as well be comfortable. The last I heard, Dassily had totally disappeared. The police have a hunch he drowned himself trying to swim the river, which I consider wishful thinking. But I don't know whether he'll get clear in time to work his way back here tonight."

"If we catch him outside, we can give him the treatment he deserves," Dick said. "After he gets in the house, we'll have to worry about breaking things. But you're the boss. Just tell us what you want us to do."

Lieutenant Keig hadn't thought much of my scheme. All the regular police and detectives who could be spared were chasing Dassily elsewhere, and my silly notion about the DeVarnay mansion received neither police assistance nor an official blessing. This vividly illustrates what Shakespeare said about the bubble reputation. Only that morning I had been awarded ceremonial congratulations for my brilliant stroke in finding Marc DeVarnay's body. In the confusion following Dassily's escape, someone had pricked the bubble.

I preferred it that way. Unless a really high police officer makes it clear who is in charge, a civilian outsider with police assistants has to explain everything twice and then argue about it whenever he wants anything done. With my own men, all I had to do was give orders.

I felt certain Dassily would make an attempt on Jolitte DeVarnay's life, and he had to do it immediately. Otherwise, his years of artful planning and weeks of brilliant execution were down the drain. Once he was arrested for Marc's murder, he knew his grandparents would write him off a second time. Jolitte, left alive, would make a new will the moment she learned that the Dolding bequest in her present one had been the cause of Marc's death.

There is always a long-shot chance of beating a complicated murder charge. If Dassily succeeded, he still might convince his grandparents he was a reformed character and worthy of inheriting the millions—provided he discreetly murdered Jolitte before he was arrested. He absolutely had to act now.

He had already lost, but he wasn't yet aware of that. Marc DeVarnay had kept his marriage so secret that Dassily knew nothing about Edie and the new heir, but this would be small consolation to us if he murdered Jolitte before he found it out.

Before I put my private army in position, Dick, Charlie, and I searched the mansion meticulously. If Dassily had already made careful plans to murder Jolitte, as I suspected, he had taken the preliminary step of discovering a way to get into the building.

We checked every door and every window on the ground floor. It was Charlie who found it—the French doors opening onto the garden from what once would have been called a drawing room had been tampered with. The lock seemed to work, but it did not catch, and the doors could easily be pushed open when locked.

"That means he's already explored the house," I said. "Probably he prowled through it while the elderly occupants were asleep. Jolitte is lucky. He could have murdered her easily anytime after he got back from Pointe Neuve."

Once he entered the house, he would move quickly. I posted my men along the route he was likely to follow and gave them strict orders. Then I settled myself in Jolitte's room. I had borrowed a clothing store mannequin; Raina Lambert provided a wig for it from her cabinet of disguises. I had no intention of posing it in a window, but I did want to create the impression that Jolitte was home. I dressed it in one of her robes, and occasionally I moved it past a window so her shadow could be glimpsed from outside.

After that, I had nothing to do but wait. Either Dassily would come, or he wouldn't. If he didn't, we could try again the next night. Beyond that, the law of diminishing returns would take over.

While I waited, I took the time to telephone Jeff Minjarus. After congratulating him on his engagement, I handed him the problem of Dassily's legal status. I wanted to know what chances he would have had of breaking his grandparents' wills.

Minjarus promised to do some checking.

I tried to imagine what Dassily was doing. Even if he chose not to swim the Mississippi, he still had to break away from the east bank and reach an area that could provide cover. That meant slipping through the continuous line of warehouses by way of doors left open, through the truck traffic and parking lots, out through a gate, and into some kind of refuge beyond. He had to do all of that while he was wet and muddy and thoroughly conspicuous and with police searching the area for him. It sounded hopeless, but nothing is impossible for a determined and resourceful man. From there, he would try to find a telephone so he could arrange for someone to pick him up with a change of clothing. If he could manage all that, he would be functioning again.

He might not look like either Francis Dassily or Marc DeVarnay when he arrived. He had successfully disguised himself once, so it was to be expected that he might have other disguises in his bag.

As midnight approached, I moved the mannequin past all the windows and then placed it in retirement in a closet. I turned out the overhead bedroom light and turned on a nightlight. Then I turned on the light in Jolitte's private bathroom and remained there, waiting. The mansion was solidly-built for its era; It creaked a little but in a very genteel way. I left the bathroom door open the smallest crack possible and moved a stool into position so I could look through it. Again there was nothing to do but wait.

The bedroom door opened with one swift, silent movement, and a figure that looked like the Marc DeVarnay Ida Gallan had seen, with shaggy hair and unshaven chin, entered the room swiftly, poised to grab and stifle his victim. He seemed surprised not to find her in bed. As he hesitated, looking around, I reached over and turned on the shower.

He smiled. He thought he had caught Jolitte at the best possible moment.

The shower's noise was exactly what he needed to cover

his preparations. He leaped onto a bureau, threaded a slender rope through a ceiling hook from which a lamp was suspended, gauged the height of the loop at the end of it, and affixed it with a knot. He vaulted down again, checked to make sure the rope was secure and at the right height, and moved a chair under it.

Now I knew what he intended. He would overpower Jolitte, strangle her into unconsciousness, and then stage a suicide scene. She would be found dangling from the rope with the chair kicked out from under her. It was another fiendishly clever plan. Her suicide on the day after her son was found murdered would be believable and might even be believed.

What Dassily had endured that day would have totally exhausted most men. He must have suffered severely from cold, exposure, and unimaginable strain, and his escape had required a superhuman effort. Despite all of that, he looked as alert and expectant as a bridegroom. This was the climax of all his planning, and he was ready for it.

And I was ready for him. I turned off the shower, allowed a proper interval for toweling and putting a robe on, and then swung the door open. Dassily, poised to throttle an elderly woman, got the surprise of his life when I leaped at him.

He fought with animal fury, grunting and muttering. I know plenty of tricks, but his strength was incredible. I'm not sure I could have handled him for long. Fortunately my reinforcements were at hand. They had instructions to lie low until Dassily entered Jolitte's room. Then they were to wait quietly outside for the sound of a ruckus. Now they came bursting in, and the struggle was soon over. They tied up Dassily with lengths of clothesline Dick Tosche had brought. When he kept trying to pull out of the knots, Dick unceremoniously planted a foot on his throat. The more Dassily squirmed, the more pressure Dick applied. Dassily soon subsided.

But he wouldn't talk. He never said a thing from the moment I dashed out and grabbed him until the police came for him.

I called Raina Lambert. Then I called Lieutenant Keig's office. A frosty voice informed me that the lieutenant was not in at that hour.

"I know," I said. "He's out looking for Francis Dassily. If he really wants him, I have him tied up and waiting to be collected."

The voice became frostier. I interrupted. "Just tell the lieutenant that Pletcher is waiting for him at the DeVarnay mansion," I said. "Ask him whether he would rather pick Dassily up now or have me turn him loose so he can go on looking for him."

I hung up. "I think we'll keep our private army here for tonight, just in case," I told Dick and Charlie. "Dassily may have confederates who won't know the game is over. But the three of us can go out and celebrate. Where shall we go?"

At any hour of the night—or morning—there are plenty of places to choose from in New Orleans because there are no legal restrictions on the hours for selling liquor. We argued about it until the police came.

At seven the next morning, I got Jeff Minjarus out of bed. "What'd you find out?" I asked him.

"You do come up with the damndest questions," he complained.

"It's life that comes up with the damndest questions. It was none of my doing. What's the answer?"

"Louisiana law is based on French law rather than the English Common Law all the other states use. There are some quirks— to put it mildly. One of them pertains to inheritance. There is something called a forced heir. The law has now been changed, but at the time of the death of Dassily's parents, a minor or a child who was mentally or physically incompetent couldn't be disinherited. Dassily not only was a forced heir, but he was the contingent beneficiary on both of his parents' wills. In other words, both of their estates should have come to him."

"So—who did their estates come to?"

"His grandparents, I suppose."

I asked incredulously, "Are you telling me Dassily's pious, preaching grandparents stole his inheritance?"

"Be reasonable, now. His grandparents adopted him, so of course they controlled his inheritance while he was a minor.

Then he ran away and got into serious trouble, and they haven't heard from him since. They thought he was dead."

"They pretended he was dead," I said. "They simply wrote him off. They disinherited him by leaving him out of their wills and acting as though he didn't exist. Eventually it must have dawned on him that he'd been shafted. I wonder whether that was the vital factor in his decision to revenge himself on the whole family, or whether he merely saw an ingenious way to get rich and tried to carry it out."

"Or both, since his criminal propensities were well established," Minjarus said.

"Fact remains that his grandparents swiped his money. A good attorney could make that sound awful in court. Those gentle, old, devoutly religious people are actually greedy terrors. They had control of their grandson's money, and they appropriated it to punish him. The wrath of the righteous is fearsome to behold. Juries have been swayed by less potent appeals than that."

"Don't be silly. The grandparents haven't heard from him for more than fifteen years. They still haven't. They have every reason to think he's dead. For that matter, how sure are you that Francis Dassily is really Frank Dolding?"

"I'm as sure of his identity as I am of mine. Texas has never heard of him under either name, but that only means he was carrying fake identification when he was arrested. Dassily isn't talking, so the police aren't even sure Texas was where he did time. They'll get it straightened out. Fingerprints don't lie, and the hospital where he was born must have printed his feet. Any doubt about who he is won't last long. What are his chances of inheriting Jolitte's money by breaking his grandparents' will?"

"There we have another fuzzy area. I don't know whether forced heirship would apply to the grandparents-grandson relationship when the parents are dead, but the point is probably null because Dassily was adopted by them. The law has been changed, as I said, but the wills of the Doldings and of Jolitte DeVarnay were made before the new law came into effect, so the old law would still apply. The law provides for exceptions, of course."

"Of course. Otherwise, how could lawyers earn an honest living? What are they?"

"A bunch of oddball things. If the child has been guilty of a crime toward a parent or attempted to murder the parents, or if the parents were kidnapped and the child refused to ransom them, or if they were imprisoned and the child refused to provide bail, or if the child married without consent—"

"What is there that would apply to Dassily?"

"A child can be disinherited if he has been convicted of a felony, but it has to be one with a penalty of death or life imprisonment."

"Dassily's crime in Texas wasn't that serious, and anyway, it was a long time ago and in another state and he was only a minor when it happened. Of course if he's convicted of murdering DeVarnay or Old Jake, it'll disqualify him good, but Louisiana's death penalty ought to take care of that rather effectively regardless. Does the law apply to a minor convicted in another state?"

Minjarus sighed. "I'd rather not go into that. In any case, Dassily is certainly older than twenty-three, which makes him too old to claim forced heirship unless he can qualify under the provision concerning mental incapacity or physical infirmity. Since I don't know him, I can't say whether he could bring that off."

"In other words, if he were to be found not guilty by reason of insanity, he still might have a shot at the ten million. It sounds like the sort of case that could keep an army of lawyers happy for years."

"I'm afraid it is."

"Fortunately none of this will ever come up in a probate court. Both Jolitte and the Doldings will make new wills that emphatically disinherit Dassily. The point may be important in the criminal case since it establishes a motive for Dassily. In that context, what the law really says doesn't matter. The important thing is what he, a layman, thought it says. Because of the fuzziness, he may have believed he had a substantial claim on his grandparents' estates regardless."

"I suppose that's possible. It's also possible that the source he consulted wasn't up-to-date, and he doesn't know that the law has been amended."

I thanked him and warned him about letting his legal research get in the way of with his keeping his *fiancée* happy. He promised he wouldn't.

I now knew enough to reconstruct Francis Dassily's actions at least to my own satisfaction. After his prison term, wherever he served it, he may have returned to New Orleans with the idea of going straight, but it didn't work out. He was extremely capable, he was a good worker, but he'd had little education and no training for anything except crime.

About the time Marc DeVarnay started his antique business, Dassily got in touch with him. He could have identified himself, told DeVarnay he was making a new start under a different name, and asked to be given a chance, but it would have been more in character to keep his identity a secret until he figured out how to cash in on it. Probably he heard DeVarnay would pay well for tips on antiques, and he took advantage of that—both to earn money and to get acquainted with DeVarnay and his business. He must have impressed DeVarnay favorably—he had a genuine knack for finding antiques—and in a limited way he became a valued assistant. He also began to dream a big dream.

He made his plans, and he matured them slowly. The street characters and criminal types he knew possessed a variety of skills, and among them were some who could do a competent job of restoring a brick and stucco tomb. This gave him the idea for disposing of DeVarnay's body. He created Ently and Company, invested in a few letterheads and envelopes, and wrote to the attorney who represented the now defunct Hormath estate, informing him that an anonymous donor was willing to pay for the Hormath tomb's restoration. The attorney gave his authorization, no reason why he shouldn't, and the letter, plus a phony work order, were convincing enough to cemetery authorities. In the meantime, Dassily had switched to the wig, let his hair grow out in its natural color, and had it cut and combed the same way DeVarnay did. And he practiced forging DeVarnay's signature. Probably he had been practicing it for years. The only other preparation he needed was to get acquainted with Old Jake, perhaps offering to cut him in on some get-rich-quick scheme.

That done, he was prepared to murder DeVarnay at the first opportunity, and the trip to St. Louis provided one. Since Dassily was so good at finding antiques, it was to DeVarnay's advantage to further his education, and he probably told Dassily all about the St. Louis auction and what he expected to accomplish there, thus preparing Dassily to take the trip himself.

Of course it was Dassily who telephoned DeVarnay and offered him a ride to the airport, perhaps on the pretext of telling him about some discovery he had made. At that point, I could write my own scenario for what happened.

Dassily, knowing about DeVarnay's culinary hobby, had already discussed cooking with him, and DeVarnay may have given Dassily his own jambalaya recipe. As they drove along, Dassily told DeVarnay about the fancy new pan he'd bought to cook jambalaya in. He wanted to know what DeVarnay thought of it, so he reached into the back seat for it and handed it to him still in its bag so he wouldn't get his own fingerprints on it. When DeVarnay had admired it—putting an adequate number of prints on it in the process—Dassily took advantage of a quiet stretch of road and shot him in the head.

Dassily's accomplices would have been following. They took charge of the body and proceeded with the plan to restore the Hormath tomb and hide DeVarnay next door in the DeVarnay tomb. The jambalaya pan was returned to its bag—with a gloved hand—to await planting on a second murder scene. Dassily went on to St. Louis in DeVarnay's place. He impersonated DeVarnay at the auction—not well, but he got away with it. Then he laid a trail to Seattle, returned to New Orleans under an assumed name, and, again impersonating DeVarnay, established his presence in Pointe Neuve and committed a second murder.

Probably he made the jambalaya after Old Jake was dead, mixing it in another pan and very carefully adding it to the pan Marc had fingerprinted. Then he left the *cabon* in Old Jake's boat, taking his pirogue with him as an added mystification. He sank both of them when he reached the place where accomplices were waiting.

He returned to the French Quarter, donned his wig and false goatee, and went about his business. At some point he put into circulation the rumor that DeVarnay had been seen down at Pointe Neuve. Otherwise, he had nothing more to do but pretend surprise at DeVarnay's disappearance and wait for an opportune moment to murder Jolitte.

Only one thing went wrong. Dassily hadn't expected private detectives. He put a watch on my hotel and on the store to try to figure out what I was up to. When I began to inquire about DeVarnay's actions the night he left for St. Louis, he became uneasy. We were supposed to think DeVarnay disappeared much later than that. He decided I was dangerous and arranged the street attack on me. Thanks to Dick Tosche, all of the attackers landed in the hospital.

His escape from the flea market showed again how resourceful—and dangerous—he could be. Now, because he couldn't resist one last attempt to make himself heir to a fortune, he was in custody and his criminal career was finished.

Unfortunately, its aftermath still had to be dealt with. At eight o'clock, I called at the hotel suite that served as Jolitte DeVarnay's refuge. New Orleans has magnificent modern hotels. Not only are they opulent, but the facilities of some of them are so futuristic they almost haven't been thought of yet, at least not by me. When Jolitte had been persuaded—with difficulty—to seek a safe haven from an assassin, I expected her to choose one of them.

But no. She insisted on Le Pavillon Hotel, splendid enough but built in 1905, because she had many happy memories of banquets and celebrations held there.

Jolitte was nowhere to be seen when one of the detectives Raina Lambert had hired admitted me to the DeVarnay suite. Raina was conversing with a small girl who looked vaguely familiar.

Suddenly I recognized her. I had last seen her working with Dassily at the flea market, but then she'd had black hair, and her clothing—patched jeans and a baggy shirt—looked a mess. Now she wore a red wig and a stylish dress. They looked good on her. Raina Lambert had lent them to her as a disguise.

"This is Cele Rundley," Raina said.

"We've already met," I said.

I congratulated her on the transformation, and she smiled shyly.

"She was in terror for her life," Raina said. "She still is even though she knows Dassily has been arrested."

"He won't be bothering you or anyone else for a long, long time," I promised her. "Probably never."

"She'll be the state's number one witness," Raina said. "Even though Dassily never told her what he was up to, he did let slip just enough."

"Mr. DeVarnay was very kind to me," Cele said. "When I gave him tips about antiques, he wouldn't pay Francis for them, he insisted on paying me. Once he gave me four hundred dollars. I'd never had so much money at one time. Francis took it away from me afterward."

"Some of Dassily's remarks made her think DeVarnay was in danger," Raina said. "So she put a *gris-gris* on his door."

"I bought it to protect him," she said simply. "He was already dead, but I didn't know that."

"Then you found out and you put the memorial in the paper," I suggested.

She nodded again. "He was such a kind man. I thought I had to do something. Francis had some photos of him. Francis looked a lot like him when he wasn't wearing his wig and goatee, and he made me study the photos and fix his hair like Mr. DeVarnay's. When I realized Mr. DeVarnay was dead, I stole one of the photos for the memorial. I also stole money from Francis to pay for it."

"That's poetic justice," I said. "It probably was money Francis took from Mr. DeVarnay when he murdered him. What did Francis say about the Memorial?"

"He didn't notice it. He would have beaten me if he had."

"What are you going to do now?" I asked.

She shrugged. "If it's safe, I'll keep working in the flea market. If I can earn enough money, I'm going back to beauty college and try to finish."

"It'll be safe," I promised. Then I paused. "Beauty college? You fixed Francis's hair for him. Did you also help him with his wig and false beard?"

She nodded.

"I saw your paintings in the market. They're good. You ought to be able to earn plenty of money with them."

"They weren't mine," she said. "They were Francis's paintings. I don't know why he always told people they were mine."

"What a tragedy! The man has real talent. So that's why he had such a facility for forging signatures."

"He did it all the time," she said. "He dealt in stolen checks and credit cards."

"There's no doubt he was very good at all the wrong things." I turned to Raina. "Does she have something solid on the murders?"

Raina nodded.

"Good show. That should wind it up. How's Jolitte this morning?"

"I haven't seen her. She had breakfast in her room. She doesn't want company."

"Does she know she's a grandmother?"

Raina shook her head. "She's kept to her room, and I haven't had an opening."

"In that case, I have one last duty to perform here. Someone has got to introduce her to her grandson, and I claim the privilege."

"You're welcome to it," Raina said. "But don't be surprised if she balks. She simply wants to be alone with her misery."

The woman operative who had pretended to be Jolitte's secretary was guarding the bedroom door. I crossed to her and said, "Please tell Mrs. DeVarnay Mr. Pletcher would like to see her."

She looked up from the book she was reading. "Mrs. DeVarnay doesn't want to see anyone."

"Even a duchess has obligations to fulfill," I told her sternly. "Whether she wants to see me is irrelevant. I'm her employee, and I'm here to report. Please tell her."

Resignedly she got to her feet.

A moment later she looked out of Jolitte's room and beckoned to me. She had a look of surprise on her face. After having been Jolitte's bodyguard for several days, she should have had a better understanding of royalty.

She may have been confused by the fact that her employer wasn't looking much like a duchess. Jolitte greeted me sitting up in bed. She hadn't been near a mirror, and her hair was a mess. Her nightgown was of genuine duchess quality, but she looked like a lush with a hangover.

She said, "I wanted to thank you, Mr. Pletcher. Lieutenant Keig told me you were solely responsible for finding Marc's body. He said it was a brilliant piece of deduction. Except for you, no one would have found Marc until—for months or even years. I don't think I could have survived that."

She was more right than she knew. Dassily would have made certain she didn't survive that.

I said, "I'm sorry I couldn't find him alive for you, but as we now know, he died the night he was supposed to leave for St. Louis. Investigators brush elbows with tragedy all the time, but this case has been one of the worst in my career. Once in a great while, though, I have the privilege of bringing good news. I have some for you now."

"Good news?" She sounded as though she never expected to hear any again and wanted no part of it.

I nodded. "Marc had been married for several years. Night

before last, his wife gave birth to a son. Your grandson. Marc, Junior."

She went rigid. "I don't believe it. Marc wouldn't have married without telling me."

"But he did."

"There's something wrong with the girl, or he would have told me."

"There's nothing wrong with the girl. If I'd met her under different circumstances, I would have been tempted to marry her myself. She's beautiful, she's highly talented—both in music and art—and she has a good head for business. She runs her own piano bar."

Jolitte gestured disgustedly. "An entertainer!"

"So what? Vladimir Horowitz was an entertainer. Ignance Paderewski was an entertainer. Don't say that with a sneer until you've heard this girl play Beethoven and Chopin."

"What's her name?"

"She was Edith Gwendolen Aronska. Now, of course, she's Edith Gwendolen DeVarnay. Marc always called her Edie."

"How did you find her?" she demanded. "Did she come to you? Does she want money?"

"In the course of our investigation, we had to track down as many people as possible who'd been in contact with Marc. It shouldn't surprise you that we found his wife. Miss Lambert will tell you how we did it in her report. To answer your question, Edie was desperate for news of Marc, but she was trying to stay out of sight because she thought he would want her to. She doesn't need or want money. She has a good income from her painting and she owns a highly successful business. Also, Marc certainly willed everything he owned to her."

"Then there's no reason for me to see her," Jolitte said.

"But there is. Marc was only an extension of your life. He was all of hers. Now he's gone. She's been deprived of her husband. Her son, your grandson, is left without a father. Surely that's reason enough for you to see them. They need you. You are left without a son, and you need them."

She looked at me steadily for a long time. Then she said, "I'll get dressed. Where are they?"

"As far as I know, they're still in the hospital. I'll find out while you're dressing."

I telephoned Karl Aronska and told him to warn Edie I was bringing her mother-in-law. When Jolitte was ready, I escorted her myself, driving her in my rental car. Raina Lambert came with us. Along the way, Jolitte kept her lips sealed. Neither Raina nor I felt like talking, so we rode in silence.

When we reached the hospital, Raina decided to wait downstairs. "Edie is Mr. Pletcher's discovery," she told Jolitte. "I've never met her. I would be an intruding stranger."

I introduced Jolitte to Karl Aronska, who also decided to wait downstairs. Then the two of us, Jolitte and I, rode up in an elevator, found the room—which had the door slightly ajar—and knocked. I stepped aside and let Jolitte enter.

Edie had been sitting on the edge of her bed. She got to her feet uncertainly. She wore a beautiful quilted dressing gown that probably was a present from Marc, and she looked as lovely as any rational mother-in-law would think her son's wife ought to look. Jolitte faced her for a long moment.

Then the two women fell into each others' arms, weeping.

I was the interloper, and probably I should have left them, but I half suspected Jolitte might need further convincing. The climax came when Edie turned to the crib beside her bed, lifted out Marc Junior, and placed him in Jolitte's arms. If he had screamed in horror at his first glimpse of his grandmother, he might have spoiled everything, but fortunately he was in an angelic slumber.

He slept on, there were more tears, and at that point I quietly made my departure.

Down in the waiting room, Raina and Karl were talking like old friends. Karl looked up at me.

"Do you think it'll be all right?" he asked anxiously.

"Yes. I'm sure it'll be all right. There'll be problems, of course. Jolitte is accustomed to managing everyone and everything, and I have the impression Edie doesn't take well to being managed."

"She's a pretty good manager herself," Karl said with a grin.

"Jolitte will put pressure on her to move into the family mansion and share in the DeVarnay heritage, and Edie will want to stay in the home Marc provided for her. Both of them will have to make compromises, but they'll work it out."

I turned to Raina Lambert. "I'm packed."

"And ready for Savannah?" she asked.

"Well—no. I had a talk with Charlie Tosche last night while we were waiting for the police. He has a vacation coming up, and he rents a *cabon* down on a waterway called Lonesome Bayou. He's invited me to stay with him for a week. Dick will join us part of the time. There'll be fishing, hunting, lots of raw nature to enjoy, including alligators, plenty of homespun Cajun cooking, which Charlie will do himself, and an unlimited supply of Blackened Voodoo Lager Beer. Charlie even shares my aversion for jambalaya. He thinks it's a mixed up mess and unworthy of a genuine chef. He's right, of course. But there'll be shrimp Creole from an old family recipe and an assortment of rémoulades and étouffées. I'm looking forward to it."

Raina was staring at me. "What about your lifelong desire to visit Savannah?"

"It's like this," I said. "Savannah is a fine old historic place and a great tourist town—just like New Orleans. I'm beginning to feel sympathetic toward the attitude of my friend from San Francisco. There can be too damned many tourists. After chasing a murderer through the flea market, Lonesome Bayou sounds just about right to me."

ABOUT THE AUTHOR

LLOYD BIGGLE, JR., science fiction and mystery author and musicologist, was born in Waterloo, Iowa in 1923. Relocating to Michigan, he received degrees from Wayne State University and the University of Michigan. With the publication of his first novel, *All the Colors of Darkness*, he became a full-time author, a profession he continued until his death in 2002.

Biggle introduced aesthetics into science fiction, utilizing his musical background and his interest in artistic themes. His mystery stories include the Grandfather Rastin and Lady Sarah Varnley short stories, two Sherlock Holmes novels and the J. Pletcher/Raina Lambert series.

He was the founding Secretary Treasurer of Science Fiction Writers of America and served as Chairman of its trustees for many years. Biggle also founded the Science Fiction Oral History Association to preserve a record of science fiction notables' speeches and interviews.

He died after a courageous twenty-year battle with leukemia and cancer.

CPSIA information can be obtained at www.ICGtesting.com
Printed in the USA
BVOW041646161212

308240BV00001B/53/P